LORETTA STINSON'S NOVEL about one lonely young woman's harrowing coming of age rings true at the same time it astonishes. *Little Green* is tender and tough, equal parts grit and grace. It's a riveting and unforgettable debut.
Cheryl Strayed, author of *Torch*

LORETTA STINSON'S *LITTLE GREEN* had me in its grip after the first sentence, and didn't let me go until the end. Stinson's characters are vivid on the page and Janie in particular is a character I won't soon forget. We're dawn into a gritty world of drugs, booze, and horrible abuse along with this vulnerable teenager, and we watch in anguish as her dreams fail and her illusions shatter. Even though the circumstances are harrowing, Stinson does well to infuse love and hope and community into Janie's story, so that we're able to witness a lost young woman take the first triumphant steps toward self-discovery.
Debra Gwartney, author of *Live Through This: A Mother's Memoir of Runaway Daughters and Reclaimed Love*

A ROAD MAP charting the many turns and unexpected triumphs in the hard territory of men, *Little Green* is also a story about bad habits that can't be broken, the chief of which is love. Moreover it is a moving story about the road some feet must travel in the pursuit of all that is true and lasting.
Gina Ochsner, author of *The Russian Dreambook of Color and Flight*

IN LORETTA STINSON'S capable hands, the coming-of-age story of Janie Marek – one of those bedraggled kids you see at a highway truck stop – becomes a clear-eyed tale of both bravery and luck. Reminiscent of Kaye Gibbons' *Ellen Foster*, this harrowing view of Oregon drug culture in the mid-1970s is both beautifully written and spiritually redemptive.
Jane Vandenburgh, author of *A Pocket History of Sex in the 20th Century*

LITTLE GREEN IS an engaging novel about the kind of people who can save you from your own life and the kind of people who will starve you of it. It's about the people and the things that get a hold of us and won't let go. It's about Janie, a young girl who finds all of this in a dark bar on the first page and stays with the reader long after the last one. Stinson has written an accurate and honest portrayal of people trying to find their lives or leave them behind.
Jill Talbot, author of *Loaded: Women and Addiction*

Library of Congress Cataloging-in-Publication Data

Stinson, Loretta,
Little Green: a novel /
by Loretta Stinson.
p. cm.
ISBN 978-0-9790188-1-7

1. Runaways—Fiction.
2. Abused wives—Fiction.
3. Self-realization in women—Fiction.

I. Title.

[PS3619.T57L58 2010]

813'.6—DC22

200902752

Hawthorne Books
& Literary Arts

9   1221 SW 10th Avenue
8   Suite 408
7   Portland, OR 97205
6   hawthornebooks.com
5   *Form*:
4   Pinch, Portland, OR
3   Printed in China
2   through Print Vision
1   Set in Paperback.

First Edition,
Spring 2010

BELIEVE YOU ARE FAR MORE THAN THE EXPERIENCES you've lived through and the labels you've been given, even those labels you've worn with pride. Take your one sweet life and live it large.

This book is for Ben Killen Rosenberg, who shows me by example how to be an artist. You encourage me to dream big and follow my heart. Thank you for all the practical ways you show me your love.

Acknowledgements

THIS BOOK WAS LOVED INTO BEING BY THE TEACHERS, friends, and family who believed I could do it even when I couldn't yet. To Julie Ajalat, who said that when I was ready, I would leave and to Brad for helping me pack. To Mary and Armond for a place to stay and a fresh start, and to all my family for their support.

To my mom, Helen Stinson, for all the stories; and my dad, Choppie Stinson, who taught me to read and made it fun.

To Tony Wolk for being a true teacher, a careful reader, fellow writer, and most of all, a friend.

Thank you Rhonda Hughes (the She-Ra of editors) and Kate Sage, the fabulous independent publishers of Hawthorne Books, for the enthusiasm you bring to your work and the care you've taken to make this book real. And thank you to the brilliant designer, Adam McIsaac, for making my book look so pretty. To Adam O'Connor Rodriguez for his insightful comments and sharp proofing.

To my second family, The Rosenberg/Broide/Vanderzwann/ Killen connection!

To my family of friends – Pat, Vern, Kurt, Anja, Kelly, Bill, Francisco, Ray-Ray, Jody, Keri, Liz, Lolly, the other Ben, Wendy and Lee, Molly, Mandee – thank you, yes you.

Thanks to the English Department at Portland State University, especially AB Paulson, Michael McGregor, Carol Franks, Susan Reese, Lorraine Mercer, Craig Lesley, Liz Ceppi, Jennifer

Ruth, Michelle Glazer, Nancy Porter, Greg Jacob, Dennis Stovall, Karen Kirtley, and Lake Boggan.

I also want to thank the fabulous and dedicated professors, instructors, and staff of Portland State University. Clevonne Jackson and the Educational Opportunity Program, my adviser Frosti McClurken-Talley. To Professors Ken Ames, Tom Biolsi, Michelle Gambourd, Sharon Carstens, and David Johnson for the self-confidence they fostered in me.

Thank you Mike Bales for your careful reading and editorial skill.

Thank you to Joni Mitchell for her amazing music.

Thanks to Oregon Literary Fellowship for their generous support.

To Zora Neale Hurston, Alice Walker, and Toni Morrison, your books changed my life.

Little Green

HAWTHORNE BOOKS
& LITERARY ARTS

Portland, Oregon | MMX

A novel
Loretta Stinson

Introduction
Robin Givens

COMPELLING. SO DEEPLY TOUCHING. I WAS CAPTIVATED by Loretta Stinson's *Little Green* from the very beginning because it is written with a simplicity that only the truth permits. Loretta has captured the very essence of an abusive relationship: the stench of the abuse, the subtle hint of hope, and finally, the sweet satisfaction of triumph. This triumph is not a victory over one's abuser, but over our own insecurities, inadequacies, and the emptiness that longs to be filled and that created the vulnerability in the first place. Loretta has also created completely believable, authentic characters that illustrate the reality of entering into, living with, and agonizing over a relationship that is defined by violence.

The main character, Janie Marek's, thoughts and actions are consistent with what I see and hear from in the thousands of women, to whom I am blessed to speak. Her journey from lonely teenager to living in an abusive relationship to ultimately finding her voice and discovering her value resonates with many victims of domestic violence and is also consistent with my own experience. Despite the emptiness in our hearts that might suggest otherwise, we are not alone and unless and until we make the choice to be whole, to be healthy, to be healed, the ache grows over time and the longing gets louder. This book is for you and, certainly, this book is one I will treasure.

The power of literature and Little Green in particular is that it serves to connect readers to common fears and universal feelings that create the human experience. I find that sometimes we are too close to a situation to see or hear its truth; all too often we haven't heard the voices of wisdom and we don't have the role models. This lack of guidance can be seen in the decisions we make. Just one conversation with a wise woman courageous enough to share her own experience could help another woman make better informed and more enlightened life decisions. This sort of guidance could also help her avoid the stumbling blocks that she struggles against; the pitfalls from which she will have to climb; the pain and suffering that may be avoidable, thus allowing for personal triumph and transformation. In the absence of such support, books can provide wisdom. In this novel, Janie chooses books and education and therefore serves as a symbol of hope and inspiration to readers. I hope that my words here, along with Loretta Stinson's, may make a difference in readers' lives.

Hopefully, my own life experiences permit me to make some small contribution to others who have experienced domestic abuse. All too often we feel as if we are alone and that our thoughts and experiences are unique to us but as I cross the country speaking to women, I realize that it's always the same story: the utter disappointment, the agonizing uncertainty and the absolute struggle to survive. I have not transformed from victim to survivor of my own accord. I have drawn on the strength of all who had come before me, women of vision and courage, women of pride and purpose. I come from three generations of survivors of domestic violence, my grandmother, my mother, and myself. I had been unaware of what it took for the women who came before me to simply stand. But I have come to realize that standing isn't so simple. I did not realize the challenges that they faced simply to go on. And I have come to realize that going on is not that simple, either. Experiences are the only things that can make appreciation and compassion part of our very essence. Through our own experiences, we come to appreciate all that it took for others to survive. And through our own experiences, we grow in compassion for others. Without a doubt, the only reason I even had the opportunity to stand tall was because of them. If I did not pull myself up and accept the challenge, if I were to sink into despair and destruction, I would not be worthy of their defiance and their courage.

I serve as the spokeswoman for the National Domestic Violence Hotline because it is an important source of support to women seeking assistance in dealing with domestic abuse. I am grateful to be part of this organization and grateful for the opportunity to touch lives in a way I had not imagined. The hotline receives more than 21,000 calls per month from victims, survivors, friends and family members, law enforcement personnel, domestic violence advocates, and the general public. Hotline advocates provide support and assistance to anyone involved in a domestic violence situation, including those in same-sex relationships, male survivors, those with disabilities and immigrant victims of domestic violence. All calls to the National Domestic Violence Hotline are anonymous and confidential. If you are reading this book and are a victim of domestic violence, please know that you are not alone. Call 800-799-SAFE (7233) or TTY 800-787-3224 or go to www.ndvh.org for help.

LITTLE GREEN

Gimme Shelter
March 1976

JANIE HUNCHED UP HER BACKPACK AND TILTED HER HEAD down to keep the rain from running into her eyes. It would take hours to dry the contents of her backpack let alone her sleeping bag. She crossed a gravel parking lot and headed for a windowless building with a lone silver El Dorado parked in front. She'd seen only fir trees through the rain since she started walking from the freeway about a mile back. This morning she'd caught a ride on the Oregon side of the river because in Washington you couldn't hitch on the freeway. An older guy picked her up after only a few minutes. He drove a sedan and looked like a businessman. He had a briefcase and a suit hung on a hook covering a window in the backseat. He said he'd drive her all the way to Seattle. For awhile it was fine. They made conversation about the weather and what he did and where he lived, and then he asked her if she liked to party. He asked if she wanted to get it on. After she said no a few times, he pulled over on the shoulder and kicked her out, leaving her in the middle of nowhere in the rain.

A neon sign flickered above the building's door – *The Habit*. A bar. The parked El Dorado made it possible somebody was inside. Maybe she could use the bathroom and dry off, maybe get something to eat. Janie wiped the rain off her face with a damp blue bandana. She shook herself and opened the heavy door.

From the back a man yelled, "We're closed."

Janie walked toward the voice, her cowboy boots thumping on the threadbare carpeting. "Can I use your bathroom?"

"I guess," said the man. "It's back here."

She passed two pool tables near the door, a dartboard, a cigarette machine, and stocky wood tables. Captain-chair stools stood around a curved stage. Burgundy curtains hung to the floor. In the mirror behind the wooden bar, she saw herself come into view, wet and bedraggled as a stray dog.

A fat man with a ponytail stood behind the bar stocking a case of imported beer into a cooler. "Back there." He jerked his head toward a beaded curtain.

"Thanks." Janie took off her pack and set it on the floor. The beads rattled as she stepped through into a narrow hallway. The bathroom door stood open. She washed up and dried off as best as she could with paper towels. Janie was a stickler for hygiene even when it was only powdered soap and paper towels.

When she came out, the man at the bar was sitting on a stool working a crossword puzzle.

"What's a four-letter word for 'stop'?"

"Halt."

"Yup. You're right." He looked at her for the first time. "Why you so wet? You walking?"

"Yeah. It's raining pretty hard out there."

"Springtime in Washington." He chuckled.

"You got anything I could do around here? I'd trade some work for something to eat."

He shook his head. "Nope. Pretty slow until the afternoon when the plant lets out."

Janie sighed and stooped to pick up her pack. She didn't want to go back outside until the rain let up. She'd have to walk for miles to get to a better hitching spot.

The bartender scratched his chin. "You dance?"

Janie had heard you could make good money dancing. If she thought about what it meant – to dance around without any clothes on – she wouldn't be able to do it. She could at least buy a little time. "Sure."

"You're eighteen, right?"

"Right." She hoped he wouldn't look too closely at her fake ID.

"Go ahead and let's see you dance then. Dressing room's next to the bathroom."

Janie found a towel in the dressing room and undid her braids, drying her long brown hair as best she could. There were some robes on hooks. She slipped out of her jeans and plaid work shirt, draping them on chairs in front of a wall heater and pulled on a white silky robe. Embroidered blue letters spelled *Champ* across the breast pocket. She'd had to do some unpleasant things since she left home. No good thinking too much about what she did to get by. She'd make some quick cash and get a Greyhound to someplace – someplace warm and dry, maybe LA. She looked in the dressing room mirror. She walked out and up to the stage, the music started, and she dropped the robe.

Janie danced. She closed her eyes tight, moved her head from side to side, her damp hair slid across her bare back and shoulders. She knew the fat man behind the bar suspected that she was underage – a runaway – jailbait. Mostly, she figured he just wanted to see her naked.

Marvin Gaye's voice spun from the speakers. She listened as she danced. She tried to look like what she imagined an exotic dancer looked like, but because she'd never seen one she was having trouble. She felt awkward and bigger than she was. Not just big. She felt fat. Janie bobbed her head around trying her best to look seductive.

The man yelled, breaking her attention. "What are you doing with your arms?"

"What does it look like I'm doing?" Janie stopped dancing and glared at him, hands on her hips.

"Well, if it looked like you was dancing I wouldn't be asking." He shook his head. "Look, just don't wave your arms around so much. It looks like you're playing airplane." He wiped a glass with a dishtowel and put it on the shelf, then looked back up at her. "Go ahead."

She closed her eyes again, trying to imagine dancing in her room back home in Yakima. From her bedroom window she could see the trees in the cemetery. Her mom and dad shared a plot just inside the back entrance where the street dead-ended. Mama wrapped her car around a tree in Mabton on an icy December morning in 1966, a few months shy of Janie's sixth birthday. Two years later, her dad met and married Norma, a cashier at the Giant T drugstore. Janie was twelve when her dad had the heart attack, leaving Janie with Norma. Norma hadn't been so bad at first, but they were never close and when Norma started dating Janie started leaving. She learned to skip school before her thirteenth birthday and began hitchhiking out to the Naches River to avoid going home. The times she was there she hung out in her room. She wore her hair like Janis Joplin's and learned to swear like her, too. Posters of Jim Morrison hung on the ceiling above her bed. With his leather pants slung low on his hips, he looked down on Janie like the Dark Angel of Sex. She burned sandalwood incense from the only head shop in town to cover the smell of the pot she smoked. She started staying out all night and leaving for days at a time. The last time she'd been home she was fourteen. She'd been gone a week and Norma had already redecorated her room and boxed up all her stuff. When Janie overheard her on the phone talking about turning Janie over to the state, she knew her days were numbered. It made it easier to leave knowing that to Norma she was already gone. It felt more like checking out of a Motel 6 than leaving home. That was two years ago.

Janie stopped dancing and looked down at the bartender. "Forget it. I can't do this." She picked up the bathrobe off the stage floor.

"I didn't say you couldn't dance."

She slipped on the robe and stepped off the stage. "Didn't say I could either."

He pulled a cigarette from a pack. "You really eighteen?"

Janie looked him dead in the face. "Yep."

He stared her down. The trick was not to look away.

"Okay. I'm probably going to be sorry. Oh, what the hell." He lit his cigarette. "You look like one of them hippie chicks, but you got a nice ass. Tell you what – you got something that says you're eighteen?"

Janie nodded yes.

"You can go on at four and we'll see how you do. I'm Ernie. Me and my business partner own this bar. You got any problems take it up with one of us."

Janie pulled the robe around her. "Thanks."

"You ought to meet Stella too. The girls you'll meet later." Ernie yelled down the hall. "Hey Stella – you back there?"

A man appeared from the back of the hall. He was tall and black. His head was shaved and a ruby shined from a pierced ear. He wore a sleeveless white T-shirt, and on his right bicep a tattoo of three stars balanced on a slipper moon.

Ernie introduced them. "Stella, this here's the new girl – What'd you say your name was?"

Janie looked up and up at the giant in front of her. His arms were bigger around than her head. "I'm Janie."

Stella nodded and walked away.

Ernie took a drag off his cigarette. "Don't take it personal. Stella's not much of a talker."

After Janie put her clothes on, she helped Ernie while waiting for four p.m. She wiped down the tables, cleaned the bathrooms, and vacuumed. He made them each a sandwich of bologna and white bread with Thousand Island dressing and barbecued potato chips smashed into the bread. Janie had been on the road long enough to eat whatever was in front of her and not complain. The sandwich was actually pretty good.

At about three, a woman came through the door. She wore a green scarf tied around her red hair and a pair of dark glasses. She went to the cooler behind the bar and took out a can of tomato juice not looking at Janie. "Who's this?" she asked

Ernie as she popped open the can and poured the juice into a cocktail glass, garnishing it with a lemon slice.

Ernie was doing another crossword puzzle. "New dancer. Delores, this here's Janie. And vise versey."

Delores took off her sunglasses and squinted hard at Janie. "You ever done this before?"

"Strip? No ma'am."

"Baby, we aren't strippers here. Stripping's different from the shit Ernie pays for. We're dancers. You just get naked and dance." Delores smiled. "She'll do. She's respectful." Delores picked up her juice and took Janie by the elbow. "Let's get you ready for show biz."

Janie followed her to the dressing room.

"How old are you?" Delores asked.

"I'm eighteen."

Delores snorted. "Sure. And I'm really Ann Margaret."

Janie spoke softly. "I'm sixteen."

"Anybody out looking for you?" Delores asked.

"Nope."

Delores shook her head. "You have a place to stay?"

"I'm just going to be here a couple of days."

"You can stay at my place tonight."

A blonde girl in a pair of tight jeans burst into the dressing room. "Hey Dee! Look what I got at the Bargain Barn. Don't you love this little top? I love pink. Maybe I'll do my nails to match." She noticed Janie. "You going to be the new girl? I'm Amber. You'd look good in blue – baby blue! Set off your eyes."

Amber tossed Janie a pair of ice-blue bikini bottoms from a box on the floor. Janie wondered how a pair of blue panties on her ass was going to make her eyes look blue, but she didn't say anything. Delores handed Janie a tube of lipstick. "You better get ready. You're up first." From her purse she took a metal box and opened it. She handed Janie a pill. "Take this. It'll make your life easier."

Janie swallowed the rocket shaped pill and looked at her face in the mirror. Whoever she was once was just about gone. She smeared on lipstick, took off her clothes, and pulled on the blue bikini bottoms, licking a pair of pasties and sticking them on her nipples. She put on the white robe and cinched it shut. She'd be Mohammed Ali and float like a butterfly. Nothing would touch her.

Music blared from the bar. The voices of men and the occasional crack of billiard balls reached the dressing room as the place filled up.

It was almost four.

Delores smiled at Janie. "You look real sweet, honey. Don't worry. Today's payday for most of those monkeys out there. They just want to see some fresh tail. Shake your ass around and you'll be fine. Dance three numbers and then come on back. You can pick out your own music on the jukebox. Okay?"

Janie walked to the jukebox and looked at the playlist. Patsy Cline's *Crazy*. Lots of Rolling Stones, some Marvin Gaye. Janie peered over her shoulder. The men in the bar wore work boots and denim jackets; they smoked cigarettes and drank beer; their loud voices erupted into even louder laughter. Janie looked at every song twice before picking out her three.

Ernie yelled from the bar. "You're up."

Janie took the stairs one at a time. There were only two steps.

Her first song started with Keith Richard's guitar solo, *Can't You Hear Me Knocking*. She'd loved dancing to this song since the *Sticky Fingers* album came out when she was twelve. She dropped her robe, and somebody whistled. Men yelled up at her. She couldn't move. The men were so loud she couldn't think. She thought she would throw up or pass out.

Stella appeared at the edge of the stage. "Come on down." His voice was deep. Janie took the steps quickly this time, pulling her robe on as she went. The crowd booed. Stella handed her a pair of sunglasses. He motioned to the room full of men. "You going to let them mess with you? Get your Zen on, girl. You'll be fine."

She put on the black-mirrored Ray-Bans. "Can I start over?"

Stella walked to the jukebox and pushed some buttons. Keith Richards started playing again, then Charlie Watts on the drums, and finally Mick Jagger. Janie took a deep breath. You could do just about anything if you thought about it right. Janie jumped up on the stage like a fighter coming out strong from her corner. She remembered watching boxing matches with her dad a long time ago. The boxers would always dance in their corner throwing punches at the air. Janie pretended she was a boxer. She threw punches at an invisible opponent. The crowd yelled and catcalled. She took a deep breath and dropped her robe. Somebody whistled. Somebody shouted. She kept her shades on and danced the set, glad the songs bled into each other and she'd be through soon. She concentrated on the music, singing along in her head and ignoring everything going on around her.

As abruptly as it started, it was over. The music ended and Amber came out.

Janie stepped off the stage.

Ernie yelled over to her from the bar, "You got the job. We'll call you Shady Lady."

Janie pulled the robe around her and went back to the dressing room to wait for her next set. She wondered how she could do this again but knew already that done once, it would be easy enough to just keep going.

Sympathy for the Devil

"HEY, ERNIE GIVE ME A BIRD AND A BUD." PAUL JESSE pulled a bill from his money clip. He carried a roll of bills sorted by denomination with the presidents facing the same way. He placed a Jackson on the bar and sat down. It was still early and only a couple regulars, old men with nothing much to do sipped beer and waited for the dancers to come on.

Ernie took a bottle of Wild Turkey off the shelf behind him and poured Paul a shot glass, grabbed a bottled Bud from the cooler and put the change on the bar, counting it off out loud. "Where you been hiding yourself?"

Paul took a sip of beer and wiped his Fu Manchu. "Went down to the city to see my kid and do a little business."

"You take your bike?"

"Yeah. Twelve hours straight. My back is killing me."

Ernie laughed.

Paul Jesse thought of The Habit as his office. He'd never been a grunt; never done more than a cursory pass at a straight job. He liked to think of himself as a Mongol trader from faraway times running drugs between Seattle and San Francisco – occasionally a trip East with a carload of dope. He'd known Ernie and Stella growing up in San Francisco where their families all lived within blocks of each other. Paul kept the dealing at The Habit low-key and mellow, gave a good deal, and never much looked at the women. He believed in the Golden Rule: deal unto others as you would have them deal unto you. He didn't so much sell the drugs as they sold themselves. He merely delivered them. His bags of dope were never short; whatever he sold was guaranteed to get you high; he never ripped anyone off, didn't sleep with their women, and if he stayed overnight on a long trip, he turned his hosts on to whatever he was selling. Dope was business and pleasure. Dope was a way of life.

Ernie called out. "Let's go, Shady. You're up."

A girl's voice called back. "I'm just looking for some decent music, Ernie."

Paul lowered his shades and glanced at the mirror behind the bar. A new dancer. She had long hippie-girl brown hair. A loosely belted robe revealed the curve of a breast. She wore old scuffed cowboy boots and mirrored sunglasses. Paul sipped from the shot glass.

Ernie smiled and yelled to the girl as she climbed the steps of the stage, "Soon as you learn to dance, baby, we'll get you some new tunes."

Brown Sugar came on the jukebox, and Paul turned on his stool to see what the new girl would do. It seemed like she was looking right at him, but it was probably Ernie she was looking at when she stuck out her tongue and shook her ass like some little kid. It made him smile. Paul turned his back to the stage and watched from the mirror. "Who's the new girl?"

"That's Janie. We been calling her Shady Lady. Cute, ain't she?"

Paul nodded. "A little young."

"We're calling her eighteen."

Paul shook his head. "Yeah, and I'm calling myself Miss America."

"I'll get your tiara, Your Highness."

Paul watched the girl dance her set and finished his beer. When she walked off stage, he stood and called to Ernie. "Later, man."

In the parking lot he climbed on his Harley Davidson '58 Panhead and kicked her on. He hadn't caught a shower or any sleep for a couple days. The road wound up a hill to a gravel road where he turned in. Paul rented a trailer parked behind Ernie's house. He showered at Ernie's and sometimes used the kitchen, but mostly the trailer was just a squat to sleep in when he needed. Paul unlocked the back door of the house and left it open while he got a clean towel from his trailer. He could smell Ernie's through the open door – beer, cigarettes, and dirty socks.

Paul's long hair was braided for riding. In the bathroom, he cut the rubber band that held the braid together at the bottom and loosened it with his fingers. His hair was stiff from the long ride and held the waves of the braid even after he brushed it. He undressed and turned on the shower, waiting for the water to run hot before he stepped in. He turned and let the steaming water pound the sore muscles in his shoulders and back.

This last trip to San Francisco had been tough. He wanted to see his six-year old son, Pauly, but little Pauly didn't want to see him. Paul sat on the floor outside the kid's closed bedroom door and talked to him for an hour, trying to get him to at least come out and say hello or goodbye. Little dude wouldn't go for it.

Mia, his ex, said Pauly was scared of him. He and Mia had been strung out on the crank he'd been selling the last time he'd seen Pauly. The kid still remembered all those bad fights. Paul got paranoid and jealous. Mia got mouthy. Their last fight he'd held her by the throat and slapped the shit out of her. He looked up and saw little Pauly, almost three then, in his cowboy pajamas, wailing for his mom. Paul let go of Mia and walked out. A few months later he rode his bike to Seattle, which reminded him of San Francisco. He didn't come back for over a year. When he did, Mia had sobriety and a straight old man. She'd even gone and married the guy. Now she, her husband, and Pauly lived in a nice house in the Avenues. The kid had his own room and a chance. Sometimes Paul thought the best thing he could do was forget about the kid. Mia's husband wanted to adopt him. Paul wasn't so sure. Thinking of his son was like running his tongue over a sore tooth. Nothing he could do about it now. Best thing probably was to cut the little dude loose.

Paul stepped from the shower and wrapped a towel around his waist, wiped the steam from the mirror and looked at himself. Getting old. He was going to be twenty-six this year. Closing in on thirty. Sometimes when he saw himself he wondered where the altar boy had gone. He trimmed his Fu Manchu and shaved his cheeks.

After he combed his hair, Paul cooked a bowl of Ramen noodles and poached an egg on top, dousing it with soy sauce. He took the bowl to the porch to eat. The spring sunshine felt warm. He liked it quiet like this. A Cooper's hawk circled over a nearby pasture. One of the neighbor's cats, a scrawny calico, crawled out from under the trailer and rubbed against his legs. Paul put his bowl on the ground for her. The cat lapped up the broken yolk, arching her back as she ate. Animals made better company than most of the people he knew. Paul yawned, stretching as he stood to go inside for a nap. He left the bowl for the cat.

BEFORE LEAVING THAT night for The Habit Paul bagged up an ounce of pot. He threw the baggies into a small paper bag and tucked it in the inside pocket of his leather jacket. He didn't like to take more than an ounce. During the evening, he made several trips outside to do business with his regulars.

He sat at the bar nursing his second round. Every now and again he'd glance at the mirror to see who was dancing.

Delores slid onto the stool next to him, tugging on his ponytail. "Hey, stranger. When did you get back?"

"Yesterday." He didn't look at her. Delores acted like the breeze.

She picked up his glass and took a drink. "How's the city?"

"Still standing. You going to buy me another drink?"

"Not hardly likely."

Ernie came down the crowded bar with a rack of clean glasses, a cigarette hanging from his mouth. He frowned at Delores. "Who's up?"

"Janie's sick. Amber's working her set. She'll go on in a minute."

"What's the matter with Janie?"

"She got her visitor."

"What are you talking about? Her period?" Ernie asked.

Delores pursed her lips. "A period comes at the end of a sentence. The girl's bleeding like a stuck pig. She ought to go lay down. Can Stella or you run her over to my house?"

"It's Thursday, Delores – payday. So now I'm short a dancer and you want one of us to take her home?"

Paul started to ease himself off the stool.

Delores grabbed his arm. "Wait a minute, Paul. Can you drive her back to my place?"

Paul shook his head. "No way, Dee. I don't even know this girl. Besides it'll take me an hour. Hell. She probably can't even ride."

"If you can stay on a bike, she can too. Look Paul, it'll only take you a half an hour and I'll buy you another damn drink when you get back."

"I don't suppose it matters if I don't want to."

Delores smiled. "Be a good boy and do what Mama tells you."

Ernie laughed. "Might as well give up. Delores has spoken."

Paul stood and zipped up his jacket. "Let's get this over with. I got business to finish tonight."

Paul waited by his bike until the girl came outside. She looked pale and young. She didn't look like any dancer he'd ever seen. "I'm Paul," he said. "You ever been on a bike before?"

"Not by myself, but I can stay on."

"What's your name?"

"Janie. Thanks for this."

Paul handed her a clean folded bandana from his back pocket. "You better tie your hair back or you'll have a real mess by the time I get you to Dee's." He kick started the bike and she climbed on behind him. "Just hold on to me and when I lean, you lean." She nodded and looped her arms around him as they lurched forward out of the parking lot and onto the road. She held him tight and leaned into him as they took the curves. The smell of dairy cows and sweet grass filled the air. She didn't try to talk, but now and then he could feel her shiver with cold. The ride seemed not to take as long as he thought it would. He slowed the bike and turned into the driveway of Dee's place. The porch light glowed yellow. He turned off the engine.

As she got off the bike, Janie fell to her hands and knees retching. Paul stooped behind her and held her shoulders, helping her to her feet when she stopped throwing up. Her eyes watered. "I'm sorry."

"Don't worry about it. Let's get you inside. You're pretty sick, huh?"

She nodded. "You don't have to stay. I'm okay now." She fumbled for a key in her pocket.

"Delores would knock my dick in the dirt if I went off and left you before you're settled." Paul steered her up the steps. He took the key when she missed the lock and opened the door. She ran down the hall to the bathroom, leaving Paul standing in the living room.

Paul liked Dee's place. He'd met her after Mia and before he left California for Washington. They lived together a couple of times when he'd needed a place to crash and she wanted help with the rent. Nothing romantic, though they did get in the habit of sharing a bed. Delores had been business on his part.

From the bathroom Paul heard Janie running water. He started a fire in the woodstove for something to do. Now that he was there, he wasn't in any hurry to leave. He looked in the kitchen for teabags and bread, put the kettle on for tea, and put some bread in the toaster. Mia used to get sick with her periods. Paul always liked the feeling of taking care of her with little things like tea and toast.

By the time he carried everything in from the kitchen, Janie was sitting on the couch in a plaid bathrobe and longjohns. He put the cup and plate on the coffee table.

"You didn't need to do all that." Janie's cheeks flushed.

"Now I can tell Delores you're all tucked in." He thought for a minute. "You mind if I hang out for awhile? The quiet is kind of nice for a change. Want to smoke a joint?"

"I better not."

The fire crackled, filling the silence. Paul felt more relaxed than he had in a long time. This girl didn't try to make small talk or flirt with him. He looked her over as she licked the butter off her slender fingers. He surprised himself by reaching over and picking up her thick, wet hair. "You put conditioner on it?"

"Yeah."

"Ought to comb it out before it dries." Her hair was wavy with flecks of red from the firelight. "You have a comb?"

Janie pulled a wide-tooth comb from the pocket of her robe and handed it to him.

He put a pillow from the couch on the floor in front of him. "Now, I'll deny I ever did this if anybody asks." He smiled at her.

Janie moved to the floor. "How do you know so much about hair?"

He worked the tangles with his fingers. "I had a mean big sister. She used to make me comb her hair out and roll it up in orange juice cans. Besides, I got my own hair project going on."

Janie leaned back against the couch. "You've got nice hair." She said it matter of fact, no extra message.

"There's an old hippie saying, 'It's not the hair, it's the head it grows on.' "

He pulled through the tangles, careful not to hurt her. They didn't speak again. He felt her nod off. He helped her up on the couch and got a blanket from the closet. He carried the dishes to the sink, banked the fire with a big log, and put on his jacket. Her eyes were closed. She looked peaceful. For a second time Paul surprised himself. He crossed the room and bent low over her. Her hair was now almost dry in his hand. He bent down and put it to his nose, breathing her in. Her eyes blinked open, blue as fresh water, but she didn't speak. He brushed her cheek with a calloused thumb and left before he could embarrass himself.

Simple Twist of Fate

FOR THE NEXT FOUR DAYS JANIE STAYED TUCKED UNDER a crocheted afghan on Dee's couch. She slept, ate bowls of Cocoa Puffs, and watched TV with the volume off so Dee could sleep. Time slipped by. Janie was waiting for Paul.

The day after he brought her home from the club, he showed up on his motorcycle. He didn't knock, walked inside carrying an armload of wood, and built a fire. Then he stood in the living room shifting from foot to foot until she asked him if he wanted to watch *Bonanza* with her. It turned out Paul Jesse had a thing for Westerns.

That first night Janie had been too sick to notice more than his kindness. The next afternoon she took in his features when he wasn't looking. His hair was long and the color of taffy, worn in a thick braided rope that hung down to the middle of his back. He was tanned and had some weather to his face. His Fu Manchu was neatly trimmed, and dimples framed his mouth. His warm brown eyes had crow's feet from laughing or squinting too hard in the sun.

Every day he showed up just after Delores left for work and stayed until Janie fell asleep on the couch during Johnny Carson. He didn't offer to comb her hair again. He didn't touch her at all. He talked very little, but the silence between them was comfortable.

Janie didn't mention Paul's visits to Delores. They were small in themselves and probably didn't mean anything to anyone but Janie. She found herself holding her breath waiting for the sound of his bike on the gravel each afternoon.

On Monday Janie knew she'd be well enough to go back to work. She hoped going back to The Habit wouldn't end whatever was happening between her and Paul. That morning she made spaghetti like her dad used to make using a page torn from her mom's cookbook. She almost never got a chance to cook and the times she had were special to her. Once she had her own home she would cook every day and love it.

PAUL HAD NO idea what he was doing. Every day he told himself to get back to work and quit going to see that girl. Come three in the afternoon he'd get restless. He couldn't sit still. Couldn't concentrate. He'd get on his bike with every intention of heading over to The Habit to do some business, yet somehow he'd find himself pulling into Delores's driveway to see the girl with the blue eyes, and the four freckles across the bridge of her nose, and the lips that needed no extra color, and the acres of wavy brown hair that smelled clean and shone like polished wood.

When he walked through the door, his intentions disappeared. She felt familiar as old tunes on the radio. She didn't talk much, but when she did she wasn't coy and didn't come on to him. She had a habit of twining her hair around her fingers when she watched TV. Anybody would think he had a crush on her but she was at least ten years younger than him.

He parked his bike and went inside through the backdoor to the kitchen. She stood at the stove stirring red sauce. Her hair was pulled back, her face without make-up. Her worn shirt was almost the same blue as her eyes.

"I hope you're hungry." She smiled at him. "I made my mom's secret sauce. The secret is bacon. Don't tell." Janie lifted the spoon to her lips, blowing on it before she held it out to him. "Want a taste?"

He couldn't speak. He couldn't look away from those eyes. Paul put his hand over hers, bending to bring the spoon to his mouth. He didn't let go of her hand as he brought the spoon down. He didn't look away.

THE SMELL OF coffee and Delores stomping around woke Paul in the morning. Janie slept next to him, her breath deep and even. He got out of bed to go shut Dee up and get a cup of coffee to bring back. He'd like to lie beside Janie and watch her sleep awhile longer.

Delores sat at the kitchen table tapping her cigarette into an ashtray. She stared as Paul poured himself coffee. Her voice was harsh. "What the hell are you doing here?"

"Getting some coffee. What's wrong with you?" Paul leaned back against the counter.

"Are you sleeping with that girl?"

"Is that your business, Dee?"

"What happens in my house is my business." Her voice rose.

"Look, I didn't plan on spending the night, and I didn't figure it'd piss you off so much if I did." Paul picked up his cup. "It's too early for this. I'm going back to bed."

"Not in my house you're not."

"Lighten up Dee. It was just a night. I'm not looking for an old lady. You want me to say it was mistake? Okay. I got carried away or some shit. Now can I go back to bed?"

The clock on the wall clicked. A drop of water splashed in the pan left to soak overnight in the kitchen sink. Delores looked past him down the hall. Paul knew before he turned that Janie was there. She didn't say a word. Before he could stop her, Janie was gone, the door to her room shutting behind her.

JANIE WORKED THE rest of the week, staying for the payday crowd to top off her savings from the past two months. Paul came to The Habit twice and never looked at her. She felt more alone than she had in a long time. She thought something real had happened between them. She'd learned that when she gave her body away she lost a piece of herself, so she didn't do it often.

She'd bartered with sex as a trade for something she needed before, but that was different. When she was in bed with Paul, she felt as if she belonged there with him. She thought she'd be alone forever. The only cure was the road. She didn't talk to Dee about Paul or about leaving. She just wanted to go. At the health food store on their way to work one afternoon, Janie read the bulletin board while Dee bought some Tiger Balm. The Oregon Country Fair was in Veneta, outside Eugene, two weeks and three hundred miles away from The Habit and Paul Jesse. Janie had almost five hundred dollars stashed. She'd leave that week.

Friday morning she packed her things and asked Delores for a ride to the freeway. Dee didn't seem surprised and didn't try to talk her out of it. The past week had been strained. Delores kept trying to bring up Paul and Janie stayed quiet.

Delores pulled over on the shoulder of the northbound on-ramp to I-5. "Well, here you go. Take it easy."

"See you." Janie felt lighter than she had in a week. She faced the direction of traffic and extended her thumb, hoping for a gypsy trucker who wanted company and might be going straight through to Eugene. Nothing like miles and a new scene to get your head back. She'd moved on from so many places and people over the past two years that staying put, no matter how much she thought she wanted to, scared her, made her feel trapped.

There wasn't much traffic so she waited, standing patiently, wondering if she should have gotten a ride from Dee to a different on-ramp. Hitching from small towns could be hard. A station wagon slowed down but didn't stop. Finally, as despair was setting in, a white delivery van with Oregon plates pulled over. The driver, a youngish guy, got out and adjusted the passenger side mirror. "So, where you headed?"

Janie looked him over. "Down to the Country Fair in Eugene."

"I'm going to Portland. That's about halfway." He opened the door for her. Fast food wrappers and a metal clipboard holding some papers were on the seat. "Go ahead and put your stuff in the back."

Janie didn't usually ride in vans. Somebody could be hiding, but when she pulled off her pack and slung it in the back she didn't see anybody. He seemed like a regular worker on the job wanting company. The guy slammed her door and got back in, stepping on the gas and merging with the afternoon traffic.

The heater rattled. Janie tried to roll down her window but saw that both the window and door handles had been removed. Her heart started thumping and her mouth turned to sand. She stared out the window, pretending to be fine as she went through escape routes in her head.

"You want me to show you something?" His voice was wet like he didn't swallow enough.

"No, that's okay."

"I really want to show you my special place." He took the next exit onto a county road. They were out in the middle of nowhere. "You're going to be my pretty girl."

"Can you pull over? I get car sick and I think I'm going to throw up."

"And you lie, don't you? Pretty girls always lie."

"I'm not lying. Can you let me out?"

"No. We're going to have a party in my special place and then maybe I'll let you out."

The van was hot with the windows rolled up and the noisy heater running. He turned onto a dirt access road in a tree farm and slowed down. Nothing but acres of Douglas firs as far as she could see. Janie threw her weight against the door hoping to pop it open. It didn't budge.

He laughed. "You can't get out till I say so." He backed the van around in a pullout on the single-lane dirt road and stopped.

"Please. Let me go. You can leave me right here."

"Not yet." As he got out of the van, Janie jumped across the seat and locked his door. Running around to her side, he opened the door and came after her, forcing her into the back of the van.

She screamed and beat at him, her arms and legs ineffective. He caught her by the hair, wrapping it around his fist and slamming her face into the metal door until all she could taste was blood. He dragged her down, turning her over and pinning her body to the cold metal floor. His breath was hot and stank of old food and cigarettes as he grunted into her ear. "You won't be pretty anymore." He punched her face until she gave up and lay still. She could smell the sour sweat of his body. Blood filled her mouth, making her choke. Her eyes swelled shut. She couldn't breathe. She couldn't move. Nobody knew where she was. Nobody would be coming to get her.

HOURS LATER HE pulled her from the van and pushed her body into the underbrush. Janie watched through one swollen eye as he dug through her pack, scattering her belongings and taking her money before driving away.

She lay on her side afraid to move until silence filled the dark. She focused on a tree trunk a few feet away. She knew she should be cold. She wasn't. She knew she should hurt. She didn't. She touched her face, examining the damage by fingertip. Her face felt misshapen. She couldn't see out of her left eye. Her nose was huge and she had trouble breathing. Her lips were split, but she didn't think she was missing any teeth. She pulled herself to her knees and began to gather her clothes. Standing up to dress, she felt dizzy and thought she might pass out. She stood still and concentrated on the rough feel of the bark beneath her fingers. She knew she wasn't that far from The Habit. She would think of getting there. She wouldn't think of how stupid she'd been to get in the van. She wouldn't think of the rules she'd broken – rules she'd created from experience – when she got in the van.

1. Always check the doors before you get in.
2. Never take a ride in a van.

A phrase she remembered played in her head, and she let

it spin as she began walking. *Keep on truckin'. You got to keep on truckin'.* She repeated the phrase until she reached The Habit miles away.

Shelter from the Storm

STELLA SAT ON A STOOL NEAR THE DOOR, OCCASIONALLY
checking a college boy's ID but mostly scanning the crowd to
make sure nobody got out of hand. It had been a good night, quiet
for a Friday. Stella thought they might be able to close a little
early for a change. That would be fine with him.

In 1968, Stella returned to his hometown of San Francisco
fresh from two tours as a medic in Vietnam. He'd joined the
Navy Reserves out of high school to escape the infantry. He wanted to be a doctor, and money for medical school would be
available when he got out. At the time, so many corpsmen were
being killed that reserves went immediately on active duty.
The kicker was he'd been assigned to the infantry anyway. A fire-
fight near Marble Mountain northeast of Da Nang put an end
to his desire for college or a medical career. Stella quit making
plans for the future and concentrated on survival.

The club was Ernie's idea. They'd been friends from the old
neighborhood and ended up in the same company during
Stella's second tour. Back in the world, stateside, they'd met again
by chance at a bar in San Francisco's Tenderloin. During a
late round of drinks one night, they decided to pool their money
and buy a bar. It didn't matter to Stella what he did. Get out
of the city, buy a bar, hire some dancers, make some money. Just
like that. Now he was happy just to think about closing early
and going home to his bed alone.

Stella yawned and straightened his back. He could almost feel the cool cotton of his sheets. The doors next to him creaked. Stella stood up to give whoever it was a hand.

Standing under the neon Hamm's sign was the dancer who'd quit the night before. It took a few seconds for her name to surface – Janie, that was it. Her face was so bloody and swollen that if Stella hadn't seen her recently he wouldn't have recognized her. He grabbed her elbow as she started to sink to the ground. He didn't want to take her through the club. "Let's go around to the back door."

Janie wobbled and shook. Stella held her up and walked with his arm looped around her, half carrying her to the office. Flipping on the light, Stella looked her over. Head traumas bled a lot, but more was wrong than just her face. Blood stained her jeans. Her shirt was torn; bruises marked the pale skin of her throat. He needed to take a look at her mouth and eyes. He hoped the injuries were superficial. He eased her into the office chair and grabbed a roll of paper towels, tearing off a trail of them and blotting at her face. He kept up a patter of reassurances. "You're going to be okay. That's good. Let's take a look now." She was going to need stitches. Her nose was broken, but they wouldn't do anything about that tonight. It might heal straight. You could never tell with a nose. "I'm going to get my car and take you to the hospital."

She shook her head. "No."

"Look, you need a doctor."

"No doctor."

"This isn't anything to play around with, Janie. You need stitches."

"No doctor."

The door opened and Ernie stepped in. "Holy shit! What happened to you? We better get you to a doctor."

Janie started rocking. "No doctor. Promise."

Stella looked at Ernie. "I don't think she wants the police in this."

Janie nodded.

Ernie shook his head. "Can you take care of her?"

"Man, I don't know. I haven't stitched anybody up in a long time. It's not like I have my kit anymore."

Ernie leaned against the door. "How about Doc? I bet he'll take care of her or set you up with what you need."

Stella squatted in front of Janie's good eye. "There's this doctor we know. Doesn't ask questions or file reports. I was a medic a long time ago but – "

"You help me, Stella."

Looking at her, he couldn't say no, even though his hands had begun to sweat and tingle. "I'll try." Stella patted her leg and stood up. "Ernie, ask Dee if she has any downers on her. Get a bag of ice too. And a blanket. She could use a blanket."

Now that he'd decided, all his training came back. Stella called Doc and gave him a list of what he thought he'd need. Then he rummaged in the office cupboards for some clean rags and a metal bowl he filled with water from the bathroom. He was sponging away the blood from her face when Delores came in with a blanket, a couple of Quaaludes, and a plastic bag of ice.

Delores stared at Janie. "I knew something like this would – "

"Dee. Shut up." Stella took the blanket, pills, and ice from her and pushed her out of the office, closing the door in her face. He looked at Janie. "You're going to be fine. Let's get you out of here before we have more sightseers."

On the way to the car Janie started to shake so hard Stella couldn't keep the blanket around her. He carried her to his car, surprised by how light she felt. He helped her into the front seat and tucked the blanket around her. Her skin was cold. He needed to get her hydrated and warm. He'd ice her face later to get the swelling down, but right then she was shaking so badly he didn't want to risk it. He kept up a constant patter, calm and neutral – no questions, nothing she needed to respond to, just a voice in the dark for her to focus on. He drove to Doc's place in town and left the car running while he got a shopping bag full of medical supplies. Stella didn't stop to think about what he was doing. If he thought too hard about it, he'd be dropping this girl at the hospital emergency entrance and driving away.

As they pulled up in front of Stella's gated driveway, China, his big black and tan dog, came running out to greet him. He got out of the car, unlocked the padlock, and swung the gate open.

"Settle down, China. We've got company." Since he'd moved here six years ago, he could count on one hand the people who'd been to his home. Now he had this girl – an underaged white girl no less – sitting in *his* car in front of *his* house about to spend the night. Stella shook his head to clear it, got back in the car, drove through the gate and re-locked it. He parked in front of the house and helped Janie out of the car. She wasn't shaking so much anymore. She hadn't cried or carried on like most people would have given whatever had been done to her. He guessed that besides the beating she'd been raped. What to do about that was beyond the medical training he'd received at Lejeune.

China shimmied her back end around, wagging her tail hard and butting her head against Janie's legs. Stella held Janie's arm and stopped as she held out her hand. China sniffed the girl all around.

Stella smiled. "She likes you."

In the kitchen Stella seated Janie at the table and unpacked the shopping bag. He gave her more pain medication and a glass of warm water to sip while he rinsed off her split forehead with lidocaine and began to stitch her up. She didn't flinch, and Stella was glad for that. He was having a hard time keeping his hands steady and his stomach from flipping. It had been another life the last time he'd sewn flesh. He hummed under his breath to steady himself. He made them both some chamomile tea, cooling hers to lukewarm with cream and honey, putting a straw in the mug so she could sip it. China sat at the girl's feet, resting her head on Janie's lap.

"You feel like taking a bath?"

Janie nodded.

"You won't slip or fall, will you?"

Janie shook her head.

Stella left her with China and ran a tub. He looked in the closet for something Cookie might have left behind the last time she'd visited. Cookie Novella was the woman he loved, but she lived in Oregon and not with him because she disapproved of the club. He found Cookie's clean sweatshirt and longjohn bottoms, gathered a couple towels from the hall closet, and carried it all to the kitchen. The girl sat slumped over, holding China's head on her lap. For a minute he thought she'd passed out until he saw her back shake with a sob. Stella stood in the doorway wiping his face with the back of his sleeve. Then he helped her to the tub.

Tomorrow he'd find some clothes for her. She'd need stuff girls needed. He'd have to do his best to remember what that stuff might be. He'd call Cookie once Janie fell asleep. He'd ask her what to do. He'd already decided. Janie would be staying, no matter what her staying might mean later.

Here Comes the Sun

IN THE MORNING WHEN SHE WOKE, JANIE STUDIED THE quilt that covered her in Stella's spare bedroom. The quilt contained a thousand shades of blue, from the indigo of blueberries in August to the pale blue of a mountain sky. Each block was stitched precise as a prayer. The fabric looked delicate and felt soft as silk, but was strong even after years of wear. Stella had said the women of his family made it for his mother when she was expecting her first child – him. The idea of all those women sitting together to make something so beautiful captured Janie's imagination. She lay in bed between thick cotton sheets.

Across from her bed a large window with sheer curtains stained the room with light. She could almost tell time by the square of yellow sunlight as it moved across the quilt. Except for a dresser and the narrow bed she slept in the room was empty and it calmed her. It had been almost six weeks since she came to Stella's. The swelling had gone down, the bruises were gone, and she could eat, talk, and smile. When she looked in the small oval mirror she could pretend nothing had happened. That was the surface of it. The skin and teeth and hair of it. She'd drawn Stella a map of where the guy in the van had dumped her and her stuff. Stella retrieved what was left – a small wooden box with a few pictures, her Social Security card, a copy of *Winnie the Pooh* her parents gave her for the last birthday they were both alive. *Love to Janie on her sixth birthday, Mommy and Daddy*. That was all that was left. The girl she'd been was gone.

She didn't think of the particulars of what had happened out there in the woods. Though she knew better she didn't call it rape because she'd been stupid and had paid for it. Janie knew from the boatload of other bad things that had happened to her in sixteen years that thinking too much about any of them would hurt too much and bring nightmares and cold sweats. She chose not to look at her past and looked at the quilt instead.

This morning was already warm. Janie sat up in bed and slid her feet to the floor. China woke stretching and yawning. The dog slept on the bed beside her since the first night. Her tail thumped against the mattress sending dust motes spinning. Janie let China out the back door. She could hear a rake scraping the ground. Stella liked to work in the garden before he went to the club. Janie helped too, since the garden was big enough to keep two people busy. Some of the vegetables Janie had never seen, let alone eaten. There was okra, squashes, melons, greens of every kind, cucumbers and tomatoes, peppers, beans, a patch of corn, cabbages, and different kinds of lettuces, radishes, onions, and garlic. Stella was a good cook, and now that it was high summer, he cooked out of the garden and didn't buy much from the store. Janie checked on the tomatoes every day for a hint of red. Stella told her to hold her horses, it was only July, the tomatoes wouldn't come on for at least another month, but Janie had a particular memory of a garden – sitting on the warm dirt with her mom when she was maybe four or five, picking a red tomato, and eating it like an apple, the juice running down her face and fingers.

On the kitchen table sat a white bowl full of nectarines and a white plate of cornbread squares left over from dinner the night before. Coffee perked in the pot on the stove. Stella came in through the kitchen, slipping his shoes off at the door carrying a big bunch of beets that he put in the sink. "You sleep okay?"

"Yeah." Janie cut a piece of cornbread in half, put it on a white plate, and squeezed honey from a plastic bear over it. "Stella, how come so much of your stuff is white?"

"White always matches white. White goes with anything. It's the color of the masses."

Janie took a bite of cornbread.

Stella shook the beets over the sink and broke the tops off loosely wrapping them in a clean dishtowel. He looked over at her. "Ernie's having a birthday next weekend. He's got a big camp-site reserved up at Eagle Creek. A bunch of people will be there."

Janie sat quiet, eating the sticky cornbread with her fingers.

"I thought we'd both go. I've got a tent and sleeping bags. We're closing the club for a long weekend. Haven't done that since we bought the place." Stella poured himself a cup of coffee. "My friend Cookie is coming up. I want you to meet her. I think you'll like her."

"I don't know." She felt scared to leave the house sometimes even when Stella was with her.

"I think it would be good. You'd meet some people. Some women. I want you to come."

Janie sat staring at her cornbread for a minute. Stella never asked her for anything, and the truth was she didn't want to stay here alone. "Is China coming?"

"Of course."

"Okay. I'll go. But I've got to get something to read."

"It's a deal."

Since Janie had come to stay with Stella she had read many of the novels on the floor-to-ceiling shelves in the living room. He had a set of leatherbound books he'd picked up from the county library sale and Janie had kept herself occupied with those for the last few weeks. At night when Stella was at work reading kept her mind full of someone else's stories. She had to have a book or she'd go crazy at every little noise or shadow in the night. It helped having China, but even with the big dog, Janie couldn't sleep or turn out the lights until Stella came home and she felt safe. Some nights she still had screaming nightmares. When that happened, Stella woke her, got her water and patted her back. He said he had them too after he got home from Vietnam, but they didn't come as often and, in time, hers wouldn't either. She took comfort from that.

FRIDAY MORNING, THEY packed Stella's ancient Mercedes with a box of garden vegetables, sleeping bags and a tent Stella had aired out all week, clothes and dishes and flashlights and towels and a hundred other things one or both of them thought they might need. China sat in the backseat with her head out the window and Janie rode in the front. They drove into the mountain range northeast of Yelm, taking country roads and old highways instead of the freeway. A forest service road took them into deep woods where the air was twenty degrees cooler and smelled like Christmas trees. Volkswagen vans, pickup trucks, and a few motorcycles surrounded an old International school bus painted a bright bubble-gum pink. Grateful Dead stickers clung to the bus' bumpers and the windows were festooned with tie-dyed curtains. Janie found herself checking to see if Paul's Panhead was parked with the bikes. She was both relieved and disappointed when she didn't see it.

Stella parked the car, and China bolted out the back door, ready to investigate other dogs. A young woman was getting out of the bus, carrying a box of groceries. When she saw Stella she put her load down and came running over. She wore a peasant blouse over a bikini and had slanted bright green eyes.

"Stella – You're here!"

"Hey Cat!" Stella gave the girl a hug. "This is Janie."

Janie felt first-day-of-school nervous. "Hi."

"Did you make that top?" Cat pointed at Janie's homemade camisole.

"I can show you how to make one if you want."

Cat put her arm around Janie and led her away. "Cat is short for Catherine but I've been Cat forever. Let's be best friends starting today and make all these old men crazy with desire."

Stella laughed as they walked away. "Won't take much to

do that." He gave Janie a wink and picked up the box Cat had put down. "Do you know where Cookie is?"

"Setting up the kitchen in camp." Cat pulled Janie along by the hand. "Once Stella finds Cookie we'll never see them again all weekend."

At the top of the hill the path ended. There was a clearing among Douglas fir trees with four picnic tables and a rock ringed fire pit. A stack of firewood had already been kindled, and boxes of supplies sat on one of the tables. A woman stood at the table unpacking and organizing a kitchen area. She wore a long muslin dress that fell off her shoulders. Her black hair was coiled into a large bun that rested at the base of her slender tan neck. The woman turned when she heard Stella whistle. She smiled and held out her arms. "I thought you'd never get here."

Stella scooped Cookie into his arms and kissed her on the forehead, nose, and mouth. Janie stood waiting while Cat dug through a bag of groceries.

Stella put Cookie down, a smile lit up his face. "Cookie, this is Janie."

Cookie held out her arms, hugging Janie swift and sure. "It's good to finally meet you. Stella's been telling me about you."

Janie smiled but didn't quite know what to say.

Stella hadn't stopped touching Cookie, and now she swatted at him, eyes twinkling. "Go help set up the tipi and leave Janie with me."

Stella kissed Cookie again on the top of her head and walked down the path calling over his shoulder, "When I'm done you aren't getting rid of me."

Cookie laughed. "Who says I'd want to?"

With Stella gone it was just Cookie, Janie, and a few women she didn't know. Cookie seemed to be in charge of organizing and setting up the cooking area and she did it without acting like she was. She asked Janie to fill some buckets with water. China ended her investigation and now stuck close by. Janie found the old-fashioned water pump nearby and worked the worn red handle until cold water shot out, hitting China in the face as she bit at the stream. The trail opened into a meadow. A few small tents were already set up but Janie didn't see a tipi, just a pile of canvas and long poles surrounded by Stella, Ernie, and some men Janie didn't know. They drank cans of beer and stared at the task ahead of them.

Janie watched for a few minutes and then headed back to the picnic tables.

Cat had opened one of the coolers. The other women were gone.

"Where is everybody?" Janie asked.

"They went to the river for a swim." Cat said.

THE REST OF the day she spent with Cat and China. They joined the others at the river and swam and suntanned. They painted each other's toenails with nail polish Cat had on the bus. Cat talked and Janie figured out she was meant to listen. She didn't mind. She met most of the people who showed up over the course of the day but gave up trying to remember their names. Delores and Amber came and Janie stayed away from them. She didn't want to talk about anything connected to The Habit or Paul Jesse.

By early evening a fire roared in the pit and the smell of spices and smoke reminded Janie and Cat how hungry they were. Janie got a plate from the stack on the table and took it to Cookie who was bent over a cast iron pot spooning out food.

"Hey *chica*! Did you have a good time today?" Cookie dished beans mixed with rice and some vegetables onto Janie's plate.

Janie had never been called a name other than Janie. She kind of liked it. "Yeah. This smells good."

"*Moros y Cristianos* – that's Spanish for Moors and Christians and Cuban for black beans and rice and save room for later. I'm making my *abuela*'s *plantanos dulces fritos* – that's my grandma's recipe for a kind of fried banana dessert." Cookie served herself up a plate and handed the spoon to the next person in line. "I want to eat with you and Stella." Janie followed her to one of the tables and sat on the bench next to Cookie and across from Stella. Loaves of bread and bowls of salad made their way down the center of each table.

Stella wiped the beans from his plate with a slice of bread. "About time. I thought you weren't sitting down tonight."

Cookie laughed. "I nibbled all day."

The rice and beans were served with a salad of oranges, avocados, and some crunchy white vegetable that was cut into tiny slivers and tasted sweet. Janie had never eaten such exotic food before. "I wish I could cook like this. How did you learn?"

"My grandmother on my mom's side taught me how to make traditional Cuban food. She moved in with us after my grandfather died. I was six. I think I learned to cook to anger my *mami*. She's a law professor at UC-Berkeley. She wanted me to be one too. Or an attorney like my dad. Or at least a profession requiring an advanced degree. My mom believes cooking is demeaning. If you want to learn, I'd be happy to show you."

"I'd like that. It's really good." Janie sliced another piece of bread from the loaf. "Did you make the bread too?"

"I can't take all the credit. Alex, that big guy in the red T-shirt, he baked the bread all last week and froze it in my walk-in."

Stella filled a cup with wine from a big bottle on the table. "Cookie has a restaurant in Eugene."

"Not a restaurant. I have a food cart on campus and a kitchen I use for some catering. I aspire to own a restaurant."

Stella reached across the table and caressed Cookie's arm. "I keep saying you could do food at my place."

Cookie pulled her hand away. "Listen *mijo*, you know what I think about the way you've chosen to make your money. Sell that titty bar and then we'll talk."

Stella looked away.

Cookie reached out this time and stroked Stella's arm. "Never mind. Over this we will agree to disagree." She looked at Janie. "Want to learn to fry a plantain, *chica*?"

Janie had never cooked much before she came to Stella's.

She was so young when her mom died and Daddy cooked simple meals designed to get by. Norma preferred frozen dinners or eating out and rarely cooked. Cookie showed Janie how to slice the plantains and slip them into a skillet of hot peanut oil and just when to turn them.

She helped Cookie fry dozens sprinkling them with cinnamon and sugar. After the plantains were eaten and the dishes cleaned they sat around the fire watching the flames die to coals. As the evening ended Janie leaned against China, who slept snuggled against her back. Cat had attached herself to her ex-boyfriend. It looked to Janie like everyone was coupled up for the night. Stella sat across the pit from her. Cookie nestled in the V of his lap, his arms wrapped around her. Cookie rose and stretched joined by Stella a moment later. They waved goodnight to Janie and walked to the tipi in the dark meadow.

Janie waited awhile before she left the fire and went off to find her small tent. He'd told her that the tipi would give her good dreams but she didn't want to be in the tipi with all the couples. The meadow in the dark was beautiful. The sky looked like a planetarium show – the stars were so close and bright. She crawled into the tent with China and into her sleeping bag, zipping up the door behind her and rubbing China's forehead until she drifted off to sleep.

Late in the night the familiar sound of a motorcycle on gravel woke her. She turned over in her sleeping bag and made herself close her eyes.

Tight-Wire

JANIE UNZIPPED THE TENT AND STEPPED OUTSIDE. CHINA stretched and shook herself, happy to be released from the small space. Early morning light filled the sky. Janie had been awake, waiting for morning to come so she could sneak away without seeing Paul. She dressed and crept through camp, hoping she wouldn't wake anyone. Yesterday she had noticed a trailhead at the campground entrance and she headed there now.

Janie walked to the makeshift kitchen and saw Paul's bike. She took some fruit, a jar for water, and part of a loaf of bread. She'd stay away all day. Maybe by sunset he'd be gone. As she walked down the path to the main campground, she began to relax. Being near Paul made her feel as if she couldn't catch a breath.

The lower campground looked like a suburban neighborhood transplanted into the woods and smelled like bacon. Janie used the cinder block bathhouse to shower. There weren't any tipis down here. People camped out of motor homes and trailers; only a few had tents. Although it was still early, people were up. When she'd been on the road before Stella's, she liked wandering around neighborhoods checking out houses from the street, looking in windows, seeing what people did. It made her sad but she could never resist a glimpse of regular families, eating meatloaf and watching *Gunsmoke*.

Janie found the trailhead. An official looking notice encouraged hikers to write their names, time they left, and destination in a battered notebook chained to the post. Janie dug in her pack for a pen and wrote, *Saturday morning early*, then paused and scratched it out. She wished she'd left a note for Stella. Nobody else would miss her.

PAUL SAT AT the picnic table sipping his coffee, waiting for Janie to appear. He had tried to get there earlier, but it didn't happen because Ernie wanted him to cop enough acid to light up this birthday party. Paul was happy to oblige, but he didn't have it on him and had to see the twins in Seattle. They didn't get off work until late. That was the thing about dealing, you could spend hours just waiting to score. You had to be patient, had to have time to kill, had to be willing to wait. Now with a pocketful of acid tabs, the rest of the weekend was his.

He wanted to talk to Janie. He had stayed away from her, going to the bar only to do business. He stayed away hoping he'd forget her. Before if he stayed away long enough most memories lost their sharpness leaving behind a dull ache, but he couldn't stop thinking about Janie. He'd gone down to San Francisco to do some business, and when he got back he'd stopped by Dee's place. Janie wasn't there. He went to The Habit. Dee said Janie was living with Stella. She made it sound like they were together, but Ernie told him Janie had been beaten up pretty bad, maybe raped, trying to hitch out of town. Paul wanted to ask Stella how she was but he couldn't. Stella never liked him and wouldn't give Paul anything, not even information. He hoped he'd see her. Make sure she was all right. She'd come around sooner or later.

Ernie, shirtless and sunburned, came down the path from the tipi. "Hey Paul! When'd you get here?" He belched and rearranged his shorts.

"Late." Paul took a joint from his shirt pocket and lit it, taking a hit and passing it to Ernie. "Happy birthday, man."

Ernie took the joint and examined it, smoothing the seam with his finger.

"Let's see what you got."

Paul took a baggie with a sheet of paper stamped with tiny purple pyramids. He handed it to Ernie.

Ernie cut two squares from the sheet with his Swiss Army knife, popped them in his mouth, and handed Paul two squares. "Let's get lost."

JANIE ROLLED ON her back and stretched out in the sun. Sometime today, unless she didn't go back, she was going to see Paul. Unless he left. That was a possibility. Thinking about him made her stomach feel tight and a little sick. She wondered how much he knew about what had happened to her. That's how she thought about it *the thing that happened to me* and she did her best not to think about it. She wondered what she would say to Paul if she saw him and why she thought about him at all.

Nobody was on the trail when she'd started out, and she didn't see many hikers as the day wore on. She and China had the mountain to themselves. She hiked all morning and they stopped in a sunny clearing for lunch spreading a towel on the grass. Janie fell asleep with China's head resting against her stomach.

When she woke, the light had changed. Maybe Paul would be gone by now. She hiked down the mountain to the swimming hole. She stayed there watching the light retreat slowly behind the mountains listening to the sounds of the nearby campground, the wet thunk of wood being chopped, and kids playing. When the light changed to shadows on the water she climbed the hill to the camp, and her heart began to pound. She rehearsed what she would say. She repeated her lines like a mantra. As she cleared the top of the hill, Paul Jesse was the first person she saw, standing there like some hippie version of Paul Bunyan, swinging an axe, cutting up a stack of firewood. Nobody else was around. Her stomach dropped. Paul looked right at her. She wanted him to hold her and she wanted to hurt him. Janie kept walking. He followed her.

"Wait up a minute." He was right behind her, touching the back of her arm.

She stopped, trying to control her voice. "What?"

He didn't take his hand off her. "Look, I heard what happened –"

All she felt was the place his fingers met the bare skin of her arm. Her words dried up, and whatever she'd planned to say was lost.

Amber trotted toward them from the meadow. She slung her arms around Paul, and he dropped his hand from Janie. "Hi Paul, I'm so high, Paul." Amber giggled. "Janie, you have any of that cherry lip gloss?"

"No, I don't have any lip gloss." Janie started walking to the meadow.

"I want that cherry kind. I could eat a stick of it, you know? Janie, where you going? Don't just walk off. It's okay about the lip gloss. I'll ask Dee."

STELLA SWUNG THE croquet mallet while he waited for his turn. The game had broken down now that it was getting dark and just about everyone was high. None of them could remember whose turn it was anyway, or even how to play. Janie hadn't been around all day but Stella wasn't worried. China was with her. Ernie turned on everybody who asked for a hit of the acid. Stella didn't do any himself. Just being around so many hippies all lit up at the same time made him think of San Francisco, 1968, the year he'd come home. He'd met Cookie that summer.

Wandering around the UC campus, feeling lost and alone, he'd seen a group of protesters in Sproul Plaza under a sign that read, *Vietnam Veterans Against the War*. Long-haired men in army fatigues, amputees in wheelchairs, all of them united by the same broken look. The crowd wasn't big, and there were only a handful of women. Stella stood at the edge of the crowd listening to a former captain – now a double amputee in a wheelchair – speak. Stella didn't realize tears were running down his face until he looked into the eyes of the petite Latina standing next to him. She put her hand on his arm and led him away to a house she shared on Prince Street. She made him tea with honey and brought it to her room. They talked the rest of that day and well into the night. By morning he was in love with Galletas Novella. Everyone called her Cookie.

Here in the meadow with the sun on her brown skin, she looked no older than the day they met eight years ago. One of the girls had painted a butterfly on her cheek, and her thick hair floated in waves to her hips. She knocked the ball through the hoop with her mallet and laughed at Ernie. Wearing Dee's pink kimono and a pair of Hawaiian print swim trunks, Ernie carried a can of beer in one hand and a parasol in the other. Delores hung on his arm, trailing a feathered boa behind her.

From the edge of camp Stella saw China come bounding through the tall grass with Janie close behind. He put down his mallet and waved her over. Her face was pink and her eyes looked as if she'd been crying. "You were gone a long time."

"I went for a walk up the mountain and fell asleep."

China crowded around them snorting and chuckling. "Looks like China had a good day. I'm glad you took her with you or I would have been worried."

"Can I sleep in the tipi tonight?"

"Sure." Stella patted her back. "Bad dreams?"

"I just don't want to be alone."

JANIE MOVED HER sleeping bag to the tipi and walked back to the fire. Cat, her face painted with tiger stripes and whiskers, stood at the picnic table chopping tomatoes. Across from the table, Paul sat on an upended log, smoking a cigarette. He watched while Janie pretended not to notice.

She stuffed her hair into a ponytail. "Want some help?"

Cat handed her a bag of avocados. "Cookie said there's enough beans left to make burritos. You make guacamole. There's limes and garlic in that box."

Janie sliced an avocado, removing the pit and putting the fruit in a large wooden bowl.

Cat chopped the tomatoes. "See they look like baby turtles when you turn them over. You should get some acid from Ernie and catch up with me. You look kind of sad."

"I'm just tired. I hiked all day." Janie used a fork to smash the avocados with some juice from the limes.

"Yeah. But you should do some acid anyway. Acid cleans out your psychic blockages – like a laxative." She laughed.

"I'll pass."

Cat shook her head. "That fork's not really doing it for you." She stuck her hands in the bowl and began to squeeze the avocados. "I don't know why we're making all this food. Everybody's so high they're not going to eat."

Amber trotted over to Paul and stood in front of him, shaking her head back and forth like a bobble-head doll. "Has anybody seen my brush? When you got hair like mine you got to brush it a lot or you get rats in it."

"No shit? Rats?" Cat licked the avocado from her finger.

"Not real rats. Of course not," said Amber. "Rats are a special word for the tangles girls like me get if we don't detangle and condition and all like that." She leaned over close to Paul, her breasts peeking out of the halter top she was wearing. She giggled. "You want to brush me out, Paul?"

Cat wiped her hands on an old towel. "Thought you said you didn't have a brush?"

Paul smiled and looked at Janie.

Janie chopped garlic.

Amber tossed her head like a pony. "Paul wouldn't need a brush to take care of my tangles."

"Find yourself another stylist." Paul stood up. "I'll see you later." He walked away toward the meadow. Amber trotted after him.

The thirty or so people congregated around the picnic tables as the smell of Cookie's black beans filled the air. Tripper,

an older guy who kept telling anybody who'd listen that he'd
been to Woodstock, brought out a large pan of brownies. He offered
one to Janie. She could smell the pot from them and declined.

Ernie grabbed a handful from the pan. "Just what the doctor ordered."

Tripper put the pan on the table. "Watch out. They'll sneak
up on you."

Despite Cat's prediction, everybody ate. Janie took her plate
and sat next to Stella and Cookie. Stella had taken off his shirt.
Painted in gold and silver body paint across the broad canvas of
his back were several stars. "What are the stars for, Stella?"

Ernie, sitting close by heard her. "You never told Janie how
you got to be Stella?"

"It never came up." Stella wiped a bit of bean from the
corner of Cookie's mouth.

Ernie took a swig of beer. "Well, it's kind of more than just
your name, Clarence."

Janie tilted her head, confused. "Who's Clarence?"

Ernie grinned. "Janie, let me introduce you to Clarence
Stubbs."

Delores plopped herself down next to Ernie and took a bag
of pot from her jacket. "Look what I've got."

Ernie grabbed the bag, opened it and smelled the contents.
"Nice looking bag of bud. Let's break it out."

Delores grabbed it back and emptied the bag of pot on a
clean plate. From her wallet she took a plastic card and began sift-
ing seeds and stems from the buds.

Paul sat down next to her and took the plate. "You can't
roll for shit, Dee."

Ernie cleared his throat. "So, I was telling Janie Stella's
name and all."

Ernie leaned back against the table, scratching his belly
before taking a hit from the joint that came his way. "We all
came up from the city. San Francisco. Me and Clarence met in

Sister Mary Joseph's second grade class. Paul was two years behind us. Still is.

"Anyways, me and Clare were friends from school and the neighborhood. Paul's sister, Cathy, and my sister, Tina, were best friends so we knew each other. After high school, Clare wanted to go to college so he enlisted and went off to be a medic. He shipped out pretty quick cause of how many casualties the corpsmen were taking that year." Ernie stared into the fire.

Stella shook his head. "Man, do we really have to talk about this?"

Ernie didn't answer.

Ernie's voice sounded like it was coming all the way from Vietnam itself. "You know, they don't train you for war. I mean, you go to boot camp, but everything's out of a book. It's all clean there. Nobody's really trying to kill you."

Stella stood up and walked away. Cookie followed him.

No one spoke for a moment. There was only the sound of fire popping and the wind in the trees.

Ernie poked at the fire with a long stick stirring up the coals.

"As you get off the plane seems like everybody and their mother wants you dead. I got assigned to Lima Company and Stella was already there. He was our corpsman – our medic. Man, I was so happy to see somebody from home, somebody I knew. He'd already done one tour. At first I couldn't figure out why he re-enlisted, but by the time I left I got it. You just change so far you don't recognize the you that you used to be. You can't see yourself back in the world." Ernie took a sip of his beer.

"Nobody tells you how to survive heavy fire. They don't tell you that if you're six foot four and a medic – like Stella – you're a prime target. Stella made it through his first tour 'cause he hung around the fire team and moved with them the first three months. Stella did the same for me. He showed me the ropes.

"You know how in the movies if a soldier gets hit some asshole always yells 'Medic'? That never happened in 'Nam. Medics had code names so Charlie wouldn't know to shoot you.

Sometimes they'd get a man down and wait for someone to come give aid. That was the motherfucker with Stella's job most of the time. Sniper'd be off in the razor grass waiting for a kill.

"So Clare got the name Stella because our platoon leader was a wop and a fucking Brando fan – I guess 'stella' means star in Italian. At night all you could see was his teeth. By the time I met up with him, he'd been Stella for some time. We were stationed out of Nui Kim San. Close to Marble Mountain and Da Nang. By then he'd learned shit they don't teach at Lejeune. I seen him stop a sucking chest wound with the cellophane off the dude's cigarette pack. And when he ran out of morphine, he'd give dudes M&Ms and tell them it was some righteous dope. We all thought Stella had some kind of special top-secret government drugs on him. Man, you had to be missing a body part or so wasted you were going home in a bodybag to get one of those M&Ms." Ernie looked up and shook his head. "Enough. We were both lucky motherfuckers. I'm going to see a man about a horse." Ernie got up, got another beer from the cooler and walked out into the night.

Delores sat next to Paul. "I met Ernie and Stella through Paul. Paul and me were living in the Haight on Piedmont. Remember that little studio we had, Paul? It was in the basement, but the windows faced the courtyard. This was back when you could rent a place in the city for pretty cheap." Paul didn't smile or nod. He looked at Janie and she wouldn't look back.

Delores's hair was piled up, and her skin glowed in the firelight, the auburn in her hair reflected the fire. In this light, she looked like the beauty she must have been ten years ago. "I was dancing at the Spanish Moon over on Exeter in the Tenderloin. Paul came by to pick me up and he sees this fat dude with a ponytail at the bar. Turned out to be Ernie and they knew each other. After my set, we all had some drinks and Ernie says I should get a friend and come dance at his place. It's going to be in Alaska, he says. The pipeline and all. Turned out they never made it to Alaska, and I ended up in bumfuck Washington with Ernie dancing at The Habit. Now you know everything, Janie."

Janie could see it wasn't Dee's intention to be friendly, or to just tell a story. Delores was marking her territory.

People began putting food away, nibbling on leftovers as they cleaned up.

Stella and Cookie came back with Ernie. Stella carried a set of congas roped together over his shoulder. He put them down and started to play. Janie had never seen him play anything. He popped out a rhythm, making the skins sing. Someone played a guitar. Moon had a harmonica. A girl called Pickle had a flute. It seemed to Janie everyone could play something.

Cat and Cookie started dancing with a black-haired girl named Demetra. She was belly dancing to the music. She wore a red velvet skirt that twirled out like a big red flower as she danced. Tiny bells sewn to her halter-top jingled to the music. Janie stood at the edge of the crowd watching the girls dance. In another life she had been fearless. Since the rape she didn't wear girl clothes, didn't dance, didn't do anything that would make men notice her. She missed the dancing. More people were moving with the music. As she swayed into the crowd, Janie closed her eyes for just a second and pictured herself stepping off a rock cliff five hundred feet above a cobalt sea.

PAUL WAS HIGH, definitely high, but he didn't think that even if he were straight he'd be able to stop looking at her. Janie was dancing. She moved like a storm coming in fast across the mountains. Her face was flushed pink in the firelight, her eyes wide open. She spun, she strutted, she barely missed colliding with other bodies. She was consumed by grace. Janie was dancing, and her face was so open with joy it hurt Paul to see the inch-long scar on her forehead and the bump from her broken nose. He had never wanted to touch a woman the way he wanted to touch Janie.

EVENTUALLY THE DANCING stopped. Cookie and Stella had gone off to the tipi. Janie went to clean up at the pump, trying not to stumble in the dark. From the path she could hear Tripper playing alone on the guitar. She felt Paul behind her before she could see him.

"Janie, can I talk to you?"

"It depends on what you have to say."

"Look I feel bad about what happened – "

"I don't want your sympathy." Words she didn't know she wanted to say kept coming. "If you love me, say it, if you don't, then leave me alone."

Janie knew it was true once she said it. The words hung between them. A breath, a sound, the falling away of sound, leaving a deep silence neither moved to fill.

A flashlight beam interrupted them. Janie left Paul standing at the pump and almost ran into Delores on the path as she hurried to get away from him.

COALS STILL BURNED in the small stone ring in the center of the tipi, giving Paul enough light to find her. He'd looked in her small tent but it was empty. He'd sat by the fire for an hour waiting until he knew what he would do. In the crowded tipi, he unrolled his bag. Janie didn't move. The dog whined once and moved to the bottom of the bag. For a long while, he lay next to her, propped up on one arm looking down at her in the dim light.

Her eyes blinked open.

Paul touched his fingers to her lips. She lay still, her breath warm against his fingers. He outlined her lips slowly, wanting this moment to make up for everything that had gone wrong before now. He traced the scar on her forehead, his fingers above her eyes and down across the bump on her nose. He could see everything in her eyes. His hand cupped her face and he mouthed silently, "I'm sorry." She nodded, kissed the palm of his hand, and turned on her side.

Paul lowered himself down next to her, his face buried in the back of her neck. He pressed his face into the hollow, breathing deeply.

Slipping into Darkness

SHE COULDN'T GET CLOSE ENOUGH. WHEN THEY WERE together, she had to be next to him, touching him, his hand on the back of her neck, her hand on his thigh, his eyes like fingers against her skin. When they weren't together she was waiting.

Her routine stayed the same. She knew Stella didn't exactly approve of Paul. They never talked about him. She was always home before Stella got home from work. Things hadn't seemed to change. She sewed and cooked and read her books, but most days after Stella left for work, the roar of Paul's Panhead on the gravel, or the softer sound of his little red Opel, announced his arrival. He called her his running partner. He called her his naked angel.

Going with Paul while he dealt had been fine, at first. They were alone – traveling, talking, telling each other versions of their lives, or often not talking. He didn't ask the usual questions about why she'd left home, and he didn't ask or care what she'd done to survive before he came along. He understood that whatever you did to get by didn't have to do with who you were.

They traveled between the same low-rent houses and apartments while he dealt. She sat on dozens of couches, stained with spilled beer and bong water, watching muted TV with Pink Floyd or Led Zeppelin on the stereo. The refrigerators in these places held empty condiment containers and moldy food. Encrusted dishes sat stacked in rusted sinks. Water ran tan and metallic from the taps. After hours of sitting around talking, money and dope would change hands, and they would leave for the next place. But later, alone in the car, when he reached across the seat and rubbed her thigh and she slipped her fingers through his belt loop, there was no place else she wanted to be.

GRAY CLOUDS HUNG low in the sky. Fall had come on overnight. Janie sat at the kitchen table waiting. Stella was at work when Paul finally rolled in the back door about noon.

"Hey, baby. Get your stuff and come with me."

"Where are we going?"

"I want you to meet Betty." China ran around Paul sniffing at him and wagging her tail. He slipped her a dog biscuit from his pocket. Paul now kept a box of dog biscuits for China in the car so she wouldn't bark at him so much. "Betty's kind of like a mom to me." Paul sat down at the kitchen table and scratched China behind her ears. "I met her kids at a bar in Seattle. I stayed with them for a couple of months when I was coming down. She's good people."

"Promise to bring me home before it gets too late."

"When are you going to stay out all night with me?"

"When I know."

"Know what?"

"Something."

"What if I said move in with me – "

"But you didn't and you only have a trailer that smells like socks and you said you didn't want an old lady – "

"*Mea culpa.*"

"Drop the Catholic talk, choirboy, I'll go with you." Janie grabbed a jacket and locked up.

DRIVING THROUGH A subdivision outside of Seattle, they wound their way through looping streets with names like Elm and Pine lined with nearly identical ranch-style homes. Janie looked out the window, wondering how Paul could navigate through the maze of lookalike streets. She'd depended on freeway signs for directions and hadn't stayed in a place long enough to know it well. Eventually he turned onto a cul-de-sac and pulled into the driveway of a house with a seagull windsock floating from the porch. Janie followed him up the steps. He knocked once, and the door opened as if someone had been watching them from the window. A wrinkled little woman in cateye glasses pulled him in and hugged him. She wore a flowered scarf over her curly white hair and orange pedal-pusher pants. She grabbed Paul's face between her hands and pulled it down, kissing both his cheeks. Her kisses were the wet noisy kind.

"Here's my boy! Get in here. Who's this you've brought with you?"

"This is Janie." He stepped aside, and the little woman grabbed Janie by the face and pulled her down to eye level. She must have been four foot eleven, tops.

"Well, so this is the Janie I've been hearing about. Honey, I'm Betty. You just come on in and make yourself to home." She planted a kiss on Janie's cheek. She smelled like Jergens lotion and talcum powder. "Come on back to the kitchen. I'm right in the middle of feeding my babies."

This house wasn't like the places they usually went to. It was more like the kind of house Janie daydreamed about. They stepped through a swinging door into the yellow kitchen. Cages holding at least a hundred birds lined the counter. The birds began making a racket.

"Are you hungry, babies?" Betty said. She picked up an open can of dog food and a pair of tweezers. "Make yourself useful, Paul. Start at the other end. Show Janie how."

Paul picked up another can from a case by the back door. He opened it and got tweezers from a chipped mug. At the opposite end of the counter he reached inside a cage containing a solitary robin. White gauze held the bird's wing at its side.

Paul gently lifted the bird out and examined the wing. "This one been here awhile?"

"Not too long. I had some trouble setting the wing." Betty placed chunks of dog food in a starling's open beak.

Paul unwrapped the bandage and straightened the robin's wing. He blew softly, ruffling feathers for a closer inspection. "Looks pretty good." He rewrapped the gauze and placed the bird back in the cage.

Betty held a small brown bird in her hands. "You have a gift with the birds, Paul. You should be using it."

"Now, Betty—"

"Don't 'Now, Betty' me."

Janie watched as Paul picked up the tweezers. "Can I feed one?"

"Let me show you." With the tweezers he positioned a chunk of dog food above the robin's beak. The beak opened wide, and Paul dropped the food in. He handed Janie the tweezers. "You should see this place in spring."

Betty opened the next cage. "Every little child finds some nestling on the ground. They touch it and poke at it until the parents won't come around, and then they don't know what to do with it. So, they bring them here to me. Right now, I've got mostly sick or injured birds. Some'll winter over. I started this place after I retired for something to do – something helpful to do. I'm busier now than when I was working."

Janie fed bird after bird, cleaning the tweezers between each cage. "They're so hungry."

Paul sat at the kitchen table and lit a cigarette. "Don't give them too much. They don't know when to stop. This was all I did for a couple of months besides sleep. Feed the birds, clean out their cages, and repeat. When're the twins coming?" A crow, the only bird not in a cage, hopped to Paul's shoulder. When he raised his cigarette to his lips the crow pecked at his fingers. He shooed it away but it flapped back to him. "Stop that, Mac."

"They'll be here for supper. Put that damn bird outside if you want to smoke in peace. Mac will not abide cigarettes. I ought to rent him out to one of those quit-smoking places." Betty put a lid on the dog food and returned it to the refrigerator. "You kids like a drink with me?"

The kitchen might have been filled with birds in cages, but it wasn't any dirtier or smellier than a veterinarian's office. White eyelet curtains hung in the window above the sink. Janie smelled something good cooking. The cabinets were too high for Betty to reach, but she had a stepping stool she kicked into place. She took an old-fashioned glass cocktail shaker and a bottle of vermouth out of a cabinet. From the gold refrigerator she brought out vodka, 7UP, cocktail onions, green olives, and maraschino cherries. She handed Paul a beer, made herself a martini, and then made Janie a Shirley Temple without asking, as if she knew Janie was underaged.

"My dad used to make me these when I'd go to his work," Janie said.

"Your daddy a bartender?"

"Yes, ma'am."

"I was, too. Hardest working people in the world. Except for bird ladies and mothers. I must be a glutton for punishment because I've done all three." Betty sipped her drink and lit a cigarette. Mac squawked and fluttered to the window. Betty slid the window open and the bird flew to a fir tree in the back yard. "Where're your people from, Janie?"

"We lived in Yakima. But I don't really have anybody anymore."

Betty took a long look at her.

"Well, darling, now you have Paul, and you have me. And if this son of a gun gets out of hand," she nodded toward Paul, "you just let me know and I'll have a little come-to-Jesus with him."

"Man, Betty–" Paul protested, smiling at her.

"I think I hear the twins. Come on, honey, I want you to meet my boys."

The twins turned out to be over six feet tall and two hundred pounds. They slapped Paul on the back, kissed their mother and let her fuss over them, and politely nodded to Janie. Paul and the twins settled into the living room sofa with their drinks. Janie followed Betty down the steps to the basement. She opened the door to a small room and turned on a dim light. "I want to show you something, honey."

In a floor-to-ceiling cage was a snowy owl, the most beautiful bird Janie had ever seen. Perched on a tree stump, it stood at least two feet tall and was almost pure white with a few bars of dark brown feathers across his wings. The owl's yellow eyes, never blinking, focused on Janie. Long black talons poked out from the feathers of its feet.

"Betty, he's beautiful."

The owl swiveled its head, watching them.

"He came to me about a week ago. He's just a young'un." She looked at Janie. "He had a run-in with a power line, but I think he can be released this spring."

"Can I touch him?"

"No, darlin', he'd take your hand right off. Beautiful from a distance but not meant to hold on to."

Janie followed Betty out. At the bottom of the stairs, Betty put her hand on Janie's shoulder. "Let me tell you a little something I wish somebody would've told me. You don't get to choose who you love, honey. You only get to choose how you love them. Some people you can love up close, and some people you got to love from a distance, or just like that bird down there, they'll tear the heart right out of you." Betty adjusted her scarf. "Now, let's go on upstairs and have some dinner before those boys tear the place apart."

JANIE AND PAUL stopped by The Habit on the way to drop her at Stella's. Paul slipped his shades on and went in ahead of Janie. She paused at the door to tell Stella about the owl. That's when she saw the guy from the white van.

He stood at the bar buying a beer. For a split second, Janie didn't believe it could be the same guy, but as he turned to go back to his table she saw his face. Acne scars and stringy brown hair. Janie grabbed Stella's arm.

"Stella, that's the guy from the van. Right there at the bar." She took a step back against the door. Her heart beat like she'd been running hard. For a minute she thought she'd fall down.

Stella rose off his stool. "Are you sure?"

"Yes."

Stella led her out the front door to the lot. "Do you see what he was driving?"

She scanned the parking lot. "There it is – the white van by the Dodge Dart."

They went inside through the back door, where she could see the guy close enough without him seeing her. "That's him, Stella."

Stella unlocked the office door. "Wait here. I'll be right back."

STELLA TOOK A good look at the guy. Greasy brownish hair covered by an even greasier baseball cap worn backwards. The face acne scarred. Probably in his early twenties, wiry build. He wore a gray delivery jacket with a red and white name patch. Stella had seen him a few times but not often. Stella leaned across the bar next to Paul and signalled Ernie over.

Paul looked over the top of his shades at him.

Ernie asked, "What's up?"

Stella spoke quietly. "Janie saw the dude who beat her up."

"Where?" Paul began to stand.

Stella put his hand firmly on his arm. "Sit down. Don't go spooking him."

Ernie's eyes scanned the crowd. "Who is it? It wasn't a regular?"

Stella kept his hand on Paul's arm. "I've seen him here

before, but he's no regular. Get Dee to watch the bar for a minute. Janie's in the office. Let's go."

Ernie yelled over to Delores. "Dee – watch the bar."

Stella steered Paul in front of him to the office. He tapped on the door. "Janie, it's Stella. Let us in." The lock clicked open and Janie stood there shaking.

"Are you sure it's the same guy?" Ernie asked.

"Positive."

Paul put his hand on the doorknob. "I'm going to waste him."

"Hold on, man." Stella stepped in front of the door, blocking him in. "You waste him and you might as well say goodbye now 'cause you'll be doing time until your kid grows a beard."

"I'm not going to get busted."

Stella shook his head. "You got 'busted' written all over your goddamn face."

Janie looked at Paul. "Don't go."

Ernie lit a cigarette and sat down on the desk. "So what are we going to do? I don't want some freak coming around fucking up the women."

"I have an idea." Stella looked at Paul. "You got any of that acid?"

"What the fuck for? I'm not wasting perfectly good acid – "

"Hear me out." Stella looked at Janie. "Let's say we dose him. Dose him good and take him for a ride. Let his karma catch up with him out there in the dark."

"It's not on tabs. It's liquid 25." Paul shook his head. "He's going to get off like a rocket."

"It's kind of perfect." Ernie smiled. "You remember Willy? Far as I know he's still in the nuthouse from a bad trip back in '72. His old lady was giving him a blowjob and he started freaking out thinking she was a cannibal. He put her in a fucking coma and tried to burn down their house."

Stella looked at Janie. "What do you say Janie?"

Janie nodded. "Let's do it."

PAUL CARRIED A glass of beer laced with a dropper full of LSD 25 to the guy's table. "Hey man, the woman at the bar said to give you this." Paul motioned to Delores and put the beer in front of him.

The guy looked at Delores and nodded. "Far out."

Paul sipped at his beer and sat down. "I'm Paul."

"Name's Larry." Larry stared at Amber as she spread and re-spread her long tanned legs at the edge of the stage. "Man, I'd like to get me some of that." He picked up his beer and took a drink.

"So, what's your gig, Larry?" Behind his shades Paul's eyes narrowed. Liquid acid was a fast rush. Any minute this dude was going into orbit.

"I deliver parts for Rock's Auto. It's not bad." Larry took a longer pull off the beer, downing half.

Paul waved Ernie over to the table. "I'm into delivery myself."

"Oh yeah?" Larry rubbed his eyes. A red flush crept up his neck and over his face. "What do you deliver?"

Amber held her breasts in her hands and licked her lips, squatting down in front of Paul.

Ernie made his way to the table through the crowd.

"Altered states of consciousness." Paul sipped his beer. "You okay, Larry? Not feeling too good? Maybe you need some air."

"What was in that beer?"

Ernie clamped a hand on Larry's shoulder and lifted him from the chair. "You've had enough for one night, pal. Come on. Out you go. Give me a hand, Paul."

Paul and Ernie muscled Larry through the crowd and out into the night.

STELLA WATCHED AS Paul and Ernie walked the guy through the bar as if he was a regular drunk they were 86ing. After the door closed behind them, Stella went back to the office. He knocked twice. Janie had her jacket on and clutched it tight, holding on to the edge of the world.

"You sure you want to come, Janie? It won't change anything."

"I don't care. Let's go."

Stella and Janie were in his car. Paul drove the guy's white van. Stella couldn't see anyone in the passenger seat. He hoped Paul hadn't done anything stupid. Paul had a short fuse and he usually carried a piece in his pocket. Stella pulled out first and Paul followed in the van.

Janie stared straight ahead.

Stella drove out to the tree farm where he'd found Janie's stuff after the night that brought her into his life. He wished it had never happened for her sake, but she wouldn't be living with him if it hadn't. The drive seemed to go on forever before he reached a rutted logging road and the spot where he assumed she'd been raped, though she'd never said and he'd never asked. He stopped the car. Showtime.

Stella reached across the seat and squeezed Janie's hand. "You ready?"

She nodded and opened her door, swinging her legs out.

Paul got out of the van and left the headlights on. Stella helped Paul pull the guy from the back of the van, letting him fall to the ground. Janie stayed near Stella's car.

The guy pulled himself to his feet and wobbled around rubbing his eyes. "Oh man, oh man. Something's wrong here."

"Yep. You're damn straight on that one, Larry." Paul took hold of his shoulder. "Don't be in such a rush. All will be revealed. Stella, this here is Larry."

"Can't say it's good to meet you, Larry," Stella said. "But you're right about something being wrong. Something here is wrong and I'd say it's you."

"Why are you fucking with me?" Larry's voice shook. "Take me back. I need to go back. Take the van. I don't have any money–"

"Oh, this isn't about money, Larry." Stella kept his words slow and simple. "This is about karma. Let me explain."

"Man, I want to go … " Larry was near tears. He looked around, waving his hands in front of him.

"Karma is like that saying – what goes around, comes around." Paul tossed the van's keys back and forth in his hands. "Larry, I wanted to just plain off your sorry ass, but my friend here said we should let karma have a go at you."

Larry shook his head. "What did I ever do to you?"

Janie stepped up to him. Stella could hear her breath sharp and panicky, but her voice was steady. "It's what you did to me." His face was blank. He didn't remember a thing. "You picked me up hitching a few months ago. Remember?"

"Aww fuck." His eyes swam around in his face. "Look, man, I don't know what she said, but she wanted it."

Stella's fist met Larry's face so fast there was only the sound of bone on bone. Blood spurted from his nose. "I shit you not. Shut the fuck up or you will lose all your fucking teeth. I put this girl back together. I saw what you did to her. Nobody asks for that. I bet she's not the only one."

"I'm telling you – " Larry backed away, wiping the blood from his face. He staggered, digging through the air with his fingers. He covered his head with his arms and dove to the ground. "What's happening?" Larry flailed his arms at the sky and covered his head again.

Paul shoved him against the van, rabbit punching his kidneys and slamming his face into the metal. "Paybacks are a motherfucker."

"Stop, Paul. Nothing can change what he did." Janie's voice sounded quiet and calm. "He should have to take off his clothes like he made me."

Larry was sobbing. He knelt in the dirt. "I didn't know – "

"You heard her." Paul shouted. "Get your clothes off and throw 'em in the van."

"It's cold – "

Paul pulled out a gun from inside of his jacket and aimed it at Larry. "I won't tell you again."

Stella held his breath. He was hoping Paul would control himself. That would be a first.

Larry took off his clothes. Stella exhaled. When his shoes and clothes were in the van, they left him. Paul drove to the road and parked. He wiped down the steering wheel and door handles with a bandana, and wiped the keys off before throwing them on the front seat. He locked the door behind him.

Stella waited with Janie in his car. The heater hummed. Paul climbed in the back and shut the door.

They drove in silence back to The Habit.

Janie looked at Stella. "What's going to happen to him?"

"Probably nothing, honey. He'll wander around until he comes down in a few days. Nothing as bad as what he did to you. I wish we could make all that disappear."

"It's over. I just want to go home."

Stella patted her hand.

Paul reached over the seat and rubbed Janie's neck. "I'll take you home."

Stella pulled into The Habit. After shutting off the motor, he twisted around in his seat. "Why don't you stay at my place tonight, Paul. I won't get out of here for a few more hours." Stella squeezed Janie's shoulder, got out of the car, and headed through The Habit's heavy double door.

Court and Spark

PAUL PUSHED A SHOPPING CART UP AND DOWN THE aisles of the Goodwill. *Raindrops Keep Falling on My Head* played on the sound system. He felt sleepy from the music, the buzzing of the overhead lights, and the joint he'd smoked in the car on the way over. He wanted to buy Janie a present. She'd been a little blue the last week.

Paul pushed the cart with one hand and with the other shopped by touch, his fingers grazing a row of ladies' sweaters. He closed his eyes. When he felt the softest sweater on the rack, he opened his eyes and an ugly green and purple cardigan appeared. Next to it was a fluffy mohair pullover the color of orange sherbet. It looked like the sweaters girls used to wear to basement dances on Saturday nights a life ago. They didn't call it dancing; they called it fishin'. Bumping and grinding against a girl in a hot, dark basement to songs by Marvin Gaye and Tammy Tyrell, Al Green, and Aretha Franklin. The girl could be any girl, but the taste of Juicy Fruit gum and stolen liquor remained the same.

He examined the sweater in his hands for stains, tears, and other flaws before putting it into the cart with his finds – an old Bob Dylan album, a pair of black high-heel shoes with ankle straps that he hoped would fit her, and a little glass fish to catch the light in her bedroom window. She was a Pisces. He hadn't remembered any of these little things about a woman in a long time.

Do You Know the Way to San Jose? blasted away over the buzzing lights as Paul headed to the cashier.

JANIE RINSED A soapy rag in a bucket as she scrubbed the kitchen floor on her hands and knees. She wore a flowered kerchief she'd made from a scrap of fabric. It looked like the ones she remembered her mom wore when she cleaned house: triangles of bright cotton stitched with seam binding or rick-rack around the edges to hold back her hair. Her mom's hair had never been as long as Janie's, but it was the same color and texture – brownish-red and wavy. After her mother died, her dad told her never to cut it, and Janie hadn't. When Paul combed out her hair, it reminded Janie of all the times her dad had done the same. It made her feel as if she and Paul were already a kind of family.

Janie slapped the soapy rag on the floor and scrubbed hard. She heard China outside barking and the rumble of gravel under the wheels of Paul's car. A minute later, the back door opened. A cold October breeze flooded the kitchen. Paul stood in the doorway holding a grocery bag. "Can Janie come out to play?"

"Don't let China in, and don't track up my clean floor."

"What kind of hello is that? I ought to take all my presents and go on back home."

Janie stood up and reached for the bag. "I want to see the presents."

"I came to invite you out for Chinese. Maybe I'll take the dog instead."

China barked from the open door.

Janie slipped her arms around Paul's neck and squeezed. "I love presents and I love Chinese food. Where're we going?"

"It's a surprise. Here – go on, get ready." He handed her the bag.

Janie pulled out a dancer's black leotard, a wrap skirt, black tights, high-heel shoes, and an orange mohair sweater. "Girl clothes!"

Paul blushed and fumbled with the door. "Hurry up and get changed. Bring your equipment. We won't be back tonight."

Janie showered quickly. She'd never been on a date before but this felt close to what she thought it would be like. She put on mascara and almond-flavored lip balm and dressed in the clothes Paul had given her. They fit perfectly. She threw a few things into her denim bag and grabbed a jacket from her room writing a short note on the pad by the phone. *Gone for Chinese with Paul. Say hi to Cookie – Love J.*

When she walked into the living room, Paul whistled. He touched her face with cold, chapped hands and gave her a kiss. She loved his hands. They were beat up and permanently stained with grease around the cuticles from working on his bike. Sometimes while they watched a movie, he'd bite his nails. With a finger in his mouth he looked like who he'd been when he was somebody's child.

He pulled a small black box from his pocket. "I almost forgot to give you this."

She took the box and opened it. Inside was a silver ring with a turquoise stone in the center. She put the ring on her finger and kissed him again. "I feel like it's my birthday."

"That's a few months down the road. You ready?"

"Yeah. Where're we going?"

"On our first real date, Jane."

THEY HEADED SOUTH. Past Portland. Past Eugene. On and on. Out of Oregon. The sun came out through cracks in the dark gray sky. Grass that had been parched white in the summer was now bright green. The forests of Douglas fir made the sudden appearance of vermillion leafed maples seem incandescent. The land changed from forest to farmland to fields. There were cows, black and white Holsteins and all-black Angus. There were crows, their silouettes stark against the sky. As they went farther south, there were sheep with mud-spotted wool. Janie loved car trips. Her favorite rides when she hitched were with long haul truckers who wanted company and conversation. She loved watching the scenery through the windshield like a private movie. The road created the chance to imagine, to talk or not talk. The only sounds for hours might be windshield wipers clicking in a sudden downpour, the heater purring, a song turned up loud on the radio.

Paul drove for hours only stopping for gas and bathrooms. As the sun set, Janie looped her hand through Paul's belt and napped. When she woke it was late, and they were stopped outside The Pinecone Motel.

Janie sat up, pulling her hand free and running her fingers through her hair. "Where are we?"

"Redding. Be right out."

The motel was an older one-level on a horseshoe drive with a grassy courtyard and a palm tree in the center. Each room door was painted a different color. Paul came out a few minutes later from the office with a blue key to a room with a blue door. The room was nice – nothing fancy, but clean and old-fashioned fifties style with a king-sized bed and free cable TV.

PAUL LEFT JANIE at the motel and went out to get food and a six-pack. The next night they'd be in San Francisco – his town. He'd take her to Chinatown and buy her dinner. He whistled as he drove, planning the trip like a tour guide deciding what she had to see this time, and what he would skip and save for the future. That's how she was different from the other women he'd known since he left Mia. He thought about what might come next with her.

Janie was sitting up in bed watching his all-time favorite movie, *Midnight Cowboy*, when he came back. She wore one of his shirts, way too big for her. He popped open a beer and sat next to her on the bed. They ate burritos and drank cold beer, watching as Ratzo Rizzo grew sicker and sicker.

"Is he going to die?" Her voice anxious.

"I can't believe you've never seen this before."

"That means he's going to die. Right?"

"It's a movie."

"But it could really happen."

He loved how her eyes changed color depending on the light and her mood. They looked so blue now. He didn't have to work too hard to figure her out. He touched her hair, and she sat back against him. They fit together no matter what position they were in. *Made for each other*, he thought. In the morning they'd leave early, taking Highway 299 out of Redding instead of the quicker, shorter I-5. They'd hook up to 101–take the coast highway into the city. He wanted to show her something he couldn't put into words. He wanted to show her who he was.

THE LIGHTS ON the Golden Gate Bridge looked to Janie like rhinestones strung across the black velvet of the bay. Fog lay on the water waiting to creep in. Commuter traffic still clogged the bridge. Paul found some music on the radio, and they snaked their way into town.

"I got to do some business tomorrow–make a little money for the trip back. We can see a few sights, too. You've been here before, right?"

"Yeah, but I was always lost and broke. Once I made it to Berkeley, I stayed there."

"There's nothing but hippies in Berkeley. And how could you get lost? This town is easy."

"People would tell me to go north or south on some street, but I don't know north or south. I only know west and east because of the sun."

"If you remember–"

"Don't tell me. I can never remember the rules that go with directions."

Paul laughed. "Don't worry. I won't lose you."

In Chinatown, they drove past markets with dead chickens and ducks hanging in the windows, and stands stacked with unfamiliar fruits and vegetables. This city, which Paul navigated with the confidence of someone who belonged, didn't look like the same place she'd been terrified of alone. She'd walked through canyons of tall important-looking buildings along streets full of important-looking people wearing business suits and carrying briefcases. She'd asked for spare change and been invisible. After two days with little to eat and no place to sleep, a man in a suit offered her ten dollars and lunch for a blow-job. She told him lunch first and the money up front. They sat in a diner in the shadow of a big concrete and steel building. He watched her eat and told her to hurry up. He had a meeting in an hour. When she was done eating, she got up to use the bathroom and skipped out on him through the back before he could try to collect. There were too many times she wasn't as lucky.

Outside in the alley she got a ride in a produce truck going to Berkeley, and once there she decided to stay. She met hippies, like Paul said, and she liked them. She found soup kitchens, where she could eat for free, and stayed places where one more runaway didn't bother anybody. For six months in 1974, she never left the area between the UC-Berkeley campus and the People's Co-op on Telegraph Avenue. When she decided to travel up the coast to Mendocino, finding her way out of the maze had been a three-day nightmare.

Paul slid the car into a parking spot and turned off the motor. "Feel like a little walk before we eat?"

Janie nodded and slipped on her sweater.

They walked a few blocks to a small red-and-gold-painted restaurant with Chinese writing on the window. Flashing Christmas lights were strung around the window, where a cardboard sign with hand-lettered English read, *Family Style Good Food*. The smell of garlic and other spices mingled with the ocean air.

"I'm taking you to Chen's. When I was a kid, my uncle would bring me and my sister after Mass every Sunday. Every Sunday for all my life. Until I left anyway." Paul opened the glass door and held it for her as she stepped inside.

He ordered for both of them, and some things that they

didn't order just appeared – egg rolls and deep fried shrimp
with dipping sauce, crispy eggplant in garlic sauce, a whole fish
deep-fried golden brown that flaked away from the bone,
dried green beans in hoisin, green tea ice cream. Two hours later
they carried white paper boxes full of leftovers through the
crowded restaurant.

Paul drove out of town to a little motel he knew in Stinson
Beach. By now the fog wrapped around them thick. He drove
slowly and told Janie about all the Hitchcock movies filmed here.
He'd seen *Vertigo* about a hundred times. They walked down
to the beach from their room and held hands, listening to the
muffled boom of the tide rushing out to sea. Later in bed,
she curled under Paul's arm and rested her head on his chest.

In the morning, Paul took her on the Paul Jesse Personal
History Tour of San Francisco. He showed her the house he
was born in, and the one he and his grandmother moved to after
his mom died, but he didn't stop even though he'd told Janie
his grandma still lived there. He drove her by the Catholic grade
school he attended. He took her to Mission Dolores Basilica,
where he'd been an altar boy until Mass changed from Latin to
English, and a priest tried to cop a feel. He told her so much,
as if he'd never told anyone else his story. He took her to places
he loved and was proud of – The City, his city.

They left the Mission District and drove to a neighborhood
with steep streets and pastel Victorian houses stacked close
to each other, almost touching like pale, sugared candies in a box.
You could see the bay in the distance, a hint of water sparkling
between the houses. Paul parked in front of a yellow house with
a wrought iron gate and no yard, just steps climbing straight
up. As they walked up to the door, Paul told her not to ask questions, no matter what she saw, until they left. Bill was the kind
of guy you were careful with.

Paul rang the bell, and a beautiful woman answered. She
was tall, tan, and blonde, older than Janie by about ten years

and dressed in a white silk blouse and perfectly worn Levis. Janie could see her nipples through the thin fabric of her blouse.

"Come in." She had an accent, maybe European. "Who is this?"

"Anna, this is Janie." Paul said her name *Ahhnahh*. "I told Bill I was bringing her."

A man's voice from inside called, "Who is it?"

"It's just Paul and his friend." Then to Paul, "Go on in." Anna walked away into another room.

Janie followed close behind Paul through an entryway into the dining room.

At the head of an eight foot mahogany table sat the most Viking-Biker looking man Janie had ever seen. He was tan with long black hair, a beard, and blue eyes. On each of his fingers he wore silver rings, some inset with colored stones. In front of him an assortment of handguns lay on a newspaper.

He stood when they came into the room and gave Paul a bear hug, clapping him on the back. "Paul. Forgive the mess. Just doing a little cleaning. You want anything?"

Paul sat down next to Bill and pulled a chair out for Janie next to him. "This is Janie."

Bill held out his hand. "Janie."

Janie took his hand, but instead of shaking it, he brought it to his lips and kissed it. She mumbled hello.

"Paul, you better watch me around this one."

With the introductions out of the way, Bill and Paul talked business for what seemed like hours. Janie figured out from the conversation that they went back a long time, and that Bill had all sorts of drugs Janie had never heard of before. Their names sounded like faraway countries or exotic diseases – Percodan, Sativa, Dilaudid, Indica, Psilocybe. She rolled their names around her mouth until she could say them out loud. She would be Indica, Queen of Percodan, and rid the world of evil. By the time she was listening again, they were discussing cost, cut, and quantity. They talked seriously, and at great length, about tiny red hairs on pot plants and the best way to sex a plant – whatever that meant. Janie knew to keep quiet and smile if they looked at her, which they didn't.

Bill yelled for Anna to get them drinks. She floated out of the kitchen carrying a tray with half a bottle of tequila, two shot glasses, wedges of lime, a small bowl of coarse salt, and two bottles of Corona. She put the tray in front of Bill without smiling or speaking.

Bill slapped her ass as she turned to go. "Thanks, baby."

He looked at Janie. "You're pretty quiet." To Paul he said, "She doesn't talk much, does she?"

Paul smiled. "Nope. She can hold her mug."

"That's a good habit to have. In this business, you better be quiet as a grave. Unless you want to end up in one."

Janie nodded in agreement. Her leg had fallen asleep from sitting too long, and she didn't find anything they said interesting enough to remember, let alone tell anyone.

Bill pushed his chair back and stretched. "There's a little store on the corner. How about you run down and get us another six-pack. Get yourself something too."

"I'm not twenty-one yet."

"That won't matter at the corner. You just wait till it's empty and tell the guy at the counter Bill sent you. Here." Bill stood and pulled a fifty-dollar bill from a roll of bills in a money clip. He held it out to her.

She looked at Paul, unsure what to do. He nodded. "Go ahead, and take your time."

Outside the sun felt warm through her sweater. Bill's house was in the middle of a block of houses on a steep hill. From the sidewalk, you could see the city spread out all the way down to the water. She walked slowly to the store on the corner. It was much smaller than the supermarkets where she usually shopped. The floors were old, black-and-white linoleum, and the door had a screen that creaked open and banged shut when she let it go. An older guy with slicked-back hair and a short-sleeved shirt sat on a stool behind the counter. He was smoking a cigarette and turning the pages of a magazine. Janie caught a glimpse of big-breasted girls on the cover. He looked up at Janie as she walked the aisles, waiting for the two other customers to leave. An old woman wearing a head scarf and bedroom slippers stood in front of the dairy case reading the expiration dates out loud. She chose a quart of milk and put it in her cart beside several cans of tuna fish.

Janie went to the freezer case and hunted for an Eskimo Pie. After the store emptied, she grabbed a six-pack of beer and went to the counter. She was going to tell the guy that Bill sent her, as if she was in one of those old movies she and her dad used to watch when she was little. Before she could open her mouth, the guy said Bill had phoned and told him to watch for her. He gave her change, put the beer in a bag, and handed her the ice cream.

She walked around the block – the longest way back to Bill's. They'd be pissed off if the beer was warm, but she was in no hurry to get back. She unpeeled the paper from the ice cream and nibbled as it softened in her hand. A big orange cat was draped over the concrete wall of someone's garden. She stopped to rub behind its ears. The gardens here were all spiky plants and bright colors. Not like Stella's place where everything was muted now by autumn, and the colors seemed more important when there were fewer of them. She wasn't sure she'd want to live here. One day she wanted a homey kind of house – a place where a family would live. Except for the drug dealing she had begun to think of Paul as her family. If she loved him enough and did everything right, he would stop dealing.

When she reached the house she didn't knock because Anna would have to let her in. Janie thought she'd save her the trouble. The door wasn't locked and she went in.

The dining room where they'd been sitting when she left was empty. She decided to put the beer in the refrigerator and sit in the sun until somebody came to find her. Janie pushed open the swinging door to the kitchen. Bill was standing at the sink, a bent spoon in one hand and a lighter underneath it in the other. Paul was next to him, a cord wrapped around his upper arm, cinched tight and held in his mouth. He buried a syringe in the crook of his tied-off arm. They both looked at her when the door swished shut.

Bill broke the silence. "Wait outside."

Janie spun around, not wanting to see what was in front of her. Paul had told her he used to shoot dope. He'd told her he didn't use anymore. She put the beer on the dining room table and went out to the front porch. The taste of Eskimo Pie was sweet in the back of her throat.

After an eternity, Paul came out with a grocery bag and threw it in the backseat of the car. He didn't say anything about what she'd seen – like it had never happened. Janie knew how this worked. If you didn't talk about bad things, hard things, pretty soon it was as if they'd never happened.

Paul drove around the city to a street in a nice neighbor-hood with more big old houses. He parked in front of one. "I called Mia from Bill's. We're going to see my son."

Paul knocked twice, and a pretty woman with warm brown eyes opened the door. She smiled at Janie. "I'm Mia. Come on in." She motioned to the living room. "Have a seat. Little Paul's next door at a friend's. He'll be home in a minute."

The living room smelled of baking. Janie sat on the edge of a chair, not sure what to say or do.

Paul dug his hands deep in his pockets. He paced around the room without talking.

Mia looked at Janie. "I just took some oatmeal cookies out of the oven. Would you like some – or a drink?"

Before Janie could answer, Paul stopped moving. "You got a beer?"

"You know I don't drink anymore." Mia spoke quietly.

"Right. You don't do anything."

Mia said nothing to this.

Janie wished she were invisible. She knew she was witnessing something private between Paul and Mia. They'd been together and had a child. Janie couldn't picture it.

Paul still had his shades on. Mia watched him for a minute. She walked up to him. She was slender and shorter than Paul by a head. Mia reached up with both hands and pulled off Paul's sunglasses. She studied his eyes. "I told you never to come here wired. You want to see your son? Come straight or don't come at all. Now get out before he comes home."

Paul said nothing as Mia handed him his sunglasses. He slipped them back on and walked out the door with Janie following him.

Janie watched his jaw clench and unclench. She walked beside him down the steps. She took his hand in hers. He squeezed and nodded.

They hit the freeway during rush hour and took I-5 out of the city. When they stopped to gas up, she bought some snacks before they got back on the road. Paul sipped a Coke, but wouldn't eat.

"Can I ask you a question?"

"Depends."

Janie knew the trick here was not to look at him – just look out the window and let him talk – or not. "Why do you shoot dope?"

"It makes me feel – I don't know – normal? I've been shooting dope of one kind or another since I was sixteen." Paul took a sip of his Coke. "I told you the truth before. I haven't been using, but Bill had some wire, and it's a long drive. When I was with Mia we were both pretty strung. She quit. Went all AA on me. That's why she gets nervous about it."

"Does it hurt?"

"Kind of, but that's part of it – part of the rush. You got any gum?" His voice was casual. He could have been talking about anything.

"I think so." Janie dug around in her bag until she found her stash of Chiclets and gave him four.

He reached over with his free hand, squeezed Janie's knee and smiled his tough-guy smile. "Turn the radio up. I'm tired of talking."

Midnight Rambler

JANIE OPENED THE BACK DOOR AND STEPPED INTO THE kitchen, dropping her bag on the floor. Cookie stood at the stove stirring chopped onions in a cast-iron skillet with a wooden spoon. "It's about time." She smiled and put down the spoon. "I thought Paul was never bringing you home." Cookie's presence filled the house along with the smell of the food she was cooking. Autumn's last dahlias filled a vase on the kitchen table. China jumped up from her bed on the floor and crowded around Janie sniffing and wagging her body in greeting.

"He took me to San Francisco for Chinese food. Can you believe that?" She stood up and stretched. "Stella still at work?"

"Yes, but he'll be home early. He'll be happy to see you."

"Was he mad?"

"No, a little worried."

"I didn't even know where Paul was taking me." China sat down on Janie's feet, leaning against her and thumping her tail against the linoleum. "I've been in these clothes too long. I'm going to take a shower and clean up."

Janie went to what she'd come to think of as her room. She'd only known Stella for a few months, Cookie less than that, but they were as close to family as she was likely to get. Coming back here after just a few days away made her look at her room more closely. Books on the bed table, plants on the windowsill, a basket with jeans she was embroidering next to a rocking chair. She wanted a place that felt like this with Paul. She picked out a change of clothes and a clean towel and headed for the bathroom with China close behind.

For the two long years between when she was someone's daughter and when she ended up at Stella's, what she'd missed most was a bathroom. A clean bathroom with a door that locked from the inside, clean towels, and her own shampoo and soap. Sometimes the best she could do was a gas station bathroom. Sometimes she'd stay at someone's place but when she did, having a bathroom came with a price. She'd slept with men she didn't like and never saw again in order to take a hot shower and get out of the weather for a night. There hadn't been anyone who cared for her like Stella did in forever. There was no outstanding payment hanging over her head now.

She ran a tub of hot water and threw in some Calgon, turning the water an unnatural lagoon blue. China settled down on the bathmat, sighing as she put her head on her paws. The hot water steamed up the mirror and turned her skin pink as she eased in, inch by inch, until she was up to her neck. She could hear Cookie in the kitchen singing along with Chaka Khan on the stereo.

Janie didn't know when she'd be with Paul next. He'd dropped her in front of Stella's place, the car running while she got out. She'd never seen him wired before and she didn't like the way he acted. He scared her. All the way back from California, he was sure the police were after him. He ground his teeth and chainsmoked. He saw things in the road that weren't there. She suggested he pull over and take a nap and he yelled at her for the first time. He called her stupid. Told her to get off his back. She knew he hadn't slept in two days but it was more than that. When she leaned in to kiss him goodbye, he turned his cheek to her and said he was going to be busy for awhile. He said he had business to do. She'd been relieved and afraid at the same time.

After her bath, Janie went to the kitchen to see if she could help cook whatever smelled so good. She looked into the big pot Cookie was stirring. "What are you making?"

"Enchiladas. Want to help?"

Cookie showed her how to soften the corn tortillas with sauce so they wouldn't fall apart when they were rolled. They worked together filling a casserole.

Janie asked, "Do you ever wonder how to help somebody change?"

"In general?" Cookie tied Janie's hair back with a bandana. "I think you almost always know inside what you need to do. The thing you're supposed to do is usually hard and simple. Like, if you ask a smoker they'll say they know they have to quit but doing it means being uncomfortable. Until the smoker decides to live with discomfort there's not much another person can do. For most of us discomfort is the scariest part and you can't really help with that."

Janie shook her head. "I've done a lot of scary stuff."

"I don't mean scary dangerous. I mean scary difficult."

FOR THE NEXT few days Janie didn't miss Paul, but she thought about him. She felt glad to be home, happy to be with Stella and Cookie, glad they seemed to want her around, glad to curl up on the living room floor and watch TV with China wrapped around her. Stella didn't ask her questions about where she'd been or what she'd seen, and she didn't offer explanations.

Three days before Halloween, Stella asked Janie if she wanted to go get pumpkins. Cookie wasn't feeling well and didn't want to go. The air smelled rich with cow manure and windfall apples. They passed a tidy farmhouse with a big plot of garden and pumpkin patch, a barn and a pasture.

Janie turned her head to watch the house as it passed out of view. "One day I want a house just like that one. A farm with chickens and maybe a horse or a cow. I'd have a yellow kitchen and a bunch of little girls and I'd make quilts for their beds."

"Would you have a man?" asked Stella.

"Maybe Paul is the man."

"I wouldn't mind having a farm. Only I'd have a white kitchen and no Paul."

"Stella, why don't you like Paul?"

Stella was quiet. A raindrop hit the windshield followed by more raindrops.

"I don't trust him. I've known him a long time and he's not a bad man. He's a weak man. He's done some bad things out of weakness and he's not dependable."

"Maybe he'll change. People change."

"It gets harder the older you get." He stared out the window for a minute. "Before you know it it's like you don't have a choice. You do what you do and hope for the best."

ON HALLOWEEN AFTER Stella left for work, Cookie and Janie carved the pumpkins on sheets of newspaper. They separated the seeds from the stringy fibers of meat and put them into a bowl. The larger denser chunks of pumpkin went into a pan to bake later for pie.

The phone rang. Cookie wiped her hands and picked up the receiver. "Janie, it's for you."

Janie wiped her slimy hands on a kitchen towel and took the phone. She knew it was Paul. It couldn't be anyone else.

"Hey, baby. I was missing you." His voice sounded funny, all slowed down and drunk. "What are you doing tonight?"

"Me and Cookie are carving pumpkins."

"Oh yeah? That sounds real sweet. Sweet Polly Purebred." He laughed, but not the way he did when he was straight.

"Where are you?"

"Taking care of business, baby."

In the background she could hear people talking loud and music playing – a woman's laugh, too close to the receiver and too close to Paul.

"When will you be back?"

She heard him inhale and hold his breath – his dope smoking voice.

"Couple days. Just wanted to 'ear your voice." He exhaled. "You have a happy Halloween, Witchy Woman. Keep it tight."

"Paul?"

The phone clicked and hummed and Janie was left with dead air. Up until that moment she had thought about Paul, but she hadn't thought about what he really might be doing. She figured he was dealing for Bill, and when he was done Paul would go back to being his old self. She didn't believe Stella knew Paul the way she did; if she was with him more she'd be able to make him change.

Cookie and Janie knew they wouldn't get any trick-or-treaters, but lit the jack-o-lanterns anyway and settled in for the night. Cookie made popcorn and toasted pumpkin seeds. Janie heated up cider with cinnamon sticks. The Charlie Brown special was on TV and then *Arsenic and Old Lace*. By the time the movie ended Cookie had gone to bed and Janie was curled up on the couch with China. She couldn't sleep yet. The sound of rain falling on the roof relaxed her. Stella's car crunched across the gravel driveway. China sat up her tail thumped on the floor until the back door clicked open, and she rushed out to greet him. Janie pulled on her wool socks and tiptoed out to the kitchen.

Stella was patting China and giving her a dog biscuit. He smiled at Janie. "Want one?'

"Stella, I was thinking about maybe asking Paul if I could move over to the trailer with him. It would give you more room if Cookie wanted to stay and I'm not making any money – "

"You don't have to worry about that. You don't need to move. We like having you around."

The kettle began to sing. Stella made the tea and sat down in the chair. "Did you meet Mia and Little Paul when he took you to San Francisco?"

"Just Mia. They kind of had a fight and we left."

"Paul was strung out in the city. He did a lot of bad things to a lot of people."

"He's not like that with me."

"I'm glad for that, I really am, but don't rush things. Take your time."

Janie stood and put her mug in the sink. She kissed the top of Stella's bald head and went to bed.

STELLA LOOKED AT the clock – 4:35 a.m. The phone rang from the kitchen. Cookie rolled away from him, still fast asleep. He pulled on a pair of boxers and stumbled out to the kitchen. The phone kept ringing.

"It's Ernie. Somebody torched the club."

"What?"

"Sheriff's office just called. I'm on my way down."

"Right."

Stella hung up the phone and threw on the lights.

Cookie and Janie stood together in the kitchen doorway.

"The club's on fire."

STELLA COULD SEE the smoke in the sky as he drove. As he pulled into the lot, flames shot out of the smoke billowing from the building. Two state police cars and a fire engine were parked close to the blaze. Firefighters moved around the parking lot, spraying what was left of the bar. Stella found Ernie filling out paperwork next to one of the police cars.

Ernie looked up at Stella. "I can't believe this."

"Do they know what happened?"

"Look over there." Ernie pointed to the back. He rubbed his temple and ran his hand through his hair.

At the edge of the lot where the forest met the concrete was a white van – Larry's van. Spray painted across the side were the words *Instant Carma*.

Stella shook his head. "That sneaky little fucker couldn't spell."

"Who'd have thought the dude liked Lennon?"

"Yeah. Anybody ask you anything?"

"They figured it's just a firebug."

"They find him yet?"

"Nah. Not yet. The fire's too hot for them to get inside. They think he might be in there."

"No shit?"

"Maybe it's time for us to head up to Alaska. Open that place we always wanted to."

"Not for me, Ernie. I'm done with this."

"What'll you do?"

"I don't know for sure. I was going to tell you this tomorrow. Cookie's going to have a baby. I'm going to be a dad." He couldn't help smiling, even with all this mess.

"I'm happy for you, Clare, and bummed for me. It's the end of an era."

"Yeah. Hey, you still carry that bottle in your glove compartment?"

Stella and Ernie sat in the car and sipped from a pint bottle of bourbon. At dawn, when the building was no more than an ashy skeleton, the fire investigator tapped on the window and told them a body had been found inside with a gasoline can and a melted Bic lighter. Later, the body would be identified as Lawrence Miller.

They Call Me the Breeze

JANIE WAITED TO PACK UNTIL ONLY HER BELONGINGS remained scattered around the house. Paul hadn't exactly asked her to come live with him, but he hadn't said no when she brought it up. Now she really would belong with Paul. Ernie's trailer was gone, on its way to Nome, Alaska, towed behind Delores's Plymouth station wagon with Ernie at the wheel. Stella and Cookie were out renting a U-Haul for their move to Eugene. They'd share a house with Cookie's brother temporarily and open a cafe. Both Stella and Cookie had asked Janie to move down with them, but she couldn't. She chose Paul. She had somebody now. She wasn't letting go.

Janie gathered her things and set them on the coffee table in the living room – a pile of books, her clothes, a sewing basket. China followed her. Janie tried not to pay too much attention to the dog. It was going to hurt when she left.

China whined and followed her from room to room. Janie found an empty liquor box on the back porch and brought it inside. At the bottom she lined up her books, like a row of wooden blocks. On top of the books she placed art supplies, a notebook, and a wooden box with the few things she could never replace – her birth certificate, Social Security card, some pictures of her mom and dad, a few pages torn from her mom's cookbook. She doubted whether Norma would have kept anything like photo albums or recipe books. If Janie ever went back she knew there'd be nothing left of her mom or dad. She wrapped the present Stella had given her at Christmas – an ornament that looked exactly like the owl she told him about from Betty's. It had tiny feathers glued to the body in the same design as the real bird's feathers and talons that attached to the Christmas tree. She put it inside the box with the rest of her things. She packed her clothes in a cardboard suitcase Stella had found at the Goodwill. Her shoes she dumped in an apple crate.

China bumped her head under Janie's hand, begging for attention. Janie took the dog by the collar and put her outside.

PAUL WANTED TO get to the city. He still wasn't quite sure how he ended up taking Janie with him. But here he was, Stella glaring at him like a big black cloud as he loaded Janie's things in the back of the Opel. It looked like no matter what he thought he wanted, he'd gone and got himself an old lady. Stella hugged Janie, and Cookie kissed her on the cheek. China kept barking and running around Janie, like a herding dog trying to keep sheep in the pen.

Paul drove straight down I-5 to San Francisco. Janie didn't talk much. Sometimes she'd look over at him and smile. She looped her fingers through his belt and kept them there. The radio static got bad in the Siskiyous and he flipped it off. Janie's face was pressed against the window. She had fallen asleep with her hand still on his lap. Paul smoked cigarettes and drove the long familiar I-5 corridor, until they crossed the Golden Gate Bridge into San Francisco.

At Bill's, Paul sent Janie to the store to get snacks for the trip and told her to wait in the living room if nobody was around when she got back. He and Bill got right down to business. In the basement garage, they took the Opel's doors off their hinges and packed five bricks of pot in the hollow shells, then screwed them back in place.

Later in front of the house, Bill checked Paul's brake lights and turn signals before they left. No reason to get stopped over something like a broken tail light, but it happened all the time. Paul liked doing business with Bill. They both thought the same way. No detail was too small. Paul would drive the dope back east to Bill's Boston connections with two stops along the way, in Salt Lake City and Aspen. He couldn't take Janie. He'd leave her at Bill's cabin in the mountains of Humboldt County. He'd do time for statutory rape if he got pulled over in some small town with his long hair and an underage runaway. They'd search the car for sure. Possesion was bad enough, but he wasn't doing time for a rape charge. As long as he didn't rip off Bill and brought the money back in time, Janie would be fine. If he didn't, Bill would get her strung out and sell her to a pimp he knew. That wasn't going to happen, so there was no reason to say anything to her about it.

Tonight they'd stay in a motel. He wanted one more night to sleep stretched out beside her. As he merged onto the freeway and headed north on I-5, Paul felt Janie's hand loop its way through his belt. She was always doing that when they drove. It was a little thing, this habit of hers, one of the many little things that made her different from other women. When she looked at him with those blue eyes, he wanted to make her happy.

In the morning they left before checkout time. The cabin wasn't far from Red Bluff. Bill had turned him on to a couple grams of crank and a clean rig for the road. He'd make up the time after he dropped Janie off. They went for pancakes. He didn't have the heart to tell her she wasn't coming along. He wanted the last few hours to be easy.

JANIE LOOKED OUT the window watching for road signs to match the map in her hand. Tiny towns zipped by – Beegum, Platina, Knob. When they were a few miles from Wildwood, Paul turned onto a rutted asphalt road and followed it into the woods to an unmarked gravel driveway that quickly became a wide, dirt, one-lane path. Deep ruts slowed the car to a crawl.

"Pretty soon you'll hear the dogs. Keep your window up."

Paul lit a cigarette. "Bill grows pot out here. I'm going to make a trip and be gone for a few days, maybe a week, and you're going to stay here. You'll like the cabin. It's real nice."

"I thought I was going with you."

"I can't take you with me. I would if I could. If I get stopped and you're with me, we'll both be screwed."

"I wish you'd told me."

"I won't be gone more than a week or two. At the very most two. Tops."

A BLUR OF dogs shot out of the underbrush on either side of the road, barking and baying as they ran alongside the car. They pulled into a clearing in front of a small cabin at the crest of the hill. A woman was sitting on the front porch pulling on cowboy boots. Her shining black hair hung straight down like a curtain in front of her face. She didn't even look up until she had both boots on. When she did Janie thought she'd never seen a more beautiful woman.

The woman stood on the porch smiling. She had high cheek-bones and wide-spaced dark eyes. Her skin was the color of caramel. "Hey Slick," she said to Paul, as they got out of the car. "Long time no see."

Janie stood back waiting.

"So's this the new girl?" Luna walked up to Janie, looking her over like Ernie did when he hired a dancer. "Looks like those hippies and whores have been dressing you." She smiled. "Time to enter Princess Luna's House of Style." Luna grabbed onto Janie's elbow and steered her past Paul. "We definitely got to do something about your clothes. When I get back, we'll go shopping."

"Where are you going?' Janie asked.

"Oh honey. I bet Slick here," she nodded toward Paul, "didn't tell you about me. Well, I owe Bill a favor so I'm helping Paul drive. You're staying here with Blue."

"Who's Blue?" Janie asked.

Luna opened the cabin door and flung it wide. Janie's eyes

took a moment to adjust to the change in light. The cabin was a big room with a ladder in the middle that led to an open loft. At one end of the large room was a stone fireplace and a bottle-green velvet couch. Rugs covered the plain pine floors. At the other end of the room was a small kitchen with a wood cook-stove and a bank of windows looking out over miles of trees and meadows.

A man who appeared to be Luna's twin sat at a wooden table in front of the windows. He had the same long black hair, thick and straight, wide-spaced deep brown eyes, high cheek bones. A guitar rested on his lap, one hand on the strings. He smiled at Janie but didn't get up or pay any attention to the commotion. Paul came in carrying Janie's box in one hand and her pink cardboard suitcase in the other. He put them down by the couch, poured himself a cup of coffee from the wood stove, and sat down at the table.

Janie followed him and took a chair. Luna disappeared up the ladder to the loft.

"How you been, Blue?" Paul asked.

"Beautiful." Blue didn't look at Paul. His eyes were on Janie.

The way he said it, Janie wasn't sure if he meant he was fine, or he thought she was beautiful. She looked down at her lap.

Paul scooted his chair back. "Let's get the rest of your stuff out of the car."

Janie followed him outside. "Why didn't you tell me about Luna?"

He opened the trunk of the car to get the box with her shoes. "Nothing to tell."

"If it was nothing you would have said something, right?"

"What kind of crazy shit is that? I don't even know what you mean. That just doesn't make any sense."

But, Janie knew what she meant. She didn't know if she had the words in the right order, but she knew what she meant.

"Look Janie, it's like this. I can't stop to sleep, so Luna's going with me to drive. We'll be gone a couple of weeks. We've done this plenty of times, and I make a good chunk of change. It'll only be a few days or so."

"But what if something happens?"

"Nothing's going to happen. Don't even worry about it. I don't like leaving you especially with Blue in there drooling all over you." Paul put his fingers under her chin, lifting her face, kissing her. "You're my girl." He let her go and picked up the last box.

Luna was downstairs when they came inside. "Let's saddle up and go rope the rhubarb, Slick. I got to get back here and fix up your girlfriend. Bye, Blue. Keep your fingers out of the cookie jar." She picked up her back pack and headed to the car.

Paul kissed Janie once more and gave her a hug. "It'll only be a couple weeks at the most. I promise. Okay?"

Janie followed Paul and stood on the porch. As Paul reached the car, she yelled after him the one thing he always said when he left her – so he'd think she was fine, so he'd be back soon. "Keep it tight, Paul."

He laughed and waved as he started up the Opel, yelling back to her out the window, "Tighter than a bullfrog's ass – and that's waterproof. Two weeks, baby – I love you."

Janie sat down on the wooden porch steps. He never said it right out like that; he loved her. She could live on that for two weeks, easy. Two and a half, tops.

Tumbling Dice

JANIE FOUND THE GREENHOUSE BY ACCIDENT THE NEXT day. It was hidden by a tangle of blackberry brambles growing along one side of the old Quonset hut building at the edge of the woods. It looked abandoned, except the door was padlocked with a chain and dead-bolted. On tiptoes she peered through a moss covered window. Long wooden tables held rows of marijuana plants in one-gallon black pots. Janie didn't tell Blue what she'd seen. Blue didn't scare her but Bill did. She would wait a month here for Paul. He said he loved her and she'd hold on to that. If Paul didn't come back by her birthday on March 4, she'd go find Stella and Cookie in Eugene.

Janie spent the long days exploring the woods surrounding the cabin with the dogs. Mala Noche, a smooth-coated brindle mixed breed, became her favorite. The other dogs stayed outside and roamed the woods nearby in a pack, but Mala preferred Janie's company. Having Mala close made her miss China less. Sometimes it seemed that all she did in her life was say goodbye to everyone and eveything she loved. She tried to keep her mind focused on Paul's "I love you." She'd lived on less. She had come to believe she would die early and alone unless her luck changed.

In the late afternoons, Janie returned to the cabin carrying little pieces of the woods. A leaf's bare skeleton, dried weeds as delicate as antique lace, a stone the color of blood. She placed these objects around the cabin.

She liked cooking on the woodstove once she got the hang
of it. At night, Blue lit the candles and hurricane lamps and
sat playing the guitar. They didn't speak and that was fine with
Janie. After the first few days, she quit thinking Blue would
try to sleep with her. He still looked at her with his sleepy stoned
eyes and called her beautiful, but she was pretty sure he just
couldn't remember her name. She slept on the couch in front of
the fire, and he slept in the loft. She read by light that turned
the pages of her books gold. In the dark, before sleep took her,
she imagined living here with Paul. They'd make babies.
She'd raise goats. She'd plant a vegetable garden. She'd have a
horse named Penny Lane and a cow named Eleanor Rigby.
She'd have chickens. She'd make Paul change through the force
of her love.

PAUL TURNED HIS coffee cup right side up so the waitress
could fill it. Luna slumped in the booth across from him pouting.
She'd been bitching for the last hour that she wanted to eat, and
now that he'd stopped at this diner in one of the Dakotas – North
or South, he wasn't sure anymore, she was mad they'd missed
breakfast. It was 11:05, and this place stopped serving breakfast
at 11:00 sharp.

The waitress wore a short, white uniform, the zippered front
open to reveal cleavage. She filled Paul's cup, and smiled at him.
"Would the lady like some coffee too?"

Luna slammed her cup around. "The lady would like you
to get your tits out of her old man's face."

The waitress straightened up, poured Luna's coffee, and
took their orders.

Paul watched the waitress's ass jiggle as she walked away.

Luna looked ready to go off. "I ought to tell her fucking
manager."

"Tell him what? That his waitress is stacked and friendly?
I bet he knows already, Luna. What's this 'my old man' bullshit
anyway? Since when am I your old man?"

"She didn't know who I was. I could be your wife for all she knows."

"Drop it." Paul stirred three sugars and two creamers into his coffee before taking a sip. Luna drove him crazy. Every step of this trip had been a hassle since she met Janie. He knew it was that *I love you* he'd yelled to Janie that'd done it. Why couldn't he keep his mouth shut? Luna wanted to know when they had met. How old was she? Were they living together? Luna made a point to act like it was nothing to her, but Paul knew better. She went on and on until he finally fucked her to shut her up. He'd known Luna for about eight years since right after, or was it before, he left Mia? He considered Luna more like one of the boys than a woman. Nothing serious on his side, and until this little burst of jealousy, he thought she felt the same. He liked her – he would even say he liked her a lot, but she reminded him of the hawks at Betty's – wild. You couldn't think about being with a woman like Luna day and night. Together they were combustible.

AT THE END of the second week, Bill came out to the cabin in his Chevy pickup. He got there before noon, bringing with him a load of well-rotted manure. He and Blue hauled wheelbarrow loads from the truck bed into the woods all morning. Janie watched them from the kitchen window as she rolled out bread dough to fry. She dropped the dough into the hot fat in the skillet, flipping it when it turned golden brown. She thought about Cookie as she dusted the hot pieces with sugar and cinnamon and let the grease drain on grocery bags spread on the counter. She was getting to be a pretty good cook. On the back burner, a cast-iron pot with bean soup bubbled away. Mala was stretched out on the kitchen floor.

"Smells good." Bill stomped his boots outside the door before he came in. "What's that dog doing in here?"

Janie flipped a fresh piece of dough and removed another. "She likes me."

"That dog is not a pet. Put it outside."

"But she's not hurting anything—"

Bill twisted her around fast by her upper arm and slapped her face hard. "You do what I say."

Janie grabbed Mala Noche by the collar and pulled her outside. Tears stung her eyes. She went back to the stove and turned the last piece of dough to keep it from burning. Bill and Blue sat down at the table, scraping the chairs across the floor. Janie dished up two bowls of soup and a plate of the hot bread, setting them on the table. She stood waiting until Bill looked up at her. "I'm sorry. It won't happen again."

He drank part of his beer in one long gulp, wiping his mouth with the back of his hand, staring at her. "While you're here your ass is mine. You do what I say the first time I ask you. Understood?"

Janie didn't blink or look away. "Understood."

"At least you aren't a weeper. Can't stand a weeper." Bill wiped his mouth on the back of his sleeve. "Blue says he wants to take you with him to do laundry."

Janie ran around the cabin getting the laundry together. She brushed her hair and stuffed the twenty-dollar bill Paul gave her in her pocket. Maybe she could get Blue to stop at that flea market for some new books. She checked herself in the mirror to see if she looked all right. Bill's handprint remained on her cheek.

Blue lit a joint once they got on the highway and passed it to Janie. She didn't usually smoke pot with men. Some guy dusted her once—put some angel dust in a joint—when she was first on the street and too young and stupid to know any better. She didn't think Blue was like that. He'd try straight out if he wanted to sleep with her. She took a hit off the joint and passed it back to Blue. Fiddling with the radio dial she found a song her mom used to sing to her. She leaned back, exhaling and turned up the radio. Patsy Cline's mournful voice filled the cab of the truck and Janie sang along. "Crazy—"

"You're a trip, Janie."

"I didn't think you remembered my name."

"Who could forget your name?"

Janie blushed. "Most of the world I bet."

Blue took another hit off the joint. "Let's get ice creams at the Dairy Queen."

"I was hoping you'd say something like that. Do you think Bill will leave tonight?"

"Yeah. His new girl's fucking around. He wants to catch her at it."

"Poor thing."

"His girls know what they're getting into. Free dope, free place to stay – they understand."

"If there's time can we go to the flea market?"

"Yup."

While the laundry dried they walked the aisles of the flea market. Blue found a banjo without the strings. Janie filled a grocery bag with yellowed paperbacks for two dollars. They each got an ice cream cone and walked back to the laundromat. Janie swirled her tongue on the melting cone.

He wiped a drop of ice cream from her lip and licked his finger. "Paul's a fool to leave you out here."

She turned her back on him and folded clothes. She felt hot all over and blamed the dryers before wondering if Blue wasn't right about Paul.

THEY RETURNED TO the cabin with dusk close behind them and Bill already gone. Dark clouds moving in made a striped sunset. When the bags of clean clothes, groceries, and books were safely inside the first fat drops of rain began to fall.

Blue opened a bottle of wine. "I'll cook tonight."

"You cook?"

"I sure do."

He looked at her with a Big, Bad Wolf smile and Janie found herself smiling right back. "Whatever we do we have to take baths. I'm not getting in clean sheets smelling like week old meat."

Blue stepped in close, and put his nose to the curve of her neck. His breath tickled. "If you smell like week old meat then give me a knife and fork. You're one of those girls who never smell bad."

Janie took a step back.

Blue bowed to her and pulled a bottle of wine from one of the bags, taking a corkscrew from his back pocket. He poured two jelly glasses full, handing her one. "I better build a fire if we're going to have baths."

THINGS HAD BEEN too simple, gone too easily all the way east and now, headed home, the Opel's transmission had blown outside Aspen near Independence Pass. Paul wired Bill his share of the money from Boston so there was no reason to hurry now, but he wanted to get back to Janie. He didn't like the idea of Blue and Janie alone in the cabin, miles from nowhere.

"My feet are fucking sore. We ought to just wait in a good spot for a ride." Luna clutched her battered cowboy hat to her head as a semi passed.

"When we get to a phone, I'll call Flea. He'll come and get us." Paul kept walking. He wasn't about to argue with her. He was tired of pulling her along behind him like some overgrown three-year-old. She'd been pissing and moaning the whole trip. She wanted something from him he wasn't going to give. Trouble was he didn't know what to do about it. He was going to pick up Janie as soon as this trip was over, and it couldn't be over soon enough for him.

Luna stomped along behind him. "I don't know why you're in such a motherfucking hurry. We'll get a ride faster if we just stop and let the drivers take a look at me."

Luna had a point but Paul didn't care. He wanted to keep moving toward town. He should have known his luck about to change. A hundred feet or so ahead a pickup pulled over on the shoulder. Paul started running and yelled over his shoulder. "Move your ass, Luna."

"He's not going anywhere without me." She strolled the few feet to the truck.

The driver gave them a ride all the way to Flea's front door. Flea was outside on a board under a Ford Fairlane. Aerosmith blared out of a cheap pair of speakers rigged in the front window. Paul didn't know Flea's real name or anything more about him other than he and Bill had done time together in San Quentin years ago.

Flea rolled out from under the car and sat up. He was covered in motor oil, his greasy hair pulled back in a ponytail. "I thought you was on your way back?"

"Car broke down. Pretty sure it's the trannie."

Flea cleared his throat with a great nose-snorting, throat-hacking noise and spit over his shoulder. "Need a tow?"

"I need a mechanic."

Luna dropped her pack at her feet. "Well, I need a fucking shower and a long nap."

Flea stood up and motioned them into his house.

After smoking a bowl, they left Luna behind and took Flea's truck out to see what could be done about the Opel. The car would have to be towed. Then Paul would need to find a used trannie and install it with Flea's help. It was about a week's worth of work, what with the hunting and gatherering that had to be done. Paul would buy the parts and turn Flea on to some of his stash for the labor.

"So you and Luna together these days?" Flea wiped his greasy mustache out of his mouth.

"Nah. She's just helping out with the driving."

"Didn't know. Hate to make a mistake like that without asking."

Paul shrugged it off and forgot about it. They stopped by a store for a half-case of Coors before heading back to the house.

OUSIDE THE CABIN it rained steadily. The light from the fire and candles cast shadows around the room. Blue took his bath first. The big metal washtub sat in front of the fireplace full of stove-heated water. Steam fogged up the windows. Janie stayed put at the kitchen table, drinking her second glass of wine. She'd only had wine a couple of times before. It made her feel relaxed.

"Janie, could you bring over some water to rinse my hair?"

Janie picked up a kettle of hot water and took it over to the tub. Blue's knees were drawn up and she avoided looking directly at him. Blue barely fit in the tub sitting down. He bent forward with his head over his knees. She poured the water over his head slowly so he could get the soap out. His hair was India ink beautiful. Janie went back to the table, putting distance between them.

He reached for a towel on the floor and toweled off his hair. "I'll make dinner while you take your bath." Blue came into the kitchen with a towel wrapped around his waist. His skin was the same perfect brown with no tan lines. "You like clams and linguine?"

"I've never had it."

"Well, you're going to tonight."

Janie refilled her glass. "Where do we dump this water? I want to take a bath."

PAUL HOPPED IN the shower when he and Flea got back from towing the car. It felt good to wash the road off. Tomorrow he'd call all the u-pulls, and take a look in the paper to see if he could find a transmission. He wanted to get away from Luna. He missed Janie. He found himself thinking about her and wondering if she missed him too.

The shower curtain opened. There stood stark raving Luna, naked except for the cowboy hat. She looked damned good in that cowboy hat. "There some room in there for me?"

"I'm just getting out."

She stepped into the stall. "You got to get by me first, Slick."

"You better take that hat off."

"Nah." She rubbed the bar of soap across her breasts and belly. "I happen to know you got a thing for Westerns."

"You're crazy, baby, but you sure are fun."

"Call me Miss Kitty, Slick. We're in the wild, wild, West."

Dark Side of the Moon

PAUL HANDED FLEA A SMALL BAGGIE OF WHITE POWDER. He'd do a line later before they left for the drive back. If Luna didn't get wasted, they'd share the driving and be back at Bill's by Monday. She insisted they should take their time. A couple of Flea's friends were over tonight. They sat on the couch while Flea cut up a gram of crank with a razor blade on a mirror. Paul watched Luna in the kitchen as she mixed frozen orange juice with tequila instead of water. She dumped the mixture over ice cubes in two large glasses. Dipping her finger in one glass, she added more tequila to both drinks and carried them over to Paul.

"What's on the mirror, boys?" Luna handed Paul a drink. "Coke or smack?"

Paul answered for Flea who had a rolled bill up his nose. "Crank. I got some for the trip back. Don't drink too much. I was thinking we'd wire up and split tonight." Paul took a sip of his drink and put it down. "Shit, Luna. What'd you put in here – lighter fluid? Slow down. You haven't been eating enough to drink like this."

"Oh, stop it, grandma. Do a line with me now." Luna sat down on the threadbare couch, sandwiched between the two grubby-looking older dudes. "I'm not ready for some long road trip. Let's party tonight and leave in the morning." One of the men held her hair back for her and stroked her upper arm with his finger, as she bent over the mirror, the rolled bill in her right nostril.

One finger held her left nostril shut. She inhaled, chasing the white powder down the mirror.

Paul took his keys from his pocket. "I'm going to the store. You want to come?"

Luna didn't answer.

Paul stood up and grabbed his jacket. "Stay if you want then. I'm going to gas up the car. If you're not ready when I get back I'm leaving you here." He wasn't about to babysit her. If she couldn't handle her shit she'd have to deal with it herself.

Luna flipped him off and did another line. The men on the couch laughed. Paul shook his head and walked out the door, glad to be out of the house and away from her.

When he got back to Flea's an hour later, the place was empty. Paul had a bad feeling. He'd never seen Luna drink so much so fast before. Those dudes had been sniffing around her. They didn't seem to realize she was acting for his benefit, not to get them hot. Paul took a beer from the refrigerator and turned on the TV. If he was lucky they'd be back soon, and even if she was trashed, he'd load her in the car and drive.

Two Mules for Sister Sarah was over and *Hang 'Em High* had been on for an hour when Flea walked in alone, carrying a half case of beer. "Hey Paul. Want a cold one?"

"Where the fuck is Luna?"

"Man, I don't know."

"What do you mean you don't know? Didn't she leave with you?"

"Look, calm down. Here have a beer." Flea held out a beer to Paul.

"I don't want a beer. I want to be on my way. Where is she?"

"Nobody thought you'd mind. I mean shit she was all over the place. You said yourself she wasn't your old lady or nothing."

"What the fuck does that mean?"

"Look, nobody thought you'd mind."

"Where is she now?" Paul was off the couch with his coat half on.

"At the barn."

"They got a phone out there?"

"Yeah."

"Well, get on the phone and tell whoever the fuck is out there, I'm coming to get her and I want her in one fucking piece."

"Right." Flea dialed the phone.

Paul left. His heart beat in his throat and the beer was stale in his mouth. He'd been in many, many biker barns and clubhouses. Women – even women who had an old man didn't ever go to a barn alone. It was the territory of men. She must have been wasted to go with those dudes – wasted and thinking he'd come get her, and here he was doing just that.

He pulled up and saw there were no cycles or other vehicles parked outside and it was dark. Paul tripped over a hubcap in the yard.

Inside, the lights were off, except one down the hall in the bathroom. Paul called out her name, heard a whimper, and headed that way. He found Luna curled up on the bathroom floor beneath a bare bulb. Her jeans were around her ankles, her shirt pulled open. She had puked on the floor. He pulled her jeans up and saw blood on the insides of her thighs. Her eyes blinked opened in fear, tears rolled down her cheeks. She spoke in a whisper how he would never love her now. He cradled her in his arms, pulling her shirt closed and her pants on. He whispered in her ear. He'd take care of her. He never should have left her like that. He should have taken care of her. This was the deal, this was the truth – she may have pulled the trigger, but he loaded the gun.

Paul scooped her up off the piss-stained floor and carried her to the car.

STORMS ROLLED IN all week, keeping Janie and Blue inside the cabin. Janie brought out her watercolors and sat at the kitchen table dipping her brush in water and paint, applying it to her paper. Blue sat across from her stoking the fire and picking out songs on his guitar. They inhabited the cabin as if they were ship-wrecked together. Janie kept track of the passing of time, hours, days, and now weeks. Paul said two weeks. Janie counted three weeks and five days. Thursday would be her birthday. Seventeen, one more year to go and she'd be legal. She had plans for the things she would do once she was eighteen – get a job, finish school, get a driver's license. Every birthday on the road brought her a year closer to the life she wanted to have. Every year also meant she'd escaped juvenile detention and foster care. One more year to go. She didn't tell Blue about her birthday. Paul had promised he'd be back by then, if he remembered.

On the morning of her birthday, she woke to rain. She got up and stoked the fire, made coffee, and started making breakfast – chocolate chip pancakes. Her mom, and then her dad, always made them for her birthday breakfast. There would always be a paper crown at the foot of her bed when she woke up on her birthday that her mom had made and they'd do something special together. She remembered once they took a picnic to Satan's Pass to watch the elk come down from the mountains to feed. There was still deep snow that year in March and there weren't other people around. A herd of thirty or so elk stood eating hay that had been dropped in a snowpacked meadow. Her dad got out of the car first and crossed the road to get a good look. Janie was a little scared because the elk were so big and she must have only been four or five, but her mom said as long as they stayed quiet and moved slow the elk wouldn't bother them. She rememebered the sounds they made – like flutes, she thought. It had been a long time since that birthday.

Blue's bare feet and low-slung faded jeans appeared first as he climbed down the ladder and came into the kitchen. His hair was loose and tangled. He raked his fingers through it and yawned. "Man, I could smell the coffee in my sleep. What're you making?" He stood behind her looking over her shoul-der. "Chocolate chips in the pancakes?"

"They're good."

"I better smoke a bowl." Blue poured a cup of coffee and sat down at the table with a small pipe. He packed the bowl with a piece of bud and lit it. The plaid flannel workshirt he wore hung open.

Janie tried not to look at him too often. He distracted her. He looked so much like his sister, Luna, and she was out there somewhere with Paul. Janie poured pancake batter in the hot skillet. She wasn't going to think about Paul or her birthday at all. She would forget all about him and then he would come.

FROM A MOTEL near Lake Tahoe, Paul called Bill and gave him the rundown on the trip, the car, and Luna. Bill's response was expected. *What the fuck do you want me to do about it?*

The Luna next to him was not the Luna he knew. She didn't talk or smile. She didn't meet his eyes. He wasn't taking her back and dropping her off like this. He wanted her to smile again and call him Slick.

He found a cheap motel with a kitchenette and an off-season special and made a deal for the rest of the week. Luna took bath after bath with the door locked. He heated soup for her and sat with her until she ate.

After that week, he drove Luna to her parents' house in Modesto. She was in no shape to come with him to Bill's. She sat next to him with her head pressed against the window. He glanced at her now and then hoping she would see something that would fire her up. She bit her nails and peeled off the cuticles until her fingers bled. She hadn't combed her hair since they left Aspen. She rarely spoke.

Paul fumbled in the ashtray for a joint he'd rolled earlier. "Want to stop and eat?"

"If you want." Her index finger found its way to her mouth.

"Get your fingers out of your mouth."

Luna dropped her hands in her lap.

"You've got to stop this shit. I'm serious. You got to put away what happened and move on."

"You think it was just that night I've got to forget? I get fucked up and I do stupid things. I get fucked up even when I tell myself I shouldn't, even when I know I don't want to. I've got years of nights like that one."

"Baby, you're twenty-four. This'll pass. You just got to live through enough time for it to scab over. You're going to be okay."

Luna stared out the window and didn't reply.

"I'm not leaving you. You know that, right? I'll be back in a few days. I'm just going to Bill's." He didn't tell Luna he was headed for the cabin after that to give Janie a ride to Stella's, if she was still there.

He dropped Luna off at her mom and dad's, kissing her cheek. She seemed not to care, but now he knew better than to trust himself to figure out somebody else's feelings.

A LITTLE BREAK in the rain brought Janie out of the house. She felt like she would go crazy sitting inside pretending it wasn't her birthday. It helped to walk. She had the dogs with her and a sandwich of cold pancake smeared with chunky peanut butter. She fed the dogs tiny pieces, making each one wait for a turn as she hiked down the hill. The forest smelled spicy and the air felt cold and wet from all the rain. It would be pretty in the summer and she hoped she wouldn't be there to see it.

She missed Stella and China. Before she left, before the club burned, back when it was just her and Stella, he had talked about her birthday. He said they'd have a cake, and he'd cook whatever she wanted to eat, she could invite people over and they'd make it special. Her birthday always made her feel like a real orphan. This year was worse than ever because she'd been expecting something more.

Janie was soaked, but she kept walking. The dogs ran off after something in the brush. Janie sat on a fallen tree so big she had to climb it to sit down. Ferns and even another tree grew out of it. They called trees like this nurse logs. Her mom had been a nurse at a hospital. She worked on the maternity floor taking care of moms and babies. Sometimes she and her dad would go pick her up from work and look at the new babies. She couldn't really remember her mom anymore, only the stories she told herself about what it used to be like. The summer after she died, Janie's dad had taken her camping. He told her about nurse logs, as if it would make her feel better about her mother's death. Nothing is ever really gone, that's what he said.

Twigs snapped and Janie looked up. Blue carried her jacket slung over his arm. He walked to where she sat on the log, looking up at her, the rain running down his face. He put his hands on her waist. Through the fabric of her wet shirt she could feel his hands, warm against her skin. He lifted her down in front of him and leaned against her, pushing her body into the weight of the log. Wiping back the hair that stuck to her forehead and cheeks, he kissed her. He slipped his warm hands under her shirt and up her back. "You're getting wet."

Later, she told him about her birthday, and he made her a bath. Nothing hurried by with Blue. Nothing about her felt unimportant. He washed her hair in the sink with lavender soap and wrapped her up in towels and then in a bathrobe. He smoothed coconut oil on her back and legs, breasts, and belly. He opened the wine and kept her glass full. He cooked pasta again, this time with marinara sauce. He brought out the rest of a hidden bar of chocolate.

They sat in front of the fire, and Blue caressed her neck. "You're not sleeping down here tonight."

"Oh yeah?" But she didn't sound serious. She dropped her head back against the couch in the crook of Blue's arm.

"Yeah." Blue loosened the belt of Janie's robe with one hand and moved her knees apart, kneeling between them, his black hair lightly touching her thighs as he bent down, his lips touching her stomach and then her hip bones. "I've got plans for you."

Can't Find My Way Home

JANIE SAT ON THE CABIN STEPS, THE DOGS AT HER FEET stretched out and panting in the early spring heat. She balanced her notebook on her knees and wrote. Inside, Blue crashed around making his coffee. She wanted to be in love with Blue because that would make it easy for her to stay here. Blue said he loved her right away, but she didn't trust his words. They didn't feel real. Paul was difficult but real. Paul couldn't really be trusted but he felt like home. She wished she could let go of the idea of Paul Jesse coming back.

Blue opened the door, letting it bang shut behind him. He sat on the step beside her with his coffee in one hand and a joint tucked behind his ear. "What are you writing about?"

Janie liked him better when he called her *Beautiful* and didn't seem to know her name or care much about what she did, let alone what she happened to be writing. "Just stuff," she said.

He leaned against the porch steps and sipped his coffee, holding the cup in both hands and stared out at the trees. "I think Paul ran off with my sister."

Janie sighed. She closed her notebook and put it beside her on the dusty wooden step.

"You should stay out here with me. Bill won't care."

"I'm heading out for Eugene tomorrow. I've got a friend there."

He put his hand on her thigh. "Eugene's a long ways away. How're you going to get there?"

"Walk out to the main road and hitch."

"It's a long way to go. What if your friend isn't there?"

"Stella's like the sun. He's dependable."

Blue got up and went inside, letting the door slam behind him.

The next morning, Janie packed up her things. She'd take just the pink suitcase. She didn't have a pack or a sleeping bag anymore. Those things were destroyed when she ended up at Stella's. She hadn't hitched since then. Thinking of being alone on the road gave her the heebie-jeebies, but she didn't want to stay here any longer. She'd leave the rest of her stuff and get Blue to mail it to her when she found Stella and Cookie. If she could find them. Eugene was a pretty big town.

Janie heard the dogs barking first and then an engine struggling up the hill. She froze and repeated some almost forgotten prayer in her head wishing it to be true. Paul's Opel sputtered into the clearing surrounded by the dogs. She dropped the hairbrush she had in her hand and pushed open the door. Paul came back for her.

PAUL DROPPED A coin into the pay phone in front of a tavern in Modesto. He called Luna and asked her to meet him there. For three weeks now, he'd been scrambling to keep Janie and Luna in their separate places. He told each of them he was dealing a lot for Bill, and he was but only because he could check on Luna and still keep track of Janie at the cabin. Janie wanted out of there. She wanted a place of their own and he wanted her away from Blue. He just couldn't leave Luna. She wasn't any better and he didn't know what he was supposed to do about it. He brought her downers when she asked and wondered what her parents thought and why it was up to him and not them to take care of her.

Paul sat at a booth in the back waiting for Luna to show up. When the door opened, he saw her before she saw him. She stood at the bar for a minute ordering drinks. Clothes hung loose on her body. She wore her hair pulled back in the same dull ponytail as when he'd dropped her off. Her skin looked sallow. Luna saw him then and walked to the booth with a double shot and a pitcher of beer. She slid in across from him. She rummaged through her pockets and pulled out a pack of cigarettes, lighting one. What he noticed then were her hands. They moved from glass to cigarette to lighter, never settling for more than a minute. Her cuticles were chewed ragged.

"Since when did you start smoking?"

"I needed a hobby." She drained her shot glass and caught the bartender's eye, holding up two fingers. "You'll have one, right? I'm buying."

He nodded.

She tipped back her beer and downed half of it. "Hey, I got some Percocets if you want."

"Great. What happened to the Seconals I gave you last week?"

"That was last week."

He took a drink of his beer. "Where'd you get the pills?"

"You the DEA or what? Fuck Paul, I got my own connections."

The bartender brought them another round and then a third. They sat silent for a time.

"You've got to get over this."

"I'm fine."

"I have eyes, baby. You ain't fine."

Luna blew smoke, lowered her sunglasses to the bridge of her nose and peered over the edge. Her eyes were flat. "Okay, then, I'm ambulatory. How's that girl you're with? What's her name? Janie?"

"Yep. She's okay. Luna, I'm sorry."

"Don't be. Never would've worked out with us. One more shot, Slick. I got to head back to the ranch." She sounded brittle.

"Whyn't you let me drive you up to the city tomorrow – see Bill – hang out up there."

"Nah – I'm done with all that."

"Luna, you got to get out of here."

She drained her glass before she spoke. "You know what?" She lit another cigarette. "I'm already gone."

The drive to her parents' house was too short. Before she got out she leaned into him for a second and kissed his cheek. "Goodbye, Paul."

"I'll call you in a week. Okay? One week."

She was out of the car in the dark. A light glowed from the porch. Her back to him, she started up the sidewalk. Paul called out to her. "Luna. See you soon. Okay?"

Facing Paul, she pointed to her eye, her heart, and then to him. *I love you.*

Only Love
Can Break Your Heart

JANIE TIED HER HAIR BACK WITH A FADED BANDANA, pulled on her overalls, and grabbed an old flannel shirt of Paul's on her way outside. She still didn't know how they came to be living here. One day they were at the cabin with Blue and the next they were driving to Oregon. Paul said a dude he knew named Judah worked at a dairy in St. Paul and the farmer needed more help. They could live in the house on the property with Judah and his girlfriend rent free. Questions sprang up, but Janie knew better than to ask. Now that they were living together, Paul had even more secrets.

Her dirty boots stood with the others on the front porch, covered thick with dried cowshit and mud. This morning not a cloud in sight, steam rising from damp ground, the day's coolness evaporating with the promise of summertime heat. The sun rose behind Mt. Hood. She liked to watch the sunrise from the porch as she put on her boots. The smell of sweet hay and the stronger smell of Holsteins filled the air. This was a big farm with two-hundred milk cows, some hop and hay fields, patches of green and gold knit together by roads.

Paul had changed, or maybe she just noticed more because they were together now. She didn't remember him drinking so much before she moved in with him. Now he would drink until he passed out, not every night, but often enough. When he drank, he sometimes lost his temper and said mean things. The night before he couldn't find his keys after drinking most of a half-case of beer. She told him he shouldn't drive anyway. That's when he yelled at her and said she must have hidden his keys to keep him at home. He wouldn't believe her when she said she didn't know where his keys were. He followed her through the house screaming at her to give him the keys. She found them at last in the kitchen and he left on his bike, coming home a few hours before he had to milk. She didn't remember him having a temper before. When he was mad like that, she got a feeling in the back of her neck – like a prickly, heavy weight – and her stomach hurt. No matter what she said or did to try and fix what was wrong, it wasn't enough.

It was a stretch to imagine Paul working on a farm, up early in the morning actually doing something besides smoking pot and watching TV, but for the past three months since they'd moved in with Judah and Shayna, he did, even on the days he was hung over so bad he puked before he left the house. Janie thought when Paul was used to the job, he'd quit drinking so much and go back to being himself. Plus, he hadn't lived with anyone in a long time. Janie thought he was stressed from having to do everything for both of them, and she felt bad for not bringing in any money. If she could do her share, he might not have to drink every night to unwind. Except for Paul's drinking and resulting bad moods, Janie liked it. The part she liked best was the house. She loved the house. It was an old farmhouse with paint cracked and flaking from years of weather. A big falling-down porch wrapped around the front of the building. The roof above the porch sagged in a low-slung V, and every step up the porch made the whole house sigh. Bare dirt skirted the house, smooth and worn hard from foot traffic and lack of water. The sweet-smelling plants of summer – meadowsweet and foxglove, morning glory and Brown-eyed Susan, Queen Anne's lace and purple loosestrife—grew wild around the yard. At one corner of the porch, a pink rose climbed up a rotting trellis and threatened to pull down the whole shaky enterprise. Up and over the eaves of the second story, the rose wound its way to the corner bedroom window where Janie had staked her claim. That summer she'd picked strawberries until her back ached and her hands were stained to buy a bed at the Christian Ladies Auxiliary in Silver Falls and a faded pink chenille bedspread to go on top of it. She also worked when she could for Henry, the farmer, whenever he or his wife needed a hand. She weeded their yard, washed their cars, and every week cleaned their house. Most of what she earned she spent on food. Paul made good money milking, plus the free rent, but he never seemed to have enough left over to buy groceries. Today was Friday, the day she cleaned Henry's house top to bottom for twenty bucks cash.

Janie stood in the sun, banging her boots together to knock loose the dried manure and mud. She wondered if she should run back upstairs and look for another pair of shoes, but just about all of them were in the same condition. Shayna came out of the house, slamming the screen shut behind her, a cup of coffee in one hand and a cigarette in the other.

"Man, can't those cows sleep in once in awhile? I closed last night." Shayna worked nights pouring beer at the Wooden Nickel. Her green kimono clung and fluttered, revealing Shayna's curvaceous body. She ran her fingers through her long shagged hair and exhaled perfect smoke rings.

"I'm cleaning Henry's today. You think these boots are okay?"

Shayna squinted and wrinkled her nose as she looked at the boots. She shook her head. "You ought to throw those filthy things out." She rubbed her temples. "Go up to my room and get my Cherokees."

As Janie disappeared into the house, Shayna yelled after her. "And put on my white cutoffs and change your damn shirt."

Janie ran up to Shayna and Judah's room. It reminded her of the dressing room at The Habit. The dressing table was spread with nail polish, perfume bottles, and boxes of jewelry. Scarves and purses hung over lamps and backs of chairs. Makeup spilled from the drawers of Shayna's bureau, and an amazing assortment of lingerie and skintight clothing covered every available space. Janie grabbed the platform Cherokee sandals and went back down.

She sat on the porch buckling the shoes. "How am I going to vacuum in these?"

"Pretend you're Farrah Fawcett –" Shayna took a drag off her cigarette.

"I bet Farrah doesn't vacuum." Janie sat back down and took off the shoes, picked them up by the straps and carried them slung over her shoulder like a backpack. "Guess I'll figure out how once I get there."

"Come back and get me when you're done and we'll do something. I'm not working tonight."

Janie nodded and walked through a neglected orchard at the back of their house and through a small pasture to the ranch house Henry had built for his wife twenty-five years ago. The ancient apple trees in the orchard and the house that they lived in were where Henry's great-grandparents had home-steaded. Small apples had formed on the upper branches of the unpruned trees. Janie hoped she and Paul would still be here when the apples were ripe.

Henry's wife, Nancy, didn't care for old things, so he built her something new and modern. Their house overlooked the farm and the Pudding River a ways off. The lawn sloped down on either side of the gravel driveway leading to a big metal gate at the edge of the road. In front of the gate was a Dairy of Honor sign. Red-and-white trimmed barns and outbuildings dotted the property under a few large oaks at the bottom of the hill. As nice and modern as it all was Janie preferred the house she lived in.

Janie bolted the gate and walked up the driveway to the back of the house. Boo, one of the black labs Henry raised for hunting, stood barking and wagging his tail to greet her. From inside, Nancy called for her to let herself in.

She went to the kitchen closet and took out the bucket she carried with her cleaning supplies. She really didn't mind cleaning their house. Usually Nancy left, and none of the kids stuck around if they could help it. She started in the living room rubbing away the smudges left from the dog's nose off the picture windows with paper towels. She had just started dusting when Nancy came down dressed for town. She had frosted hair and frosted lips and nails. Her two daughters, Lindsey and Ashley, looked almost exactly like her, but their hair was longer and feathered back, sprayed in place with a ton of hairspray. Janie liked Henry, tolerated Nancy, and hated both the girls.

Nancy stood in front of a big oval mirror in the hall checking her suit and adjusting her scarf. "Janie, I'm going into town with the girls to do some shopping. We need anything in the nature of cleaning supplies?"

"You're about out of Mop & Glo." Janie knew she was the only one who used the cleaning supplies unless some kind of disaster during the week required the use of a mop or broom.

"That it?" Nancy scrutinized her reflection in the mirror and picked a flake of icy pink lipstick from her teeth. She yelled down the hall. "If you girls want to go to the mall with me and my credit card, you better get moving." She turned to Janie. "Are you sure we just need the Mop & Glo?"

"Yes, ma'am, I'm sure."

"All righty then."

Lindsey and Ashley emerged from their rooms in a cloud of drugstore perfume. Janie bet they had to lie down and use a pair of pliers to zip up their tight jeans. She also bet that Lindsey wasn't wearing any underwear.

"Cute sandals. Where'd you get them?" Ashley said.

"Shayna let me borrow them." Janie moved a small bronze statue of a cowboy on a bucking horse onto the floor and polished the table.

"It figures," Lindsey said. "Mom, don't forget to tell her about our rooms."

"Oh that's right. Janie, make sure to vacuum the girls' rooms this week. You don't need to dust–just vacuum and do their bathroom." Janie wasn't supposed to go into the girls' rooms. Henry wanted them to have chores, including cleaning their rooms, but he was out at the barns and would never know. "Your money's on the kitchen table when you leave. Oh, and make sure you close the screen door tight. The flies are something awful this time of year."

As soon as Janie heard Nancy's car pull away, she turned on the radio and blasted it so she could listen to music while she vacuumed. She knew they wouldn't be back for hours. She finished cleaning the rest of the house and went down the hall to Lindsey and Ashley's bedrooms and shared bath. Wet towels lay in piles on the bathroom floor. Lipstick, flecks of toothpaste, and makeup dotted the mirror. The trash overflowed with dirty tissues, and wrapped tampons, and there was blood on the inner lid of the toilet seat. Janie cleaned it all. The bedrooms were just as bad. The floor was littered with clothes and garbage; pizza boxes and the remains of uneaten crusts, dishes with bits of hardened food, wet bathing suits and towels heaped on and under the beds.

As she made a path to vacuum Ashley's room, she found a bong. It amazed Janie that she was Ashley's age and only two years younger than Lindsey, though the family didn't know it. The girls didn't even do their own laundry–their mom did it. Sometimes they'd come down to the house to try to buy pot from Paul. They always offered him more money than what an eighth really cost, just to see if he'd do it. So far he hadn't, but Janie could see how tempted he was.

Janie went through their rooms until she found their pot. It was in the bottom of Lindsey's sock drawer. She couldn't believe it–the sock drawer. These girls didn't have much imagination. Janie didn't take the quarter-ounce baggie full of green bud. She just moved it to the front pocket of Lindsey's Chic jeans in the laundry basket. She left a corner of the baggie sticking out far enough that their mother would have to be blind to miss it. Janie took all the dirty clothes to the utility room, loaded the dirty dishes in the dishwasher, and hauled the trash to the cans behind the house. After she vacuumed both rooms, she picked up her twenty dollars and walked home.

Janie got back to the house just after two. Shayna still sat on the porch, but in a new outfit, and she had all the fixings for a pedicure spread out beside her and a glass of diet soda.

"How're the li'l bitches?"

"They went off to Salem with Mommy and the charge card." Janie took a sip of Shayna's drink.

"You want to go down to the river? Leave a note for the boys and go swimming?"

Janie stretched and thought for a minute. Paul didn't approve of her spending time with Shayna. He thought she was wild. He called her a slut behind Judah's back. He thought she dressed too trashy and talked too much. Janie knew this was all true but didn't see why she couldn't hang out with her.

Shayna looked her over. "Janie, when are you going to tell that old man of yours to get off your ass."

"It's not Paul. I'm just tired." Janie blushed. Shayna was a lot smarter than Paul thought.

"Come on. They're going to be working for hours still. We'll leave them a note and take some food, pick up some beer, and they can meet us at the trestle. It's Friday night, live a little."

Janie hesitated, but she could picture the river and smell the blackberry vines in the late afternoon sun. It was almost September, and in a few weeks there'd be nothing but rain and cold. She smiled at Shayna. "Okay. You talked me into it. I'll go change my clothes."

They drove down to the banks of the Pudding River in Shayna's truck. Fine white dust coated everything. Heatwaves reflected off the gravel single-lane road. The ruts were so deep that Janie bounced up and hit her head twice on the roof. Early fall gold tinted every leaf, and the bleached hay fields waited still for the tractors to come. These were the last days of sweat and cold beer and swimming in the river. Shayna parked the truck and hauled a cooler out of the back. Janie grabbed a grocery bag full of food from the cab.

A path led down a steep bank to the river's wide rocky beach. It was still early enough to get a good spot by the water, but when late afternoon arrived, kids from far away as Salem and even Newburg would make this their local night spot. Shayna said hellos to some of the people already hanging out waiting for dark. Janie took off the baggy shirt and shorts she wore over her swimsuit. She avoided eye contact with people so she wouldn't have to talk. Nobody here knew her well. Not even Shayna or Judah knew she was technically underage, a runaway, a dropout, a former topless dancer. Janie slipped into the water while Shayna stood talking to some guy.

At first she shivered, and the skin on her arms and legs puckered. After a few minutes the water didn't feel so cold. Janie swam downstream underneath the train trestle. Trains hadn't run on these tracks for years, but that didn't mean they weren't used. Mostly it was boys and a few wild girls who climbed the trestle to dive. Janie floated away from all the people getting high, getting drunk, yelling and screaming while they jumped from the trestle into the water below. She swam where the river bottom grew thick with silt and weeds. Blackberry vines tangled against the steepest banks, and from all around the gentle sound of water lapped against the shore. In a dense patch of weeds and brambles, Janie caught a glint of glass and the peak of a roof. She'd been in the water long enough to start to feel cold. She needed to get out and dry off. Maybe she'd explore that little shed. The sun still had a couple of hours before it would begin to slide behind the Coast Range. Paul probably wouldn't come to the river till dusk. For a minute, Janie felt the weight of him at the back of her neck. She shook it off like the water as she pulled herself onto the bank.

Sister Morphine

PAUL'S BACK ACHED AND THE HANGOVER HE WOKE UP with hadn't gone away. Laying irrigation pipe for Henry all day and coming home to find Janie gone with Shayna had not improved his mood. The note on the table read, *I'm kidnapping Janie. We're at the river. Bring more beer – S.* Paul hopped on his bike and rode out to find her. He didn't like her hanging around Shayna. Shayna was too wild for her own good. Janie hadn't done anything to make him not trust her. He didn't ask her about Blue because he didn't want to talk about Luna.

He thought about Luna at least once a day, usually more. Her crazy smile. That cowboy hat she always wore. Two weeks after he'd left her in front of her parents house, Paul had gone to the city, copped a pound of bud, sold it to the twins in Seattle a couple days later, and was back at Bill's to pick up another pound. He and Bill were in the garage looking at an old Indian frame that Bill got in a trade for some pot.

"So, what do you think?" Bill ran his hand over the frame of the motorcyle.

"Nice bike. You think you can get it running?"

"Yeah – the bitch'll be finding original parts. Always is with bikes like this." Bill took a sip of tequila. "You think you could stop by the cabin and feed the dogs? Spend the night if you want. I'm going to go up there tomorrow to stay until Blue gets back from the funeral."

Paul knew before he asked. "What funeral?"

"You didn't hear about Luna?"

"I just saw her–"

"Not this week you didn't. Crazy bitch went and offed herself."

It didn't surprise Paul, but for a minute he couldn't speak.

"They found her washed up on the beach at Half Moon Bay. Blue only knew because he called his mom's to see if Luna wanted to come up to the cabin."

Paul couldn't speak.

"Man, don't take it so hard. You getting sentimental on me? Plenty of women to go around. The bitch was a lot of fun–great fuck and all, but she couldn't handle her shit. You know what they say–got to pay to play."

"Yeah, they say that, don't they." Paul steadied his hand around his shot glass and downed it. "Yeah. I can go by and feed the dogs. Maybe I'll spend the night." They stood around in the garage talking about bikes and dope for another hour before Paul drove to the cabin.

PAUL MADE IT look like the work of vandals. He felt bad about killing the dogs but he felt worse about Luna. Before he left the cabin, Paul took a polaroid of Luna from the kitchen wall. She sat on the porch wearing one of his old shirts, the top buttons opened, the curve of her tanned throat so lovely, the bridge of her collarbones as delicate as a bird's wing. She had her cowboy hat tipped back, and her smile was caught in a laugh. He tucked the picture in his shirt pocket when he rode away.

Paul called Bill from a phone booth at the Texaco in Garberville that night. He was careful to say what he might have said once–*the cabin was wrecked when I got there. The dogs were gone, your whole crop torn out. Probably just some stupid kids– that's what it looked like to me. Yeah, funny about the dogs. Look, I'll see you in a couple of weeks after I unload this dope. Yeah, right.*

Paul took the job at the dairy that week. He hadn't been back to Bill's since.

PAUL TURNED THE bike onto the unmarked road that led down to the river. First order of business, find Janie. Second, get high and have a few beers while he unloaded the acid he had in his pocket. Cars, bikes, and trucks were piled along the shoulder of the road. His bike kicked up clouds of thick white dust. It hadn't rained in weeks.

Paul spotted Shayna's Toyota close to the river. She and Janie must have gotten here early. On a weekend night in high summer, there was no place to park. People had to hike in from the main road by the time the sun went down. Paul pulled the Panhead in behind Shayna's truck and stretched as he climbed off the bike. As he worked his way to the river, Paul said his hellos and sold a few hits of acid. Finding Shayna didn't take much effort. She held court in a skintight bikini, her breasts straining the thin, silky material. A few admirers sat with her. Paul didn't know how Judah could put up with Shayna. Janie was nowhere in sight. Shayna spotted Paul and sat up on the blanket, fishing around in a nearby cooler for a beer.

Paul took the beer from her and popped open the top. "Where's Janie?"

"I don't know. She took off when we got here."

"When was that?"

"Relax. Have a beer. She went for a swim."

"When was the last time you saw her?"

"I don't know. Maybe an hour ago. Relax. She'll be back. She's a big girl."

Paul didn't know when it went from having a good time with Janie to feeling responsible for her. Sometimes her love made him feel good. Sometimes it made him feel like he was in prison with no hope of parole. All he wanted was to go get high and be left in peace. He finished off his beer and split to sell the rest of the acid.

People milled around the river. A keg turned up in the back of a pickup truck. Paul bought a red plastic cup. An older dude in worn leathers stood next to the keg, pumping it up before he filled his cup. He had a "Live to Ride" tattoo on one bicep and a naked woman on his forearm.

Paul took the nozzle from him and filled his cup. "Bring your bike?"

The guy took a sip and nodded.

"What do you ride?"

"Knucklehead."

"I got a '58 Panhead."

"Nice."

"Yeah." They both stood silent before moving away from the crowd of people lined up for the keg. A pretty blonde in a turquoise tube top stepped up to the guy and gave him a hug.

"Rick! I was wondering if I was going to see you tonight. Come see me before you leave, okay?"

Rick wiped the beer foam off his mustache and nodded.

Paul held out his hand. "I'm Paul. You the Rick with the crank?"

"You the Paul with the acid?"

Paul grinned and finished his beer. "Small fucking world."

"Want to make a deal?"

"What is this, a game show?"

"Yeah. *The Price Is Right.*"

They took their bikes back out to the main road and drove miles on county roads where traffic disappeared at dark. In the middle of nowhere, Rick pulled off and unlocked a padlocked gate that led down a long, narrow driveway. Ahead was a single-wide mobile home with a porch tacked on. Behind the mobile home sat a shed about thirty feet long. They parked the bikes in front of the porch and walked to the shed. The door had a chain lock around the latch. Rick unlocked it with a key from a huge ring he pulled from his pocket. A dog barked from inside as he opened the door.

"Get back, Hooker! C'mon in. Don't mind the dog. Long as you're with me she won't fuck with you."

The dog, a black and white pit bull, continued snarling until Rick kicked her in the ribs and sent her cowering to a corner.

"Nice looking dog."

"Out here you got to have a dog and a piece if you deal."

"Yeah. That's everywhere."

The overhead lights hummed and the smell of motor oil and WD-40 permeated the windowless shed. Tools hung from hooks on the walls and ceiling. The cement floor was swept clean, and empty coffee cans acted as ashtrays half full of sand. A stained set of coveralls sat folded on top of an old barstool. Rick flipped on the stereo and opened a big wooden cabinet. Inside a triple-beam scale, handgun, shoebox with pot-filled baggies, and film canisters sat on tidy shelves. Rick took out a small foil-wrapped square, a syringe, a silver spoon, a lighter, and a cotton ball from a first-aid kit.

Under the metallic glare of the overhead lights, Rick put an old Traffic album on the turntable on the workbench. "After you," Rick said, handing Paul the square of foil.

The first time you shot dope with someone, they were watching to see what you did – if you were a lightweight, if you knew how to tie off your own arm, if you had tracks from a long relationship with the needle. Paul could taste the crank in the back of his throat and feel his scalp begin to tingle before he slipped the needle into his left forearm. It was always like this. Like the best fuck of his life. Like going home. He had to be careful not to use the same spot too often, or the vein would collapse and abscess. An abscess made it harder to find a sweet spot the next time. Lately, Paul couldn't fool himself as well as he used to. He knew there would always be a next time. His arm burned as the speed made its way into his blood supply. His heart beat in his throat and his ears filled with the sound of the ocean. He knew he was sweating, and for a minute it felt like his heart would explode. But it didn't, and the peace of being wired and invincible settled over him.

JANIE WOKE UP to darkness. It took a minute to remember where she was – in the little shed under all the blackberry bushes. She'd slept through the last of the afternoon light and now it was dark. She'd crawled in wet and cold hours earlier to look around and stayed to dry off and warm up. She stretched out on the floor in a pool of sun. Her body felt heavy with the long swim and heat. Through the walls she could hear the buzz of bees in the bushes. She had closed her eyes, just for a minute, to rest before she went back. Paul wouldn't come down to the river for awhile.

She must have been asleep for hours. She sat up and left the shed, down the bank, and back into the river. The water felt colder than it had before. The moon hung in the sky, a shimmer of light on the water. Her stomach growled. She hadn't eaten today. The swim back against the current was more difficult and took longer. She could see a campfire from the bank, and silhouettes of people milling around laughing and talking too loud. She aimed for the fire, where she'd be most likely to find Shayna, her dry clothes, and Paul. Janie felt she was in trouble again. She spent a lot of time these days trying to figure out how to avoid Paul's anger. She knew he'd be wondering where she was.

She pulled herself out of the water, wading as soon as she could stand. Some dude whistled at her and yelled, "Look at the mermaid." She shivered with cold as the water ran down her legs. She found Paul by the keg with an older dude. They were talking and drinking beer. Janie didn't know if he'd seen her yet, didn't know whether she should find her clothes and dress first or go right over. Then Paul looked at her and he didn't smile or call out.

Janie walked over to them knowing she was already in trouble, and it was her fault. "Sorry I wasn't here when you got here. I went for a swim and then I fell asleep." She sounded lame even to herself.

Paul didn't look at her. The muscles in his jaw clenched and unclenched the way they did when he was wired and pissed off.

"I'm going to go get my stuff from Shayna," she said. "Have you seen her?"

The older guy looked confused for a minute "So is this your old lady?"

"I don't know." Paul's voice was colder than the river. "Are you my old lady, Jane?"

Janie nodded. He'd never used to talk to her like this.

Paul glared at her. "Well then, you better get dressed quick and get yourself home."

Janie nodded again. Her face burned with shame. She'd been dismissed and knew it would only make things worse to say more, but she couldn't stop herself. "I'm sorry, Paul. I found a shed downriver and fell asleep, and when I woke up it was night."

He slapped her so fast she didn't believe he'd really done it. "Get the fuck out of here."

Janie stumbled past him and ran into Judah coming up the hill with the cooler.

"Hi, Janie," he said. "Paul's looking for you. What's going on?"

"Can I get a ride home?"

"I'm headed that way."

"Can you wait while I grab my clothes?"

"You okay?"

Janie ran down the bank and retrieved her clothes, pulling the shirt and jeans on over her wet suit. She rushed back up the hill. She didn't see Paul on their way to Judah's truck.

Judah pushed the lighter in and waited for it to pop out. "These always make me think of those timers in Thanksgiving turkeys." He lit a cigarette. "So, what did you do today, Janie? You know, I don't think you've ever told me your last name."

Janie looked over at Judah as he drove. He reminded Janie of those sad-eyed Jesus paintings in an old book she'd seen once. "I guess I never did tell you my last name. What's yours?"

"Greenberg."

"Mine's Marek. I don't think anybody's asked me my last

name in a long time. It seems like people don't have last names anymore."

He laughed.

"Where's Shayna?"

"She's going to hang out a little longer. I've got to milk in the morning so I'm off to bed."

"Doesn't it bug you? You know, her out here by herself?"

"I know what a lot of people think about me and Shayna. I just don't care." Judah yawned and smiled at her. "You can buy a house and fix it up the way you want it. You can buy a pair of pants and have them taken in or shortened, but people and shoes you better take the way they are."

Janie smiled at him. "Can't you stretch shoes?"

"Yeah, but only about half a size, and they'll always be the tight side of comfortable."

AS THE NIGHT dragged on, Janie knew Paul wasn't coming home. She moved around their room putting things away and listening for his bike. She picked up a book she'd been reading, but the words made no sense, and she found herself reading the same sentence over and over. Janie had plans for this weekend – Paul's weekend off, no cows to milk, no irrigation pipe to move. Since they'd been on the farm, Judah and Paul took turns having the weekends off. She'd been looking forward to sleeping in, making love late in the morning, falling back to sleep. They didn't make love much anymore. He was always tired, wired or drunk, or maybe he just didn't want her anymore. That scared her more than anything, that he would be done with her and she'd be alone again.

By first light, she had to get up and get out or go crazy. Grabbing a bucket from the porch, she walked along the back of the house picking the blackberries that grew everywhere. She listened for Paul and rehearsed what she would say if he came back. She'd begun to realize that, with Paul, the question was *if* not *when*.

The day seemed to grow longer with the waiting. The hours crawled by until it was evening and Shayna began dressing for work. Janie walked down the hall and peeked her head in the door. "Can I come in?"

"Sure. Help me with this zipper." Shayna was struggling into a black velour halter dress.

"Won't you be hot?"

Shayna shrugged as she bent to the vanity's mirror, lining her eyes with a smoky blue pencil. "The tips'll be good."

Janie sat on the bed, leaning back on her elbows to watch Shayna get ready.

"You ought to come down to the Nickel tonight instead of sitting here waiting for Paul."

"I want to be here when he comes home." Janie chewed on a cuticle and shifted around on the bed.

"You're always waiting on him. Maybe he needs a little waiting on you. You'd think you did something wrong, the way you wait around for him. You ought to teach him a lesson."

"He's not like Judah. It wouldn't work out."

"I bet he won't even come back tonight. He's off with Biker Rick, the crank freak, and you'll be sitting here alone all night waiting for him. Janie, you're young – you should be enjoying yourself. You should be dressing up and going out."

"I don't have clothes for going out."

"Well, I do. Let's get you all dressed up. Then, if you change your mind, you can come with me. Judah's coming in for a beer later on. He'd drive you home, if you didn't want to stay."

Janie looked at the fancy clothes all over the room. "You don't have time."

"I don't have to leave that soon. C'mon, take off those jeans, and let's sex you up!"

Shayna's enthusiasm was catchy. Janie let Shayna paint her face with too much makeup and spray her hair.

Shayna started digging through the clothes on the bed. "Now, what about an outfit?"

Janie giggled. "An outfit? Man, my stepmom was always trying to get me into those *outfits* at Penney's."

"Well, I didn't get this at Penney's." Shayna held out a pair of silky orange harem pants. "You need a halter top to go with."

Janie began to tie the pants on at her waist.

"Hey! Take your panties off. You're not supposed to wear these with panties."

"No way, Shayna. There's no way I'm –"

"Wear this then." Shayna tossed Janie a sleeveless black Danskin leotard with straps that crossed in the back. While Janie changed, Shayna dug through a box of jewelry and produced a pair of silver hoop earings and several thin silver bangle bracelets. "You look great!"

"I look like a whore."

Judah appeared in the doorway smiling. "Nope, you look like a whore's child."

Shayna gave him a hug. "She doesn't either and you're no one to talk. You stink like cows. Go take a bath. I have to go to work but bring her down with you later. Okay?" She kissed Judah on the cheek as he took a towel and headed for the bathroom.

Janie shrugged. "Don't count on it, Shayna. But this was fun."

After Shayna left, Janie went to the kitchen and poured a glass of milk. A moment later she heard Paul's bike in front of the house. She knew that whatever was wrong between them would be made worse when he saw her in Shayna's clothes with too much makeup. His boots hit every other step on his way up to their room, and she stood at the sink, pouring the milk out and rinsing the glass. For a minute she considered going out the back door and waiting for him to pass out or leave, she knew that would be the smart thing to do, but she realized she would never be smart when it came to Paul. She walked up the flight of stairs to their room. The door was open. Paul had dumped out the contents of all the dresser drawers on the bed and some of the clothes had slipped to the floor. Now he was digging through baskets and boxes.

"Are you looking for something?"

He spun around and grabbed her by the wrist, yanking her into the room and slamming the door. "Where did you put my keys to the car this time?"

"I don't have your keys. Aren't they downstairs? You must have just had them."

His red-rimmed eyes looked glassy from no sleep. He tightened his jaw, chewing his words as he spit them at her. "Where the fuck are you going dressed like that?" He held her wrist tight and squeezed, twisting so hard she felt the skin burn. She knew there'd be a mark later. "You going trolling for a farm boy?"

"I wasn't going anywhere. Shayna just wanted to see me dressed up."

"Right. Shayna." He let go of her wrist and went back to digging through the box he had on the floor. "You know what? I don't need this shit – wondering where you are, who you're fucking. You better be gone when I get back." He stared at her.

"Paul, don't be mad." Janie swallowed hard.

"Where are my keys?" Paul half stood and yanked her down by the hair. Her face was inches away from the open box. "Find them! You hid them, didn't you? Quit looking at me like that – "

Janie saw Judah standing in the doorway, wrapped in a striped beach towel fresh out of the shower. Nothing about Judah let on that he heard anything. "Hey Paul, you have a hang scale? I think this eighth might be a little shy."

Paul released Janie's hair, and she slipped away from him. He moved and picked up his scales from the floor. "Who'd you get it from?"

"Jeff – you know him?" Judah didn't look at Janie or appear to notice that the room had been torn apart.

"Yeah. I know Jeff. Here're the scales."

"Want to smoke some? Try it out?"

"Sure."

Janie heard Judah's calm voice walking down the hall

with Paul. "Hey, in case you're looking for them, your keys are on the kitchen table."

"Thanks, man."

Later, after Paul left in his car, Judah came up to her room. Janie had scrubbed the makeup off her face, showered, and put on her pajamas. She was folding clothes, putting all the pieces back together, making it look as if nothing had happened. Judah tapped at the door.

"You okay?"

"Yeah. He didn't really do anything." She said it loud enough to convince herself it was true. "Aren't you going to meet Shayna at work?"

"I'm kind of tired. Think I'll eat and get some sleep. Come on down and eat something. I hate eating alone."

"I'm not hungry, but thanks." Her stomach ached, and she wanted to sleep.

JANIE WOKE LATE. She went to the bathroom and ran a tub of hot water. Her body ached even though he hadn't really hurt her. The night before felt like a bad dream. Below her, the front door opened and closed. She heard the sound of boots being taken off to dry and placed by the door. She heard the low hum of men's voices, then the sound of bare feet coming softly up the stairs. The door to her room opened and closed, feet padded back down the hall to the bathroom. She got out of the tub and wrapped herself in a towel. Two taps and the door opened. Paul came in and closed the door. His eyes were tired but the madness was gone.

"Janie, I know sorries don't mean much, but I am sorry. I don't know what I'd do without you. I didn't mean what I said last night. I was crazy high. I don't even remember what happened. Judah told me this morning when I got to work."

"I shouldn't have listened to Shayna. It was my fault."

"You didn't do anything. I turn everything to shit. I should have left you with Stella."

"I don't want to be anywhere else." She stepped into his arms and felt him fold around her, warm and familiar.

He held her close telling her a favorite story. "I remember that night I first took you home, sitting on the couch at Delores's while you slept. I didn't want to leave. No girl's ever made me feel like that. I was looking at your face, wishing I could do it all over, you know–everything. With you."

Janie's eyes were closed, and his words spread inside her warm and true. He kissed her eyelids and held her face in his hands, touching her lips with the tip of his tongue. She heard herself say *I love you*. He faced her to the mirror with her eyes still closed, his body a nest behind her, creating heat in the small spaces between them. He crossed his arms over her. No pressure, no force, his body an invitation to come home. He combed his fingers through her hair, letting them travel across her throat, her shoulders, and down her arms to her hands that still held the towel around her. His hands so warm and dry against her body as he pressed the towel from her hands, releasing it to the floor. His voice in her ear. "Open your eyes, Jane. See what I see when I look at you."

Janie opened her eyes, taking in the reflection of herself dizzied by love and need. Paul's face in the crook of her neck behind her, and Paul's hands calloused and real against her suntanned hips, traveling slowly up the contour of her waist, her ribs, the undersides of her breasts. He looked at her eyes in the mirror. "You're home."

She turned toward him, opening his shirt and stepping into his skin. His teeth and lips met on the ridge of her ear. "Don't ever leave me."

She could feel his heart inside her beating. She wasn't going anywhere.

Pretzel Logic

PAUL DIDN'T EVER REMEMBER IT BEING SO HARD TO CUT back on the booze and drugs. Summer passed into fall, and he couldn't seem to make it through a day without something to take the pressure off. He'd stopped drinking before, or at least slowed down every now and then, but this time, telling himself that he should take a break for a day or two wasn't happening. Waking up hungover, he swore to himself that today would be the day he didn't drink, didn't get wired, didn't take whatever handful of pills he could find or was offered. Every afternoon, he told himself that a couple of beers would be okay, and the joint he smoked in the afternoon wouldn't be the same without an ice cold tall can of beer. Nothing would ever get him to give up the pot he smoked. He'd been smoking a joint first thing in the morning and last thing at night every day since he was thirteen and that wasn't about to stop, but he wished he could stop the drinking. When he drank and got wired, something inside snapped. It wouldn't matter so much if Janie wasn't there with that look when he first woke up. Sometimes when he drank he couldn't remember what he'd done. He'd look for clues, hoping the house would still be standing, and there'd be no blood on his car or bike. Sometimes, in the moment before he blacked out, he could almost see out of the corner of his eye what he was about to do. Once he stepped across that line nothing mattered but to keep on going.

When Paul teetered on the edge of a blackout he believed

that a demon lived inside him. It never rested. It was always there
waiting for the alcohol or crank to kick in and let him loose.
Finding out he slapped Janie didn't surprise him. That was how
he'd lost Mia. He'd be high and snap for whatever reason. After
it happened the first time, it just kept happening.

This morning the alarm clock rang at 3:00 a.m. as usual.
He could hear rain beating against the window as he picked his
clothes up off the chair and dressed. Janie started to wake up, but
he whispered for her to stay in bed. The house was freezing.
As he pulled on his boots in the dark to go milk a herd of shit-
covered Holsteins in the rain, it occurred to him that this
particular way of life might not be conducive to staying straight.
Throughout the morning as he hooked up the waiting heifers
to the mechanical milking machine, he built an argument convinc-
ing himself that to get straight and have a normal life, he needed
to get a normal job, working days and sleeping nights. He knew
there were people who didn't drink the way he did, or plug
themselves into a needle every chance they got. He didn't have
to quit smoking pot, just everything else–except for a few
beers. Even straight people drank a beer or two at night to relax
and unwind. No harm in that.

JANIE STOOD AT the sink washing the counter of dishes Shayna
left in her wake every day. When she had gotten up, cold
because the heater didn't work and crabby because her period
had started and she felt bloated and achy, all she wanted was
to make a hot cup of cocoa and take it back to bed with her hot-
water bottle until she could face building a fire in the wood
stove. Instead she had to wash dishes so she could heat the milk
in a pan and have a cup to put it in and a spoon to stir it with.
The lukewarm water in the sink steamed the window above the
sink. Janie shivered in her thin blue sweater and long johns.
Last week the clocks had been set back for fall and the weather
had turned cold. Farm life didn't seem like as much fun as it
had a month ago. The house was drafty, and the roof leaked. Mold

was growing in all the dark, unventilated places, like the closets and bathroom. It was cold and dark when Paul got up to go milk in the morning, and cold and dark when he went to milk in the evening. Today all Janie wanted was to be warm and dry, but with the rain coming down in sheets and an east wind blowing hard, she doubted this was possible. She heard Paul clomp up the porch and take off his boots. He brought an armload of wood into the kitchen and crumpled newspaper to stuff inside the woodstove with the dry kindling.

"How're you feeling?" Paul lit the fire and stood up. "It's colder than a motherfucker in here. Why didn't you start a fire, baby?"

"I wasn't planning on being up. Shayna left the dishes again."

Paul filled the teakettle with water and put it on the stove. He stood behind Janie, holding her tight and rubbing her arms through the thin sweater. "You're like ice. You know, I've been thinking all morning about this. What if we got our own place in Silverton or Mt. Angel, and we wouldn't have to put up with all this."

"You work here. I work here."

"I was thinking about that. I could get a regular straight job. I know a couple of the foremen at the mobile home plant. It pays pretty well. I've been thinking maybe it'd be good for us to get a normal gig."

"I couldn't get a regular job right away."

"You wouldn't have to. I could take care of you. What do you think?"

Janie replied with a kiss.

By Friday the next week, Paul had a job hanging sheetrock at Silversides Mobile Home Factory. His foreman, Jim, knew of a little one-bedroom house for rent–cheap, only $200 a month, near the IGA market and close enough to walk to Suds-Yo-Duds. For rent money, Paul turned over an ounce of crank for Rick at the plant. Most of the men and women who worked there, from the plumbers and electricians to the secretary in the head office, bought crank or pot from him. Paul planned to move into the new place after work on the first payday.

Friday morning, Janie began packing up their stuff in boxes that Shayna had been saving and bringing home from work. Since the night on the river, things hadn't been the same in the house. Janie knew Paul never liked Shayna, and now she knew that Shayna never liked Paul either. Janie figured Judah must have told her about that night in August with Paul, but nothing bad had happened since then. Janie had put that night out of her mind, telling herself it was a freak accident and mostly her fault, not something that would ever happen again. She was sure this new job, with its regular hours and regular money, would help Paul stay straight. She knew he was dealing, but they needed the money to move and get settled. She didn't think he was shooting dope–just smoking pot and drinking two tall beers after work. Janie could deal with that.

She went down to the kitchen to pack the few dishes they owned.

Shayna sat at the table in front of the woodstove looking at a back issue of *Vogue*. "So you're really moving?"

"Yup. I think I know which dishes are mine." Janie opened a drawer to sort silverware first.

"Take what you want. We have too many dishes. You're going to need a few things, anyway."

"Paul says he'll take me to the Goodwill in Salem."

"Paul's a real prince."

"Shayna, don't be like that."

"Look Janie, if you wanted to stay–"

"I don't." Janie slammed the drawer shut and opened the cabinet below, pulling out a cast-iron skillet and putting it into a box.

"Don't get all pissy with me. I don't care what you do. I'm just telling you–"

"Telling me what–to leave my old man? You don't know about Paul and me."

Shayna got quiet, took a Kool from the pack on the table, and lit it with a wooden match. She exhaled a smoke ring that floated and dissolved in the air between them. "I left home after watching my dad get shit-faced every night for eighteen fucking years and beat the crap out of me, my mom, and anybody else who got in his way." She put her magazine on the table and got up, scooting her chair across the floor with the scraping sound of metal on wood. "Right now, I know more about you and Paul than you do. You think he'll change and I know he won't. I hope I'm wrong but I doubt it."

IN SILVERTON THE homes were trimmed with gingerbread and had picket fences and old rose bushes planted years ago when the town was born. Janie could walk from one end of town to the other in half an hour, but it usually took longer, because each time she saw things she hadn't noticed before. The downtown had two-story brick buildings and wide wood-plank sidewalks. For such a small town, it had everything she'd ever wanted, it was pretty and old timey, with tall oak and maple trees that changed colors in autumn and lost their leaves with every gust of cold wind. Janie liked to go to the Farmhouse Restaurant for apple fritters and hot chocolate made from scratch. On the main corner, the Silverton Music Box Theatre played movies Friday through Sunday nights with matinees on Saturday and Sunday. Janie loved going to the movies even when Paul wouldn't go. Standing in line with what seemed to be everyone in a forty-mile radius made her feel part of things.

A block away from the theatre was her favorite place of all—The Good Shepherd Thrift Store, run by ladies from one of the town's four churches. The first week in town, Janie found an old Schwinn bike with a wire basket for five dollars. She bought a kid's wagon for a couple of dollars so she could haul the laundry over to Suds-Yo-Duds every week. The ladies who ran the store were volunteers, and they all worked on different days. Janie's favorite old lady wore two-piece knit dresses in pale blue or bright red and orthopedic rubber-soled nurse's shoes. She had fuzzy white hair in a bun at the base of her neck. Her name was Lila, and she was teaching Janie to knit.

Janie had come in on a Wednesday, late in the afternoon. Paul said he was working overtime all week, so he wouldn't be home till after five. Janie had stew in the oven, slow-cooking all day, and she was bored. The days dragged without a job or anyone to talk to. She wished she could have gone to school. She used to love school especially reading and art. She'd been a good student too. Maybe one day after she turned eighteen she'd get to finish school and get a real job like regular people.

The day was clear, sunny, and cold. She'd gone for a long bike ride out of town and into the hills. Coming back, she stopped at the Good Shepherd to get warm, and there was Lila alone, sitting in one of the worn easy chairs that were for sale. Beside her sat a basket full of ivory-colored balls of wool, and in her hands knitting needles that clicked and spun. She smiled. "Hello dear." Lila had a name tag so Janie knew her name. But most of the people in town, if they called Janie anything, called her "dear" or "honey."

Janie walked over to where Lila sat. "What're you making?"

"Layettes for the babies who need them at the hospital. My, you look cold! Would you like a cup of tea? I bring my thermos from home."

"Sure," Janie said.

Lila stiffly got up and put her knitting down in her chair. "I've seen you quite a bit in the last month or so. Are you new to town?" Behind the counter Lila pulled out a large red plaid thermos and two tea cups. "I hope you don't mind it sweet and light."

Janie took the teacup from Lila's hand; it was as thin and brittle. She held the cup, enjoying the warmth of it in her hands. "I just moved here. I like your store a lot." Janie took a sip. She walked back to the chair, stooping to look at the knitting. "When did you learn to knit?"

"Oh my! Since I could hold the needles, dear. My mother used to say that idle hands were the devil's playmate. She always kept us busy. Where are my manners? I haven't introduced myself. I'm Mrs. Lila Mersereau–and you are?"

"I'm Janie." She looked at the delicate pattern of cables taking shape in the pale ivory wool. "I wish I could knit."

"It's usually so slow on Wednesdays–if you'll come about this time next week, I can teach you. You'll have to practice, and we'll have to find you some needles."

Janie smiled. "Really? You think you could teach me?"

"I learned to knit before I was five years old, and I'll be eighty-six this December. If you'll come and you'll practice, I'm sure you can learn." Lila moved to an aisle that held small vases and baskets, old teapots, and a variety of other donated things. "Now let me see. I thought I saw a pair of nice old wooden needles–" She paused and rummaged among some things in a large basket full of sewing supplies, pulling out a pair of wooden knitting needles the thickness of Janie's smallest finger. "Here they are! Now let's get you started."

At first, Janie didn't tell Paul about Lila because she hoped to knit him a Christmas gift. Lila thought she could easily make a scarf by Christmas time. In just a few Wednesdays, Janie began to realize she wanted to keep Lila separate from her life with Paul. She liked how being with Lila made her feel–simple. Nothing in the little house she shared with Paul on Chester Street was turning out to be simple.

Paul had promised her he wasn't going to deal anymore, but come Friday he went to Rick's, picked up an ounce of crank, and drove all over the valley selling it. She knew he was using too. His face broke out in pimples and he picked at them until they got infected. He ground his teeth and seemed thinner by the day. Sometimes he didn't come home until after Saturday's half-day overtime shift and then only to change and shower before going back out. Even with all the dealing and the regular weekly paycheck they were behind in the bills, and sometimes he wouldn't give her money for groceries because there wasn't any money left. Janie knew better than to ask why.

Sitting in an easy chair knitting at the Good Shepherd with Lila, light streaming in through the windows, it was easy to forget everything else. The only sounds were her needles clicking and a Benny Goodman album playing "String of Pearls" on the Philco stereo for sale in the corner.

Lila looked over her shoulder. "You've dropped a stitch, dear. Remember how to go back and pick it up?"

Janie bent over her needles, shoulders up by her ears, trying to scoop the errant gap back into wholeness. "Shoot. I'm never going to get this."

"Don't be discouraged. It's good practice." Lila stretched and yawned. "Will you be having Thanksgiving with your family, Janie?"

Janie had been dodging the whole family thing with Lila for weeks. She didn't exactly lie, but she didn't tell her the truth either. "I'm not sure what I'm doing."

Lila laughed out loud. "You know, dear, I taught high school English for nearly twenty years, and I never knew such a girl for secrets. Most girls your age spill the beans with a little prodding, but not you."

Janie blushed. "I'm not in high school anymore. I'm nineteen." Janie always said nineteen, even back when she was fourteen. It sounded more believable to be nineteen.

"I would guess you to be sixteen or seventeen at most."

Janie couldn't say a thing. Her face felt hot. For a second, she wanted to run from the store and never come back. In the next second, she wanted to tell Lila the truth.

Lila patted her shoulder. "It's all right, but if you'd ever like to tell me I'll listen."

Janie thought of the home she'd started leaving when her dad died. "I used to get up early on Thanksgiving with my mom before she went to work. She was a nurse. I'd help her put the turkey in the oven, so it'd be ready when she got home. Mostly

I just watched. The last thing she'd do before she left was kiss a tissue after she put on her lipstick. She wore this really red lipstick that smelled like ink almost. And she had wavy hair. My dad got up later, and we'd watch the Macy's parade. It seemed like that parade lasted until my mom got home, but I know that's not right. I remember we'd use candles and pretty dishes, and I remember how the cranberry sauce made that sound when it came out of the can."

Janie looked at Lila. "I haven't had Thanksgiving at home for–" she counted on her fingers, "four years. This will be five. My mom and dad died."

"Oh my, I'm so sorry." Lila took a handkerchief from the sleeve of her red knit dress and blew her nose discreetly. "That's a long time. Would you like to join me?"

Janie shook her head. "I've kind of got a new family I'm going to be with."

"That's a fine thing." Lila put her needles down and smiled. "My son is coming down with his family. Do you think you could help me clean house next week? I can't get all the nooks and crannies the way I used to."

Lila wrote her address on a small piece of paper and gave Janie directions. Janie would go over to Lila's Monday and Tuesday of Thanksgiving week, and she would be paid. Janie hadn't been thinking about Thanksgiving until Lila brought it up. Now it was the only thing on her mind. She hadn't thought there'd be any money for turkey or pie, but the possibility of making it nice–the way it used to be–possessed her. She'd never made a holiday dinner on her own, and it would be the first for her and Paul. Janie wanted to make everything perfect.

You Can't Always Get What You Want

PAUL DROVE TO PERCY'S THANKSGIVING MORNING TO watch football. Percy and a couple of guys from the plant were coming for dinner. Janie had been keyed up all week since he told her she'd be cooking for more than just the two of them. Paul couldn't wait to get out of the house. She was up at six making food and fussing around. It made him nervous. Before he left she reminded him at least twenty times that dinner would be at four. Paul figured she was padding the time so he wouldn't be late, so if he got there at five he'd be right on time.

The heater wasn't working in the car and the defroster was broken too, so Paul left his jacket on and drove with the window cracked and a joint in his mouth. This would be the first time somebody made Thanksgiving dinner for him in years. Sometimes a woman he was with would do some little thing and he'd be invited, but with Janie it was different. She was going all out.

Paul pulled into a courtyard apartment complex on the edge of town and parked in front of Percy's place. The front door swung open when he knocked and a thick cloud of incense, cigarette, and marijuana smoke emerged.

"Close the door, man, you're letting all the heat out." Percy said. On the couch sat three men: Doug, barrel-chested and banty-legged; Zippy, short and dark-skinned with an afro the size of a beach ball; Percy, long and skinny as a willow switch, his mustache and every other feature running downhill in his faded blue Veterans Hospital bathrobe. Each of the men held a can of beer in one hand and a cigarette in the other. On a palette covered with pitted sheetrock, which Percy used as a coffee table, stood a ceramic bong and rolling tray. A quarter-ounce baggie lay next to it.

Paul looked at the television. Instead of the football game he expected, Clint Eastwood and a bunch of Confederate soldiers shot at each other with a variety of guns and rifles.

"What the fuck are you watching? I thought we was going to watch the game, man."

Percy stretched his spaghetti-thin arms in front of him and picked up a Bic lighter and the bong. "Game'll be on for hours, man. This here's *The Good, the Bad, and the Ugly*, best fucking movie ever made."

Paul laughed. "Good, Bad, and Ugly–that's you here."

Percy held a lungful of smoke. "I think you must be wrong. You look like 'the Ugly' to me, Paul."

Zippy primped his afro up with one free hand. "I know it ain't me–I'm one pretty motherfucker."

Paul took the bong from Percy. "Bullshit. You so ugly, I got boils on my ass prettier than you."

"Shut up and get yourself a beer."

JANIE WATCHED THE Macy's parade while she peeled a ten-pound bag of potatoes. She knew how to make good mashed potatoes, so if she messed up something else, at least the potatoes would be there. She'd never roasted a turkey before. When she was helping Lila clean house on Monday and Tuesday, she'd asked her how to do the dinner so it would all come out at the same time. Lila had given her a list of when to do what, along with recipes for everything from the turkey and stuffing to pumpkin pie and cranberry sauce.

She told Paul dinner would be at four, but really it would be closer to five. Janie had the day planned from the moment she got out of bed. It was better if she stayed busy. Holidays were hard and they never got easier. She missed her dad and mom.

She missed Stella and Cookie and being part of a family. She wanted to believe a baby might make things better between her and Paul. A baby might give him a reason to change.

Janie dropped the final peeled potato into a pot full of cold water and turned off the TV.

WHEN THE BEER was gone, Percy opened a bottle of Wild Turkey and passed around jelly glasses full. Paul walked over to the Minit Mart and got a carton of cigarettes and a bag of Doritos. When he got back *Rio Bravo* was on. He ripped open the bag of chips, took a handful, and put the bag on the table.

Paul picked up the bong and packed it. "Isn't John Wayne in this one?"

Zippy nodded and got himself some chips. "This is the one where he murders a bunch of Indians."

"You're Indian, right Zip?" Percy poured another glass of whiskey.

"That's right, man. Not American Indian though."

"What tribe?"

"Fucking headhunters, man–Pacific Island Indian on my mom's side. She's from some little island near Samoa."

Doug brushed crumbs from his beard. "You ever been there?"

"Nah. Never been off this hunk of sand."

Paul put the bong back on the table. "Where would you go if you could?"

Doug answered immediately. "Amsterdam–legal dope and blondes all over the fucking place."

Paul had thought about this before. "I'd go to Spain."

"What's in Spain, man?" Percy asked.

"When I was in the joint, I read this book, *Don Quixote*. Took me damn near my whole sentence to finish it."

"Where'd you do time?" Zippy took a handful of Doritos from the bag.

"Vacaville–I jacked up a Circle K down in Fresno.

Supposed to do three to five but ended up with eighteen months for good behavior."

Doug laughed, spraying chips across the room. "Good behavior!"

"Yeah, man. Can't hardly believe it, right?" Paul sat back and sipped his whiskey. "That *Don Quixote* was a damn good book."

JANIE HEARD CARS pull into the driveway at 4:45. At least he wasn't late. The turkey was still in the oven, and she hadn't mashed the potaotoes yet. The minute she laid eyes on Paul and the other three she knew they were drunk–definitely drunk. At least if they were just drunk they'd eat. If they were wired they would push the food around and not eat anything. Janie wasn't sure which to prefer. Zippy carried a half-case of beer. Percy had what was left of a fifth of Wild Turkey.

Paul held out a handful of bedraggled chrysanthemums to Janie. Mud still clung to the roots of the plant. He must have pulled them out of someone's yard. Paul shook them, and a shower of dark brown droplets fell to the floor. "Here you go, baby. Flowers for you."

Janie took them. She kissed his cheek, inhaling deeply to check for the telltale odor of crank. She couldn't smell anything but alcohol, pot, and Camel Straights. "Hi, you guys. Dinner'll be ready in a few minutes." She turned to go back to the kitchen, and the men all gathered around the television as if it were a campfire. She could hear the click of poptop beer cans.

Paul yelled, "Baby, come on out and have a drink with us. Hey–and bring some glasses."

Janie brought out the smallest glasses she could find and a plate of cheese and crackers. If they ate they would slow down on the drinking, but nobody seemed interested in snacks. She perched on the armrest of Paul's chair. His hand looped around her hips and rested on her thigh. The men had grown silent and sat staring at the TV, their eyes shiny and unblinking, their shoulders drooping as they collapsed into the couch. "I'm going to go finish up, okay Paul?"

His words were thick with booze. "You bet."

From the kitchen she heard Santana on the stereo, and their voices became more animated. Paul's laugh stretched too tight and high. When he sounded like this she had to watch herself. She'd have to make sure she didn't do anything to make him angry. Janie mashed the potatoes and put them in the biggest metal bowl she had. She carried the food to the table and called out that dinner was ready. The men stumbled around the sheet-covered table she'd rigged on an old piece of plywood and two saw horses. Paul came wobbling through the door carrying the nearly empty bottle of Wild Turkey and a beer.

"Man, this is great." Zippy was the first to slide into a chair.

"Yeah, Janie, everything looks real good." Percy joined in, and everyone sat down.

Janie passed and served the food, waiting to sit down until all the plates were filled.

Paul stood, tilting back and forth. "We got to say a prayer before we eat." He picked up the heavy bowl full of mashed potatoes, lifting it above his head and looking up at it. "God, we thank you for your blessin's—righteous dope and Led Zepplin."

The men started laughing, but Paul wove back and forth staring up at the bowl.

"Hey, remember that show *Roots*? Don't he look like Kunta Kinte holding up his baby?" Doug pointed at Paul and the others laughed louder.

Janie watched the bowl drop from Paul's hands. It splattered once on the table, then hit the floor. Mashed potatoes lay everywhere. Paul fell into his chair and his face landed in his food.

Janie grabbed his shoulders to move him out of the hot food, but at her first touch Paul's arm shot out, hitting her in the torso. She tripped backward, slipping over her own chair and into the wall, falling with a loud thump. "I'm okay. Just an accident."

Percy stood up and helped her to her feet. "Maybe we better get out of here. Let Paul sleep."

"I'm fine. I just slipped, that's all."

"Oh yeah, yeah. I know. We all seen you slip." Doug got up from his chair, putting on his dirty white cowboy hat while he spoke.

Zippy stood, too. "Yeah. It'd be better to let Paul sleep. We'll get out of here."

Janie felt like she was about to cry and didn't want to. "At least let me pack you some sandwiches or something. I mean, I cooked all day."

Percy said, "I'd take a couple sandwiches." The others chorused in agreement. Janie cleared the table and made sandwiches, wiping her eyes with the back of her sleeve. She could hear them through the thin walls of the kitchen as they wrestled Paul into the bedroom and cleaned him up. She brought a grocery bag of turkey sandwiches, cranberry sauce, and pie to the three men standing by the door.

Percy said, "He's pretty wasted, Janie. He'll probably sleep till noon and have a pretty bad hangover tomorrow."

Zippy nodded. "We got most of the food off him and put him face down so if he yaks he won't choke on it. That's how Jim Morrison and Jimi Hendrix both died. Did you know that? Choked on their own vomit."

"Man," Doug said to Zippy, "That's great. Scare her to fucking death. Don't worry 'bout Paul, Janie. You got to be a fucking rock star to choke on vomit and die."

Janie looked away.

"Nah really," Percy jumped in. "That and planes. Rock stars should never fly."

Janie handed Percy the grocery bag and said goodbye as they left the house. She stood in the doorway watching their headlights until they turned a corner and were gone.

It took two hours to put everything away and clean up. She didn't want to wake Paul before he was done being drunk.

His moans and groans echoed in the small house, and she heard him struggle with his blankets. She tiptoed into the dark bedroom to make sure he was okay. The smell of stale alcohol permeated the room. She crept across the creaking wood floor and cracked the window to let in fresh air. She didn't think she could sleep in the room, in the bed with him. His arms flailed around and he stank. She got a coat from the closet, tiptoed out of the bedroom, and left the house.

The streets were dark and quiet. Janie walked through the neighborhood looking into windows. Light illuminated the families gathered together inside. She could see lamps on tables and shadows through gauzy curtains. Uncarved pumpkins sat on some porches, and streetlights lit the branches of elms, oaks, and maples. She tucked her hands deep into her coat pockets and tramped through the town.

At the elementary school, Janie peered in the classroom windows. Tissue-paper leaves and traced hand-turkeys lined the windows of some classrooms. She wandered out to the play-ground and wiped the seat of a swing dry and sat down. Two things helped when she was sad like this, moving and getting really cold. Her body couldn't think about more than one thing at a time, and if she was very, very cold the hurt she felt in her heart would be less, and then she could go back to the house. Nothing bad had really happened. Paul would be fine tomorrow. He liked to drink a flat, cold, Coke when he was hungover. She'd pop one open when she got home and leave it in the fridge, so it would be perfect in the morning. At least he didn't have to work the next day. She'd make a bed on the couch and leave the TV on all night to keep herself company. She'd get herself a slice of pie and eat it in her pajamas. Maybe tomorrow she would ask Paul if they could get a puppy. A baby might be a stretch for now.

Superstition

THE WEEK AFTER THANKSGIVING, PAUL DROVE OVER TO his friend John's place to drop off two kegs for Percy's upcoming birthday party. John lived on a farm between Mt. Angel and St. Paul that his grandmother had left to him when she died. Close to ten acres of land, an old empty barn, and no neighbors nearby made it a perfect party spot.

When Paul and Percy pulled up, John was standing on a ladder nailing up strings of Christmas lights. "Hey, Percy," John yelled. "Get over here and help me out."

Percy ambled over to the little man poised precariously on top of a ladder. "Get on down. I'll rig up the lights in the morning."

Paul took a joint out of his flannel shirt and lit it, handing it to John first. "You mind if I use your phone?"

"Help yourself."

Paul knocked on the door and went in. The heat and dirty diaper smell were intense after a day spent working outside. Paul heard children's voices and the television from the living room. John's wife called over the racket for him to get himself a beer. He grabbed one and came into the stuffy room. "What'cha all doing?" Paul couldn't remember the wife's name and hoped he could avoid having to call her something particular.

Three kids – from two to five years old, wearing dirty one-piece pajamas with greenish snot trailing from their noses – sat on the floor surrounded by empty beer cans and baby bottles, dirty dishes, laundry, old magazines, and broken toys. The kids stared at an old console TV. John's wife, her light red hair set in a helmet of pink and light green rollers, sat on the couch smoking a cigarette. Where John was short, dark, and in pretty good shape, his wife was tall and fair, with the bad skin, sunken cheeks and the missing teeth of a speed queen.

She nodded to Paul. "Hey Paul, you know Debby?"

A woman of about twenty appeared in the doorway. She had the same blue-black hair and crazy, twisted smile of Luna. She could be her twin. "Nope. We've never met. You from around here?"

Debby smiled at him, big and bold. "Nah. Just moved up from California with my dad."

"Whereabouts?"

"Pacific Palisades. Janet says there's going to be a Convention of Idiots here this weekend."

Paul laughed. "Ought to be a good turnout."

"I hope so. It'll be my first party since I got out of rehab. I've been on my best behavior."

John's old lady interrupted. "I told Debby to talk to you about copping some wire."

Paul snorted. "What am I? The district sales manager?"

Debby laughed this time. "That's what I heard."

"Well, maybe we can work something out. How much do you want?"

Debby grinned. "How much can you get?"

JANIE WANTED SOMETHING pretty to wear to the party. She lived in jeans and Paul's old work shirts. Paul didn't like it when she dressed up especially if there were men around. Sometimes she still went with Paul when he did business, but that just meant sitting around in houses and apartments while everybody else got high. Even if she'd wanted to get high now there was no way they could afford that kind of habit. Lately she had the feeling there was more on Paul's mind than the usual stuff like money or some deal, but she wasn't sure what and when she asked him he got mad at her.

Janie tried on everything in her closet twice before resorting to the Good Shepherd to buy a dress for the party. She went in while she waited for the laundry to dry and found a green velvet dress for five dollars. Lila wasn't working. Janie hadn't been in for weeks and hadn't seen Lila since she worked for her before Thanksgiving. She'd probably never see her again. Lila would ask questions and she'd have to lie to answer them. The scarf she'd been making for Paul hung from the knitting needles stuffed in the back of a drawer. Lila had never shown her how to bind off. Lila was just one more in a long list of people who came and went through Janie's life.

She stood at the kitchen counter frosting Percy's birthday cake when Paul came in the back door. He lifted the hair from the back of her neck and kissed her. "Is this new?" He fingered the green velvet between thumb and forefinger.

She could smell the crank. Janie willed herself to ignore it. "Yeah. Good Shepherd. Want some popcorn, or can I fix you something?"

Paul shook his head. "You put brewer's yeast on the popcorn?"

"I like it that way. Besides, it's good for you."

"I'm not hungry now. There'll be food at the party."

"I know, but a little snack wouldn't hurt. You didn't eat anything this morning."

"I'm watching my figure."

Paul didn't eat anything, but he didn't drink any beer either, just red Kool-Aid. He seemed distracted, but when he was wired he was usually distracted.

A VARIETY OF cars, motorcycles, and pickup trucks were parked in the pasture in front of the house when they arrived. An orange moon hung low in the sky. The steady thump of bass and drums from a local band playing in the barn.

Percy was coming out the back door. He wore a tinfoil crown

over the dark blue bandana tied around his head. He slapped Paul on the shoulder and made a short bow to Janie. "Glad you could come. Hey Paul, got my bike running."

Paul nodded. "It's about time."

Janie smiled and held up a cardboard box. "Happy birthday, Percy. I made you a cake."

"Gee, you didn't have to go and do that." Percy said. "Sure looks good."

Paul clapped Percy on the shoulder and kissed Janie quickly on the cheek. "I got to do a little business. You be my old lady's date for a minute?"

Paul was never jealous of Percy. Paul thought Percy was too slow-witted to be any threat.

Percy bowed again to Janie and offered her his arm. "My pleasure, ma'am."

Janie said, "You've been watching too many episodes of *Big Valley*."

Percy steered Janie toward the barn and the music. "Yeah. I love that show. Who's the daughter? The blonde – "

"Linda Evans. She used to date the Six Million Dollar Man. He was her brother on *Big Valley*. She's on *Dynasty* too."

"Yeah. Die-Nasty. That's right." Percy looked down at Janie under the sparkling lights before they entered the barn. "Linda's got nothing on you tonight. Let's put that cake on the table and go shake a tail feather."

Janie laughed and nodded. There was nothing she could do about Paul. He'd come find her when the grams were gone.

PAUL FOUND DEBBY standing in the kitchen. From the back she could have been Luna. Her shiny dark hair roamed halfway down her bare back. She wore a leather halter top despite the cold and a worn-out cowboy hat. Her jeans clung to every muscle of her long legs. Luna would approve of this girl's look. *Princess Luna's House of Style*. He watched Debby for a few minutes, his mouth dry from the crank he'd done that afternoon. He had the desire to spin her around and see Luna standing there, smiling, calling him Slick, teasing him. It spooked him and stirred him up inside.

Debby half turned and, spotting him, waved him over. "You holding?"

"How much do you want?"

"As much as you've got."

"You got any money on you?"

"Give me a ride to the store and I'll cash one of these." From her back pocket Debby pulled a wad of traveler checks. She unfolded one and held it up for Paul to inspect.

"Baby, you're going to get me in trouble."

She smiled Luna's same nasty, shit-eating grin. "My dad had to go to LA for business and he left me some emergency money. Too much money and not enough crank seems like an emergency to me."

Paul led her out the front door and down the driveway to his Opel.

THE BAND PLAYED covers – mostly old Stones, Allman Brothers from before Duane Allman died, and Aerosmith. Janie felt like a dog set free to run after being tied to a porch for too long. Percy got her beers during a couple of slow songs. She quit thinking about where Paul was and why it was taking so long for him to come find her. She lost track of time and danced, got sweaty and danced some more. She danced alone when Percy went off to pee. She danced with her eyes closed. She danced without seeing. But eventually she had to stop and go find the bathroom. She wound her way through people and furniture leaning against each other. The air stank of smoke, cheap perfume, spilled beer. Janie found John slumped on the couch and asked him where the bathroom was.

"There's two," he said. "Upstairs is for business. Downstairs is the toilet."

Janie inched her way to the downstairs bathroom. The line twisted around through the kitchen and out the back door. A few little kids ran in circles through the house, carrying Hot Wheels cars and plastic guns. They made car noises and shot each other as they ran through the crowded house. She decided to try the business bathroom upstairs.

Janie pushed between people and squeezed up the stairs. At the top she scanned the crowd for Paul. She noticed there were only men upstairs. Janie stood on her tiptoes and searched the packed landing by the bathroom.

Next to the bathroom, a bedroom door stood wide open. Doug came out of the bedroom, zipping up his pants as he left. He didn't look at Janie, but she knew he'd seen her. She was about to follow him and ask if he'd seen Paul when she saw a woman kneeling and topless in front of a man seated on the bed. The woman's head bobbed up and down in his lap.

In the crowded hallway, she felt pressed too close to men she didn't know. She felt a hand on her ass. For a second Janie's feet refused to move. She felt lightheaded. All the blood seemed to have left her arms and legs. Then she was down the stairs, never feeling the steps under her feet or the press of people around her, not smelling the smoke or bodies pressed in tight. She wanted to find Paul and go home.

Outside, the moon had disappeared. She started down the driveway to the car, not sure where Paul had parked. Nothing looked familiar and she didn't recognize the Opel until she stood behind it and heard Paul and a woman laughing inside. The car windows were a screen of gray. She could see two shapes. The smaller shape moved toward the larger one. Janie stepped away from the car and crouched behind a nearby van. She wanted to see who made Paul laugh like that. She wanted to be wrong about what she thought she'd see. Paul got out of the Opel first and stretched. She could see his head and shoulders over the roof of the car. She kept her eyes on the passenger side door. A second later a tall dark haired woman emerged. She looked almost like Blue's sister. Janie held still and watched them walk by. She told herself it didn't mean anything. Paul dealt with a lot of women, but something about the way Paul laughed and the way they leaned into each other made her stomach tumble.

On the car floor Janie found an old grocery receipt and wrote Paul a note. She put it on the dashboard. *Got a ride home. Janie.* She didn't want to go back to the party. She didn't want to pretend she hadn't seen Paul with whoever she was. He'd explain it all to her and somehow whatever happened would end up being her fault. She started walking. She walked for hours till blisters formed on the soles and heels of her feet. She kept on walking through the darkest part of night waiting for a sign, an omen, anything to tell her what to do next.

At 4:30 in the morning in the window of an abandoned Texaco station she saw a piece of cardboard. It read *Last Chance* in big hand-painted letters. A phone booth with a flickering light was near the door.

The phone book inside was fluttering rags tethered to a steel counter. When she picked up the receiver, it surprised her with a dial tone. She dialed the operator.

"What city please?"

"Eugene, Oregon."

"Go ahead."

"Clarence Stubbs. With two 'b's."

"I have that number."

"Could you just connect me? Collect. Say it's from Janie."

"One minute, please."

The phone rang and rang before Janie heard a click.

"Hello?" Stella's voice thick with sleep.

"I have a collect call for Stella from Janie. Will you accept the charges?"

"Hell, yes!" The sleep disappeared. "Janie? Where are you?"

She didn't think she'd cry so hard or so soon. "I'm in a phone booth."

"Where? Are you okay?"

Janie couldn't speak. For a little while she could only close her eyes and listen to Stella tell her everything would be all right and believe it. It took her time to calm down and talk. "Stella, I didn't mean to worry you. I'm okay."

"You're okay and I'm a middle-aged white guy."

Janie sniffed back tears and giggled.

"Tell me the truth, Jane."

Stella didn't interrupt, give advice, or hurry her along. He didn't say mean things about Paul when the occasion arose and several did. Sometimes he'd murmur words of comfort. She told him everything and he listened.

Every Picture Tells a Story

TOWARD THE END OF THE PHONE CALL, STELLA TOLD HER a little about his life in Eugene. He and Cookie had a baby girl now, Ruby, Stella called her Ruby Tuesday. He and Cookie owned a small restaurant near the university and a house a few blocks away. China was fine, another year older, but fine. Janie could almost see herself helping with the baby, and in the restaurant, being part of their world in a family that cared about her.

When Janie got home, Paul's car was in the driveway. The front door was unlocked. Paul sat with his arms crossed. She could see from his face that he was mad. Right now she didn't care. She felt far away from him.

He started as she walked in the door. "Where the fuck were you?"

"I left you a note in the car." She put her purse down and sat on the couch to take off her boots.

"Yeah. You left me a note that you got a ride. With who?"

"I lied." Janie peeled her tights off. They were stuck to the heel blisters that had leaked and dried hours ago. "I walked."

Paul got up and knelt in front of her, taking her feet in his hands, examining first one foot, then the other. "You walked? I would have brought you home if that's what you wanted."

"You were busy."

"I told you I was going to do some business."

"What's her name?"

Paul's face reddened and he looked up at her. "Oh, that's what this is all about. You're jealous of some speed queen I sold a couple grams to. You got jealous and thought you'd teach me a lesson." He dropped her foot and stood. "Well, guess what, I'm not playing."

Janie met his eyes. "Is that what you think this is? A game we're playing?" She gestured to the room, the house, their life together. "I may be young and not very smart about a lot of things, but I know this, Paul Jesse – I'm not playing either. This is no game of chicken. This is no tug of war. This is us you're fucking with."

Paul's voice softened. "That girl isn't anybody you need to worry about, Janie. She's just a speed queen from a party with too much money and too little sense. She's not you."

"Sometimes I think I should get wired with you."

"If I ever caught you spun, we'd be over. Only one of us gets to be fucked up at a time."

PAUL HADN'T PAID all of November or any of December rent. The landlord came to collect on a Thursday evening a week before Christmas. The guy wanted to get rid of them so bad he promised he'd give them a good reference if they left the place clean and moved before the end of the month. For all the dealing he was doing, Paul couldn't seem to break even. He knew it was because he couldn't leave the product alone. He tried to quit or cut back, but when he grammed out an ounce, most of it went into his arm or Debby's.

Paul knew from the start that Debby was going to be a problem. She talked too much at the wrong time and to the wrong people. She asked too many questions. She wouldn't leave him alone. The thought of her and all her easy money distracted him from his life with Janie. If she didn't look so much like Luna, he never would have slept with her. Luna had been wild and sweet, but Debby lived to get wired. He didn't like the way she whined when she wanted something and she always wanted something. But he did like her money. The bitch had cash and no connections except him. She was his own private gold mine.

Paul went looking for a new place to live. He found a low-rent apartment in a huge complex off the freeway in Salem. They moved on the payday before Christmas. He used his whole check to pull it off.

After they took the last load of boxes up two flights of stairs he left. Janie watched him go. He couldn't wait to get away from her. He lied and told her he had some business to do. He said he'd be back later and maybe they'd go get a Christmas tree. He blew her a kiss from the door and left her standing in a room full of boxes. He ran down the steps, skipping every other one to the parking lot and freedom. Paul hopped on his bike and rode over to Debby's to get some cash and cop some dope.

JANIE WALKED FROM room to room. She hated it. It felt like a shoebox. The complex consisted of twenty identical buildings that looked like Monopoly hotels. Janie could see the headlights of each car entering the complex from her position in the kitchen. She didn't believe Paul would be back anytime soon. She didn't believe he would remember about a Christmas tree or food money. She had five dollars she'd been hoarding, and that would have to see her through until she could get some kind of work and money of her own. Paul wouldn't be responsible for things that didn't matter to him, like food and shelter.

Paul was high most of the time on something other than just pot and beer. He denied he was back on the needle but where was he all the time? Why couldn't he look at her anymore? Why was he picking fights with her all the time? Why couldn't he wait to leave? There was more to it than the drugs, something between them had changed with the arrival of that dark-haired woman from the party.

Janie opened the kitchen boxes first and looked through what would have to pass for groceries. There was a jar of mustard, a half-jar of mayonnaise, two packets of Kool-Aid, some herb tea, popcorn, vegetable oil, beans, rice, and brewer's yeast. She made the Kool-Aid and a batch of popcorn with brewer's yeast, and began unpacking the rest of the house.

Dazed and Confused

JANUARY BROUGHT SALEM WEEKS OF RAIN. TWO MORE months and she'd be eighteen. She no longer anticipated the day she'd dreamed of for so long. The first week in the apartment complex she met Janelle, a nineteen-year-old single mom, who lived with her son, Tyler, in the apartment below them. Janelle took classes at the community college and worked part-time in the admissions office. She needed a babysitter for three-year-old Tyler, a red-haired and freckled boy who liked trains and balls. Their apartments had the same floor plans, but Janelle's was brighter and fresher – no cigarette smoke, no rolling tray or scales lying around. Janie usually watched Tyler at Janelle's place, but sometimes she'd take him upstairs to play with Eloise, the cat Paul gave her for Christmas.

Janelle didn't get high and made it plain that Tyler was not to go to Janie's place if Paul was home. That hadn't been a problem so far. Paul worked all day every day and said he had to work overtime after every shift including half-days on Saturdays. At night, if he came home at all, he picked a fight and left. Janie tried to figure out what she did to piss him off so often. If he misplaced his keys, or couldn't find an envelope he'd written a phone number on, he'd be mad at her. If there was no beer in the house, he got mad. If she used an unfamiliar word, he said she was uppity. Sometimes he didn't like the way she was dressed, the way she kept the house, or most recently, the way her face looked. She didn't know what to do about that one. The things that made Paul mad were too numerous to list. More often than not his anger ended only after he hit her. No matter what she tried to do differently, it didn't work out the way she wanted.

She sometimes thought about what her life might be like without him but she couldn't imagine leaving him. He was her home. They had history. In the moments when he was himself, she could still see the man she loved. She knew in her heart that Paul Jesse had potential. She had seen it.

But so many nights after they fought, after he passed out and she sat on the kitchen floor holding a bag of frozen peas to her bruised face, she found herself wishing they would both hurry up and die. She couldn't see herself killing him but Janie understood how you could want to kill somebody you couldn't imagine leaving.

This morning Janie let herself into Janelle's apartment, bringing a cup of instant hot chocolate and a bag with a book and her jeans for later. She walked down the short hall to the bathroom. Janelle stood in front of the mirror putting on mascara. She put her fingers to her lips, pantomiming that Tyler was still asleep. Janie took her cup to the couch and curled up, closing her eyes until Janelle tapped her shoulder.

Janelle whispered. "He had nightmares in the middle of the night. He was up for hours and so was I. Let him sleep in, but no nap today. We'll go to bed early. I've got to get some sleep tonight. I've got midterms." She paused. "I don't know if I should tell you this but I'm going to."

"What?" Janie waited.

"I saw Paul yesterday stopped at a light with some black-haired woman in his car."

Janie felt her face get hot. "Paul knows lots of people. Men and women."

"Do they all french kiss him?"

Janie didn't know what to say. She felt stupid and embarrassed, like she'd stepped in a pile of crap and someone else had to tell her about it.

"I thought you should know." Janelle picked up her car keys and headed for the door. "I'll be home at six." Janelle closed the front door and Janie turned the deadbolt.

AT 11:15 THE buzzer sounded, signaling the thirty-minute lunch break at Silversides Mobile Home Factory. Paul, Doug, and Zippy headed for Paul's car to do a line before they had to head back to work. Paul preferred to use a needle, but he didn't like to share his rigs. Syringes were more difficult to replace than the drugs that filled them. He hated using a needle with a person he wouldn't share a glass of water with.

A group of people stood in front of the gut wagon to buy pre-wrapped deli sandwiches and cans of soda. Cars squealed out of the lot and down to the McDonald's on the corner. Paul hadn't eaten more than a mouthful of anything in the last week, and he did that only to appease Janie. He hadn't slept either, and the only thing that kept him showing up for work day after day was the promise of selling some dope before he went home.

He could see Debby's black Mustang parked next to his Opel.

Zippy nodded toward the car. "Looks like you got company, man."

Paul tossed Zippy his keys and got in the passenger's side of Debby's car. "I told you I'd pick you up after work."

"I got tired of waiting. Besides, thought you'd like some lunch." She pulled a small teardrop-shaped cylinder on a chain out of her leather bag and handed it to him.

He unscrewed the vial and lifted it to his nose, snorting the white powder, pinching both nostrils shut and snorting again. His head cleared, his eyes watered, the back of his throat stung with the chemical drip, and his heart started beating again. He had no clue what to do with this bitch, but he wouldn't say no to her as long as she was buying. He gestured to his car. "I'm heading back. I'll see you at your place about four. Okay?"

She pouted as he got out of the car. "Aren't you even going to say thank you?"

"Thanks, Deb. See you later." Paul checked the clock in the Opel when he got in the car. He still had fifteen minutes left before the buzzer rang.

JANIE WALKED OVER to the grocery store's payphone after Janelle came home and called Stella's. Paul's car wasn't in their parking spot yet. Janie didn't know what to believe. If she told Paul what Janelle said, he'd have a story for it. He'd be mad at her for believing Janelle and they'd fight. She unfolded the slip of paper from her pocket, slipped quarters in the payphone and dialed Stella's number.

JANIE PUT OFF telling Paul she wanted to visit Stella and Cookie until Thursday night. She wasn't sure whether she was telling him she was going to Stella's or asking for permission. She watched Paul, waiting for the right moment to talk to him, rehearsing over and over how to say it. Paul had been wired all week. When she finally asked, it turned out to be no big deal. He said it sounded like a good idea. The only thing he wanted to know was when she'd be coming back so he could pick her up at the bus station.

Paul dropped her off early Friday morning on his way to work, with a kiss on the cheek and a promise to take care of the cat. Janie watched him pull out of the Greyhound parking lot, waiting for him to look back and blow her a kiss, or smile, or wave, but she stood, forgotten, with her backpack slung over one shoulder, as he drove away.

Inside, she bought a round-trip ticket to Eugene, along with some gum and a magazine. Janie sat on a hard orange plastic chair and waited until the announcement came over the loudspeaker for "all points south," and then showed the driver her ticket as she climbed aboard.

STELLA STOOD IN front of his blue Chevy pickup scanning the crowd filing off the bus. He saw Janie before she saw him.

She'd lost weight. She wore the same denim jacket she'd had since before they met. Her pack seemed too empty. Her smile was there though – open as the sky, and her eyes shone even with shadows under them. He smiled and held out his arms. She crashed into him as if she'd been thrown. "Janie, Janie! Look at you!" He held her at arm's length and studied her face. "This all your stuff?"

Janie nodded, her chin trembled. "I missed you so much."

"Don't start tearing up on me. Ever since Cookie had the baby, I cry like a girl all the time. Last night I cried over a damn *Little House on the Prairie* re-run." He hugged her tight and kissed the top of her head. "Let's get out of here before I get busted for white slavery. I need to get back to work until the lunch crowd thins out. Are you hungry?" Stella noticed how her cheeks had thinned. "Cookie wants to feed you before we go to the house." He patted his belly. "She'll put some meat back on you. Look at me."

Stella drove through town to the restaurant. She didn't talk much and he didn't push her. He entered the small loading area behind the restaurant. "Well, this is it. We called it *Red Light* because it's at the intersection."

Even with the restaurant door closed, they could smell garlic, cumin, and onions in the air. Stella held open the door and she stepped inside the kitchen. Cookie stood at the big stove, a pair of tongs in her hand. She never failed to amaze him. She wore a turban Carmen Miranda-style and a chef's apron over her clothes. She'd gained some weight with the baby, and if possible, looked more beautiful than ever. Cat picked up filled plates from the counter next to the stove. Stella'd hired her a few months ago, when she moved into the house down the street where Cookie's brother, Joe, lived. Cat was a space cadet, but she worked hard.

Stella let the back door slam shut. His voice boomed over the Bob Marley album on the stereo. "Look who I found at the bus depot."

Cat put the plates down and bounced across the room to Janie. "Bet you didn't think you'd see me here."

Cookie smiled and waved, holding her tongs aloft. "Let her catch a breath, Cat. Welcome home, Janie."

Janie put her bag on the floor. "Thanks, Cookie."

Cat began tying a yellow-and-red striped apron around Janie's waist. "These aprons have a good vibe. I always feel like a natural woman in them. See?" Cat hugged her. "Where's that sexy Paul Jesse? Didn't he come along?"

Janie blushed. "Paul couldn't come. He's working and stuff."

Cookie looked dubious. "Well, I'm glad you're here, *chica*. I can't wait for you to meet Ruby. She's asleep in the office. Go see."

Stella opened the office door and Janie peeked inside. A small lamp on the desk gave the room a cozy glow. Next to the desk and a shelf of books was a rocking chair and a crib. Janie tiptoed to the crib and looked down at the baby.

Ruby was curled on her belly, her rump up high in the air and her face against the sheet, fast asleep. The curve of her cheek and her long curled eyelashes were dark against her skin. Her lips were pursed in sleep as if she were ready to nurse. Her tiny dimpled fist rested by her face. Her hair was wavy and thick already like Cookie's, her skin the color of coffee with cream. Janie knelt by the crib and touched her cheek. Ruby wriggled her bottom and slept on.

"What do you think of our Ruby Tuesday?" Stella asked.

"She's so beautiful."

Cookie laughed. "Wait till she wakes up! That girl has lungs like Miles has horn."

JANIE FELT AS if she had landed on another planet. Stella, the silent, stern bouncer of The Habit–the one who had to be coaxed to speak–had disappeared and left this jovial, gregarious giant in his place. He smiled and joked with the regulars. He asked how people were and listened the way he did when Janie had

things to say. She watched him for a few minutes while she
pretended to read all the flyers on the bulletin board.

Behind the front counter, he talked to people who ordered
food. She could tell customers came in often.

When Stella had told her about the restaurant, she had
never imagined such a bustling place with Bob Marley's voice
rising above conversations and the clatter of lunch dishes, but it
suited Stella.

The tables and booths were full, and a few people stood at
the counter waiting for take-out orders. The wood floors were
worn smooth, and the furniture had seen better days, but everything was clean and cozy. On one wall hung a poster of an
Indian man with the slogan *Better Red Than Dead* across the bottom. On the wall across from that was a poster of Bob Marley
singing, his face framed with long dreads.

All the tables had baby bottles filled with homemade *salsa
verde* or *salsa rosa*. The nipples had been cut off so you could
pour salsa on your burrito or your chips. Small jelly jars with sprigs
of thyme and rosemary served as flower vases. A community
bulletin board by the front door had dozens of handmade an-
nouncements in a variety of colors. There were rooms and
houses to rent, people looking for rides all over, yoga classes, bikes
for sale, and a newspaper article about boycotting lettuce.
The menu was drawn in colored chalk on an old blackboard hanging over the counter:

> *Black Bean Burrito*
> *Tofu and Sweet Potato Burrito*
> *Guacamole Quesadilla*
> *Chips and Salsa*
> *Rice and Bean Plate*
> TODAY'S SPECIAL:
> *Black Bean Quesadilla with Pineapple Salsa*

After the lunch rush was over, the three of them ate together
in a corner booth, reaching over each other for salsa or napkins
or to hand-feed Ruby a bite of banana. Her mouth opened and

closed like one of Betty's nestlings wanting to be fed. Ruby
reached out for Stella's food, slow-moving and purposeful. Her
eyes were the color of cocoa. Janie felt Paul and her life back
in Salem melt away.

Later that night, in the small sun porch they'd fixed up as
her bedroom, Janie curled up tight next to China. She lay tucked
under the familiar blue quilt, listening to rain fall softly against
the windows. As she thought of Paul, she pictured him as a bal-
loon and practiced letting go of the string.

Walk This Way

JANIE HEARD THE CLATTER OF DISHES AND SMELLED coffee brewing and breakfast cooking, full of vanilla and spice. She stretched again and pulled on a pair of thick wool socks. She'd never slept so well. She hadn't known she was so tired. She could imagine a dozen different lives she might live as she listened to Stella and Cookie begin the day.

The room she slept in was much like her old room at Stella's in Washington. They called it "Janie's room" as if she'd never been away. To have a room for herself again made her part of their family. When she went back to Paul, she would imagine this room and it would make her feel good. China lay pressed against her, thumping her tail when Janie stretched and swung her feet to the floor. China jumped off the bed, wagging her body.

In the kitchen Cookie balanced the baby on one hip and flipped french toast with her free hand. She looked up when she heard Janie. "I thought you were never getting up! Stella went to work already, but he's closing early. There's a potluck tonight at my brother's."

Janie got a mug from the shelf and poured in coffee and cream, letting the white spirals appear on the surface before she stirred. "What can I make?"

"Want to help me make lasagna?" Cookie filled a plate with slices of french toast and took it to the table. "I'm starving. Breast-feeding makes me hungry all the time."

After a huge breakfast of french toast with yogurt and

Cookie's homemade apple butter, they dressed and walked to the co-op to get groceries. Cookie knew everybody: the neighbors on both sides of the street, the students who worked at the store, people shopping. Janie smiled when she was introduced, said hello, and not much else. This world wasn't her world though she wished it was. She had the sense that she was back on the street again, fourteen instead of almost eighteen, looking at a picture of home and wishing she fit in somewhere. At The Habit Delores used to tell her to wish in one hand and shit in the other, and see which hand filled up first. Janie could wish all she wanted, but her real life was north of here in a crappy apartment off the freeway with a man she loved but couldn't seem to change no matter how hard she tried.

They stopped by the restaurant on their way home and had lunch while Stella closed. Cookie went into the office with Ruby, and Janie helped Stella clean up.

"You sure are quiet, Jane."

When Paul said "Jane" it meant she was in trouble, but when Stella called her Jane it meant he was worried about her. "Just thinking, I guess."

"About?"

"How different this is from Yelm."

"Things change," Stella said.

"Not everything," Janie said.

"Not everything. Not everybody."

"Maybe when you want it enough."

"Not necessarily. Can't do someone else's changing for them and the longer you wait to change yourself, the harder it is." Stella scooped chopped onion into a container, covered it with a lid, and slid it into the refrigerator. "Look how long it took me to make this new life for myself."

Janie concentrated on the big metal pot she was scrubbing.

Stella untied his apron. "Just don't run out of time, Jane."

IN THE EVENING, they walked over to the house where Cookie's brother Joe and his housemates lived. Stella carried Ruby in a pack on his back and Cookie and Janie carried bags of food. Janie never got tired of looking at houses. In her notebook where she sometimes still drew and wrote things she had long descriptions of houses she liked. Someday she thought she'd see a house and say to herself that's it, that's the one for me. This house looked like one of the big Victorian houses in San Francisco. It had a wide front porch and three floors with fancy woodwork around the windows and doors. The house was already crowded when they arrived. Janie recognized a few people from Ernie's birthday party two summers ago. There were little kids and babies at this party too, but like Ruby, they looked loved and cared for. The adults were of every age and color. There was no keg of beer, no line of the wasted waiting to get into a bathroom to shoot dope or get a blow job. No one was allowed to smoke in the house, although she suspected a few people smoked pot together outside under the light of a half moon.

Janie didn't feel hungry but she fixed a plate of food because she wanted to keep her hands busy and look like she belonged. She carried her plate through the crowded rooms looking for a place to sit and eat, and ended up standing against a wall in the noisy room holding her plate with nothing much to say. The people here talked about politics and books and things she'd never considered as part of her life. She wandered around the rooms for awhile saying hi to people she'd met before, listening to bits of conversation. She wanted to go back to the house and wait for Stella and Cookie. It seemed like everyone here went to school either at the university or the community college. They lived in a world Janie didn't know a thing about. Nobody she knew in Salem went to school except Janelle, and nobody, including Janelle, read a book for the hell of it. Janie read but she didn't think she could talk to people about the books she'd read. She felt like she didn't belong with all the smart people.

She walked into an empty room with a heavy tapestry hung

where the door should be. It felt good to be away from the crowd. She looked around – bookshelves, old desk with built-in cubbies for mail, bay window, overstuffed paisley covered chair, mattress bed on the floor doubling as a couch. This was someone's room. As she turned to leave she almost bumped into a guy who looked a little like Cookie.

He smiled and extended his hand in an old-fashioned polite way. "I'm Joe, Cookie's brother. I think you must be Janie."

Janie juggled her plate with one hand and held out the other. "Hi."

"Kind of crowded out there, huh?" Joe took a sweater off the back of a chair. "You don't need to leave. Stay here and eat."

"It was so crowded. I didn't know this was somebody's room –"

"Don't worry. Really, you're more than welcome to stay and eat in here." Joe slipped the sweater on. "I've been wanting to meet you."

"I'm not really hungry. I don't know why I took so much. Do you want some?"

"Don't let Cookie hear you. My sister thinks if you aren't eating, she's not doing her job." Joe sat down. "I'll help you out if you'll stay and talk with me."

Joe was easy to talk to. He sat next to her and ate from her plate. He asked her questions, but not the usual ones. He wanted to know her favorite book, her favorite color, and her favorite piece of music. They both liked the same movies and loved dogs of all kinds. When the food had disappeared from her plate, she got up to get them some dessert. As Janie turned to leave the room, she saw a group of pictures on the wall. One stopped her: a young woman with short dark hair sat in a straight-backed chair in an empty room. She wore a man's suit and held a pair of scissors. All around her on the floor were locks of what used to be her long hair. The picture next to it was same woman's face, but her hair was bound in a braid on top of her head, and on her forehead was a circle with a skull inside. Next to it hung another picture of the woman with her hair loose. She lay on her side in an orange gown with a vine growing out of her heart and over her body into a barren desert landscape.

"They're great aren't they?" Joe said. "I'm kind of in love with them. With Frida too. Frida Kahlo. Which one is your favorite?"

Janie looked them over, deciding. "It's hard to choose. I think I'd pick the one where she's cut her hair and she's in the suit."

Joe smiled at her. He had a nice smile and a nose that reminded her of a hawk. He stood very close to her and she wondered what it might feel like to kiss somebody who read books for the hell of it and hung pictures on his wall. All of a sudden, just as she was thinking the thought about him kissing her, he touched her face, brushing a strand of hair away from the corner of her mouth and kissed her. She could feel her heart beating where their lips met.

She took a step back. "I should go now."

"I'm sorry. I got a little ahead of myself. I hope I'll see you again."

"I shouldn't have done that."

"Me neither, but I'm glad I did." He smiled. "Don't go. Wait a minute. There's something I'd like you to have." Joe went to the bookshelf and fumbled around, pulling a book off the shelf. "I already have a copy of this." He handed her a book with a picture of the same woman in the pictures.

"That's an expensive book."

"Not so expensive. I'd like you to have it. Now you'll remember Frida and me. Back to the party?"

Janie carried the book with her.

The next morning, she could hear Stella in the kitchen when she woke. She pulled the quilt up around her cheeks. Maybe Paul would be at the Greyhound station this afternoon. Maybe he wouldn't. It didn't surprise her anymore when he didn't show up where he said he'd be. Janie found herself not missing Paul and not really wanting to leave yet. She hadn't seen Stella forever and she'd only been there two days. She wanted to live like this. If Paul could see what they could have together he'd be able to give up the dealing and the crank.

Janie turned on her side and picked up the Frida Kahlo book from the floor. She found the picture of Frida with short hair looking tough and determined. On the picture were words in Spanish: *Mira que si te quise, fué por el pelo, Ahor que estas pelona ya no te quiero.*

Stella stood in the door. "Hey there, Sleeping Beauty." He came in and sat on the edge of the bed, pushing China aside to make room.

"See the book Joe gave me?" She held it up.

"That was nice of him." Stella flipped through the pages while he talked. "The cafe's closed today and I was thinking why don't you hang out here and I'll drive you back later on. Salem's only an hour away."

"Paul's supposed to pick me up."

"Is there a way to get a hold of him? Then we'd have the day."

"I guess I could see if our neighbor could give him a message."

"Go call so it's all set." Stella moved off the bed. "I'm making cornbread for breakfast."

"You don't have to bribe me."

Just for the day Janie would pretend she belonged here with nothing more important on her mind than what to spread on Stella's cornbread.

Stormy Monday

A NOTE PINNED TO THE FRONT DOOR READ: *JANIE, I DON'T need you to sit for Tyler tomorrow. Come down when you get this. Janelle.* Janie tore off the note, stuffed it in her pocket, and unlocked the door. Paul's car wasn't in their space, so she knew he wasn't home. The apartment looked clean. She guessed that had more to do with Paul not eating than with any attempt at domesticity. Eloise had left through an open window, but her food and water bowls were full.

Janie found the bottle of Nair on the ledge of the bathtub when she put her soap away. Some other woman had been here, using Nair and leaving the pink bottle and a ring of stubble-flecked scum in the bathtub for her to find. She had to get out and think about something else until she could figure this out.

Janie ran down the stairs to Janelle's.

Tyler opened the door and threw himself around her legs. "I mithed you, Janie. You coming to play trucks?"

Janelle was studying at the kitchen table. "Janie came to talk to Mommy. You take your truck in the bedroom to play and she'll come say goodbye before she goes."

Puzzled, Tyler looked up at Janie.

Janie rubbed his head. "You heard your mom, Tyler. I'll see you in a minute."

Tyler drove the big truck into the bedroom, making putt-putt noises on his way.

Janie felt like she'd been called into the principal's office.

"I'm not going to be able to let you watch Tyler anymore."

"Why? Did I do something?"

"It's not you at all. Look, you **know** I **trust** you with Tyler. He likes you and you've always been good with him."

Janie folded her arms in front of her waiting for more bad news.

"When I went to give Paul the message this morning, he didn't want me coming in, but Tyler pushed right in looking for you. Paul had lines out on a mirror and that same black-haired woman was half naked, coming out of your bathroom."

Janie looked down.

"I don't care what you do, but I don't want my son around that life."

"I don't do drugs, and I don't know who that woman was. It didn't have to do with me. I'd never do anything to hurt Tyler."

"You live with Paul and that makes Tyler too close to somebody who could hurt him. Tyler's my son and if I can do something to keep him safe I'm going to do it. I don't want him around Paul and that means you can't sit for Tyler anymore."

Janie dug in her pocket for Janelle's extra housekey. "Say goodbye for me."

"One more thing." Janelle took the key. "Don't ask me for any more favors."

The door closed behind her and Janie walked the two flights of concrete steps back to the apartment.

The rest of the day dragged more than she imagined possible. The cat didn't come back and neither did Paul. Janie paced the apartment. Her chest felt tight, constricted, as if she were holding her breath under deep, deep water. She wanted to do something bad to that black-haired woman. She tore through the apartment, and through his coat pockets, looking for something but she wasn't sure what. She ripped the sheets from the bed and carried all of it to the laundry. She poured in extra soap and plenty of bleach. She returned to the bathroom, scrubbed the tub with Ajax twice, and poured bleach in the toilet and down the sink.

Janie was remaking the bed when she heard the key in the lock. She was in his face before he had a chance to take off his coat. He caught the bottle of Nair she threw at him and looked at it.

"Tell me I'm wrong, Paul. Tell me you aren't fucking her."

"What are you talking about?"

"How stupid do you think I am?"

"Debby was over here. So what. We were just killing time before we went to score."

"Bullshit. Janelle saw her up here."

"Oh. Janelle. That bitch doesn't like me. She's jealous of you. She doesn't have an old man of her own. You ever wonder why that is? Why would you listen to her?"

"So, why was that woman in my bathtub?"

"We were waiting to score. She was bored and took a bath. Besides where the fuck were you? I'm here trying to make a good life working my ass off for you, and you come home accusing me?"

She didn't believe Paul, but she absolutely wanted to. It was probably all her own fault for leaving. Speed freaks did weird things all the time when they were tweaking. It was a stretch to believe him, but she'd do her best, because not believing him would mean she'd need to do something she couldn't, like leave him.

"Bring her to this house again and you better not turn your back on me. I mean, lock up your gun and put away the knives, because I don't know what I'd do."

Paul sighed. "You have nothing to worry about. I love you. Let's not fight anymore, okay? I got to lay down for awhile before work. Come lie down with me. I missed you."

Janie locked the deadbolt and followed Paul into the bedroom. He looked like an old alley cat these days. She could imagine him with an ear torn loose, ribs showing through a patchy coat of fur. The speed was hard on him. He kept himself pretty clean, even though the crank came out through his pores with a cat urine smell that she was used to now. She curled into the hollow of his arm, brushing his hair out of the way. She breathed him in – Camel straights, pot, Budweiser, and another woman's perfume.

PAUL KEPT HIS eyes closed and his body motionless, willing himself to at least rest if not sleep. Little white dots traveled across his eyelids. The thing that drove him crazy wasn't the meth bugs but the creepy high-pitched humming in his head that grew louder the longer he stayed up. Paul's trick to coming down off a long run like this was to buy some downers, maybe Dilaudid or Percodans or his personal favorite, morphine sulfates. Only then, could he trust himself to sleep deeply without dreams. Sleep like a coma, with none of the nightmares that could jerk him back to earth when he was starting to crash.

Paul stayed very still, holding on to Janie. How long since he had last slept? Days, maybe a week. His body jerked occasionally when he crept close to sleep – it felt like the edge of the world. Janie mumbled into his skin and went back to her own dreams. Paul squeezed his eyes to relieve the burning and opened them to look at the digital clock on the table. The pale green glow of the clock's scoreboard flipped to 5:45 a.m. Not too early to get up. He might as well. He slid out of bed, placing the warm pillow against Janie's back. She rustled but didn't wake up. He picked up jeans, a sweatshirt, clean socks, and a flannel shirt and tiptoed to the bathroom. The bottle of Nair sat next to the sink. He put it in the trash and crumpled paper on top. Better if Janie wasn't reminded. He couldn't believe Debby had left her shit here. He knew it wasn't an accident. He didn't like what he was doing with her, but he couldn't stop. Her dad was going to be out of town for a week. She'd be flush with cash and looking to score. He wasn't going to turn down such easy money.

He pulled on his clothes, grabbed his keys, and headed to work.

JANIE PUSHED A thumbtack through the Queen of Hearts, sticking the playing card to the outside of the front door. Eloise bounded up the concrete steps ready to come inside at last. Janie hadn't seen Paul for three days this time. He'd never been gone so long before.

She thought they had had a good week together. No fights. He crashed Monday night and stayed home from work on Tuesday. She made soup. He watered all the plants and played with the cat. They stayed in their pajamas all day, like it was a snow day, like it was home. Thursday night he didn't come back, and it was Saturday night and he was still gone. She was hoping he wasn't with that woman. That's why she'd tacked the playing card to the door. Hoping for a little magic.

She was in the kitchen cooking up the last box of macaroni and cheese when she heard someone knocking. She looked out the peephole. Under a dim bulb on the landing stood a woman with black hair. Janie unlocked and opened the door, willing her heart to slow down. "Yeah?"

"Paul here?" The woman fidgeted with the dozen jangly bracelets on her wrist.

Janie stepped aside, letting the woman in. "I thought he was with you."

The woman sounded like a crow when she laughed. "I didn't think you could be as stupid as he said. You're Janie." She put her hand out to shake.

Janie just watched. Didn't offer anything.

"I'm Debby." She put her hand down. "He took off with my money to score on Thursday and he hasn't shown up yet."

"Nothing I can do about that." Janie shrugged. "You might as well sit down." She perched on the edge of the couch watching Debby fumble through her leather bag, pulling out a cigarette and lighting it. "So how much money did you give him?"

"Seven hundred."

"Seven hundred dollars?"

"Yeah. Paul said he could double the money and we'd get wired."

"That's a lot of money. He might not be back for awhile. You got any pot?"

Debby opened a gold cigarette case, took out a joint, and lit it. She handed it to Janie. "I'm going to be so fucked if I can't replace at least part of that money before my dad gets back."

Janie took a long hit, letting her mind go blank for a minute. Her heart felt like a block of ice. "When does your dad get back?"

"Not till next week, but that's a lot of money, and I don't have another connection. Just Paul."

"Me." Janie took another hit off the joint. "You've got me."

Landslide

JANIE FOLLOWED DEBBY TO THE CAR PARKED IN PAUL'S space. The few lights working in the parking lot sputtered in the winter dark. They drove through town as the streetlights blinked on just ahead of them to a street in a neighborhood full of big houses with manicured hedges and trimmed trees on a sea of sloping lawns. Debby parked in a driveway.

She punched in a security code on a panel of numbered buttons that unlocked the front door. Janie followed her inside. The rooms were bare of personal things like photographs and knick-knacks. The living room furniture was black leather and glass and chrome on plush white carpet. Janie stood still for a minute calculating the kind of money that bought all this.

Debby took two stairs at a time up a curved staircase, dumping her bag and coat on the way. She called down from the top of the stairs. "Come on up. I've got to pee. There's a phone up here."

Debby's room looked like a picture in a decorating magazine. Everything matched – white and gold furniture. A canopy bed. The only sign of Debby was a small mirror with the residue of white powder clinging to it, a rolled bill beside it on the vanity.

Janie couldn't keep the awe out of her voice. "How's your dad make the money for all this?"

"Oh, this is nothing like we had when we lived in Pacific Palisades. Before the divorce and all that." Debby stood at the sink. "Salem is such a hole, but Daddy was scared I'd relapse and my mom is definitely out of the picture, so he moved us here."

"Why don't you just leave? I mean how old are you anyway?"

She gestured to the room. "Why would I leave? You can use the phone in my dad's room. Come on."

In the room next door an unmade bed took up much of the space. Empty glasses and filled ashtrays sat on the floor. This was obviously where Debby was sleeping, maybe Paul too.

Debby pulled a painting away from the wall, exposing a small wall safe hidden behind it. She dialed the lock back and forth. From inside she pulled out a business-sized envelope stuffed full of bills. "Are you going to be able to get me a good deal?"

Janie's voice was tight and level. "I'm going to get you another connection, but when this is over, I never want to see you again or hear you've been with my old man. I'll help you move it if you want, because I know this whole damn valley. You might make back part of your dad's money. At least I won't be jacking up the price to make a profit off you like Paul does. We clear?"

Debby handed her a slim black phone. "I'm going to hop in the shower. No long distance. Nothing my dad will see on the bill. Okay?"

Janie nodded and dialed Paul's main connection, Jeff in Keizer. Long distance. Too bad.

He picked up on the third ring. "Yup?"

"Jeff. This is Janie."

"Your old man just left. I imagine he's a bit peeved with me."

"Oh yeah?"

"Yup. Told him only salvation is free in this fucking world."

"Well, I'm not calling about Paul. There's someone I want you to meet."

"Oh yeah? Is this person female and fine?"

"Paul seemed to think so."

He hooted. "So, that's how it is! You know the old Bible verse don't you? *Vengence is Mine sayeth the Lord.*"

"You want to meet her or not?"

"Oh, I definitely want to meet. Give me half an hour. See you at the Flight."

"Make it Denny's on 99."

At 7:00 p.m. Debby and Janie sat in a window booth watching for Jeff. He pulled in driving a muscle car and circled the parking lot twice before he parked.

Janie nodded at his car. "He's here."

"How come he doesn't just park?"

"He watches too many cop shows."

Jeff got out of the car, dragged a comb through his long hair, and stuck the comb in the back pocket of his black Levi's.

Debby looked him over. "Looks kind of like Johnny Winter."

Jeff found them and sat across from Debby, next to Janie.

Debby leaned forward across the table, pushing her breasts together. "So, you're Jeff. Janie says maybe we could do some business."

He took a cigarette out of the pack in his jacket pocket. Debby leaned closer, lighting it. He cupped his hand around hers and inhaled the smoke, looking at Debby over the top of his mirrored shades. "Finish eating and we'll see what we can do."

When they left Denny's an hour later, ice had begun to form on puddles. Janie felt stiff with the cold. She crawled into the backseat. Debby sat next to Jeff in the front. He drove the backroads out of town, did a stint on the freeway, then doubled back the long way, all the time talking over the radio. Janie wasn't even pretending to listen. She'd heard this same old shit from every two-bit dealer she'd ever met, and given enough time they all ended up busted. Janie pushed her face against the cold window and watched as the scenery flashed by. She had never felt so mean and ugly in all her life. They were outside town where the houses thinned out and grew unkempt.

Jeff edged the volume down as they pulled onto a gravel road. "I told you Paul might be by later?"

"That's cool." Janie didn't flinch.

Debby grumbled. "He'd better have my money."

Both Jeff and Janie laughed.

Jeff shut off the motor in front of a house that spindly trees partly hid from the main road. No other houses were nearby. "You going to cut his throat?"

"If I can."

"Man, I'm glad you're not my old lady. But shit – you two can go round and round – I don't care as long as I get my money up front."

Debby piped in. "It's my money."

Jeff looked at her. "But they're my drugs, darling."

He opened the car door and gave Janie a hand as she struggled out of the back, her foot asleep. He smiled at her as Debby got out of the car and walked to the front door. "She's going to be fun for awhile. A regular roller coaster. Hours of entertainment."

Janie nodded. "I was hoping you'd feel that way."

The house had the cranked up smell of cat pee and aluminum that Janie had grown accustomed to. The baseboard heater didn't work. Jeff turned on a space heater in the middle of the living room and went upstairs. Janie waited with Debby on the couch while Jeff went upstairs to get a bag of fresh powder.

He came down a few minutes later and tossed a baggie full of white powder to Janie. "You want a taste?"

"I do." Debby grabbed the bag. "How many times I got to tell you it's *my* money – *my* gig."

Jeff shook his head. "Let's get it straight, Debby. This is my gig. Got it?"

Jeff gave Debby a coke spoon filled with the powder. She snorted it in one nostril, refilled from the bag, and then did the other. Jeff had a taste too. Janie watched, waiting for Debby to decide. There was a fair amount of coughing and snorting, and a trip to the kitchen for water.

Debby flushed beet red. "Let's do it."

Jeff had an ounce of some powdered baby laxative to cut the

methamphetamine with. Janie listened while he told her how to cut the dope on the mirror with a brand new razor blade, how to weigh it out on the triple beam minus the weight of the bag, how to wrap it up properly in small foil squares.

At 10:00 p.m., Janie and Debby left Jeff's. Janie planned to sell grams to every person Paul knew for five dollars less than he did. By the time she was done, Paul wouldn't be able to sell anything to anyone.

They drove for hours, stopping every few minutes at another house or apartment. Debby waited in the car with the heater running and the radio tuned to the all-night rock show. Janie ran in and out of homes, turning over dope as fast as she could, feeling like she was in a race with Paul. Somewhere out in the night he was trying to get somebody to front him an ounce until he could sell it and replace all that money. Janie knew all the places he knew, and she got there first.

At 3:00 a.m. Saturday, they were back at Jeff's. Jeff and Debby were in the kitchen doing lines on a mirror under a light-bulb that hung in the middle of the room. In a month or two, maybe three if Debby was lucky, Jeff would be done with her and she would be more strung out than even she could imagine. She'd wanted to teach Paul a lesson and get rid of Debby once and for all. She'd done that, but there was no pleasure in it, no glimpse of green.

A car pulled up outside, setting the dogs to bark. Jeff came out of the kitchen holding a .357. He pulled the curtain away from the window and peered out. "Party's over, Janie. Your old man's here." He unlocked the door, opening it wide to the night. "Man, I can't believe it. It's snowing."

Large white flakes drifted down. Thousands piling up, around, and on top of one another. Janie walked outside to Paul's car, a handful of stolen bills stuffed into her pockets.

If You Want Me To Stay

PAUL SLEPT FOR A WEEK. COMING DOWN HARD WITH
the snow outside, he burrowed into Janie. He quit his job by
default, simply didn't show up and didn't think too much about
it. The rent was paid for February and all he could do was sleep.
Janie stayed in bed with him. Her arms around him, the heat of her
body against his back. Lots of women had tried to change him,
they screeched and shouted, cursed and yelled. Eventually they
left or he left. Either way, same thing. But here was Janie
whispering in his ear, stroking his hair while he was coming down.
"Come back to me. I need you back." No one had ever loved
him this way before. The tenacity of her love amazed and terrified
him. He'd never wanted to change for anyone, never felt inspired
to try. She asked him to get straight and try to live for everything
he loved. Paul didn't want to tell her that at the top of the list he
loved getting high.

They moved again. He found them a tiny one-bedroom
rental across the street from a park in Salem, close to a health
food store that she liked. It had a yard in the front and back and
trees everywhere. He'd never noticed before how much she
loved trees. The house itself was so small you could sit on the toilet
and put your feet in the shower, and the kitchen was only big
enough for one person at a time, but Janie loved it. He used the
rest of the money to move them and sold his car. He was still
dealing – only pot in small quantities, no chemicals, absolutely

no more wire. Paul spent the mornings making coffee, smoking pot, and taking care of the houseplants.

Staying away from crank was harder than ever. He missed it, the anticipation when he scored, the sting of the needle, or even snorting, with the taste in the back of his throat metallic and harsh, the lopsided beating of his heart, the sweat when you first got off. More than that, he craved the feeling of invincibility, the all-out rush of it, the feeling that everything he did was all right. Everyone he knew did crank. If he gave it up, he'd be like those AA guys who never hung out with their friends anymore. People would know he was strung out if he stopped using. It would show weakness if he couldn't use like he always had. Mistrust would hang over him like a stink in the wind, and people would say things about him that he could only put to rest by doing a bump. He tried hard to remember what life had looked like before he started getting high, but that time was short and far gone. Seemed like getting high and dealing were what made him Paul Jesse. If he could just stop with the crank, maybe douche out the old brain with a couple hits of acid – get his shit together. Yeah. That seemed like the right thing to do.

FINALLY THE MORNING Janie'd been waiting for since the day she left Yakima in 1974 had arrived. March 4, 1978. Her birthday. Sun streamed in the window. She took it as an omen that things were going to change for the better. She could hear Paul singing in the kitchen to an old Al Green song. Snuggled next to her, Eloise allowed her belly to be rubbed.

Paul appeared in the doorway holding a jar full of daffodils and a cup of coffee. Standing there in only jeans, his hair clean and loose to his waist, his Fu Manchu trimmed neatly and his brown eyes sparkling and clear, it was easy to forget the other Paul – the one with the needle in his arm who hit her sometimes and scared her always.

He smiled. "Happy birthday, Janie."

"You got me flowers." She sat in bed propped up with pillows and took the coffee from him.

He sat beside her, putting the jar of flowers on the table. "Yup." He picked up her hairbrush. "Scooch up, honey."

Janie moved forward, straightening the soft flannel shirt she slept in. She loved it when he brushed her hair. It made her think of that first night at Delores's. Paul climbed in bed behind her and began brushing out her hair, first working out the knots and tangles with his fingers, and then with the brush. He wove his fingers in and out of her thick brown hair, french braiding it, taking his time.

"Where'd you learn to braid like this?"

"I told you – my sister taught me all about hair when we were kids. I should've gone to beauty school."

"Am I ever going to meet your sister?"

"I don't know, baby. We fell out hard when I left the city. I haven't seen her in years." He tied the end of the braid with a piece of yarn. "Looks real pretty." He kissed the curve of her throat. "Get dressed. I've got a surprise for you." He tumbled her out of bed and left the room.

When Janie came out of the shower, Paul had laid out some clothes for her on the bed. He was dressed in his leathers so she knew they were going for a ride. "Where are we going?"

"Get what you'll need for a couple of days and don't ask questions."

Janie put a few essentials into her pack and carried it to the front room. Paul waited for her on the couch, rolling joints and filling an empty Camel pack with them. "Ready?"

"Come on, Paul, where're we going?"

"I'm not telling. You're going to need this." He picked up a garbage bag stuffed full of something and duct-taped to hold it closed. "It's not wrapped very well, but – here."

Janie took the bag and tore it open. Inside were a set of biking leathers – black jacket and chaps. He'd been telling her he wanted to get them for her, but until he sold the car they hadn't ridden the bike together very much. She never told him she didn't want leathers. She hated being on the back of the bike when he was high. They weren't new, but they were in good condition. Paul looked so proud of his gift. She smiled. "Wow! These're great." She kissed him.

"Rick turned me on to them. You like them?"

Janie looked at his face, beaming with pride. She loved that he wanted to have her on a bike behind him. "You bet. Let me put them on." She struggled into the chaps and put on the jacket.

Paul slipped on his shades. "Let's go."

They rode west through the farm country of the valley, to the foothills, and then to the mountains and forests of the Coast Range. The highway ran through the forest beside a river for a time, then up to the summit of the mountain pass and down-hill as quick as water into the flood plains of the Oregon coast. She could smell the ocean before she could see it. Paul headed south from Lincoln City. They rode leaning into the curves together. Janie felt as if they were chasing something they would never catch.

They pulled into a row of weathered cabins on a bluff above the beach. Paul paid for two nights and they carried their stuff to a cabin close to steps that led down to an endless stretch of sand and ocean.

He unlocked the cabin door and they stepped inside. It was nothing fancy, but it looked clean. "Go on down to the beach for awhile. I have things to do."

"Paul, this is enough. Don't spend money we don't have."

"Don't worry about the money. I have it covered. Go on down and I'll meet you on the beach at the bottom of the steps at sunset. Okay?"

"Okay." Janie took off her gear and went down the wood steps to the beach below. She stretched, working the kinks out of her back from the long ride. The beach was empty. She walked through the sand to where it was hard, and farther down to the water. Once she started, she didn't want to ever go back.

She wished it was possible to start over. When you were a kid, you could get another chance by calling out, *Do Over!* Above her a row of ocean birds flew low, skimming across the incoming waves. The tide boomed in. Janie felt much older than eighteen today. Loving Paul was an Olympic event. A marathon. She wished he hadn't spent so much money on this trip. Janie knew the cost of things now – a bag of groceries, a bag of dope, a month's rent, another woman – everything had a price.

THEY STAYED AT the beach for three days. Paul couldn't wait to leave. He couldn't sleep. He drank a six-pack every night and smoked pot all day and still couldn't relax. He didn't want to yell at Janie again, but she watched him with a look of doubt in her eyes. By the time they left the beach for home, they were both pretty miserable.

As soon as they were back in town, he dropped Janie off at the house and went to Doug's. He couldn't wait to get away from her for a little bit, see if Doug wanted to buy some pot, drink a few beers. He felt more like himself, less rattled, less confused. He banged on the aluminum screen door.

Doug stomped through the house and unlocked the door. "My man! Where the fuck've you been?"

"The old lady's birthday so I took her to the beach."

"Prince Charming, huh?"

"That's right. You got a beer?"

"You got a joint?"

"Yup." Paul followed Doug to the kitchen. On the stove was a bent spoon and a lighter. The point of a a syringe stuck out from under a piece of junk mail.

Doug opened the refrigerator and pulled out two Hamms, handing one to Paul. "Here's to you."

"So, you score lately?" Paul nodded toward the paraphernalia.

"Yeah. You want a bump?"

The tracks burned in Paul's arm and his mouth dried up.

Just a taste wouldn't hurt anybody. Janie wouldn't have to know. "Sure."

It felt like going home. He wanted to cry it felt so good. The doubt and craving left him. Paul was Paul again, and he knew in that sting of the needle and the first rush of speed that he would never give this up for anybody.

JANIE OPENED THE wooden box where she kept her most important things. It was under her side of the bed. It held no real secrets, but she had never shown it to Paul. Inside were things she could never replace: her Social Security card, her birth certificate, a rose Paul had given her on their trip to San Francisco, some coins minted in her birth year, and a few photographs she'd taken from an album before she left home:

Janie about six months old in her mother's arms on the front porch of their house.

Janie at four on the beach with her dad sitting in the sand, a sandcastle in front of them.

School class pictures from first, second, and third grade.

The straight A report cards from each of those years.

A picture of her dad and mom the Christmas before her mom died. Her mom on her dad's lap. Her mouth open in a smile and her dark hair tossed back. His arm around her waist.

Janie took out the birth certificate and Social Security card and slipped them into her purse. She had taken them when she ran away knowing one day, if she didn't get caught, she'd need them to get a job, to get a driver's license, to start her life. She was ready for that now.

PAUL STOPPED AT a Minit Mart for a six-pack, deciding to go drink a few with Rick. He'd wait awhile and mellow out before he went home. Janie could always tell when he was wired. He felt sharp and on top of things, but something he did when he was wired always tipped her off.

As he rode out of town, a police cruiser pulled out behind

him. Paul only had a few joints on him, not enough to get busted over, and he hadn't had a beer yet. But he felt like the cop knew what he was up to. Maybe he'd get pulled over or worse, followed to Rick's and people would think he snitched him off. The cop finally made a turn and passed out of Paul's view.

Rick was in the shop parting out an old Moto Guzzi motorcycle. He worked like a surgeon, meticulously taking apart the bike and lining the parts on a tarp. Rick nodded to Paul. "Hey."

Paul ripped a beer from the six-pack. He popped the top, took a drink, and set the rest of the six-pack on a work bench. "Thought I'd stop by. Brought you a beer. Here you go, man."

Rick wiped his hands on his coveralls, got up off the floor, and grabbed a beer. "First beer of the day is always the best."

They drank in silence and soon Paul lit a joint. "Well, Rick, I got a business proposition for you."

"Yeah?" Rick took the joint from Paul with his black-stained fingers.

"What would you say about a front."

"Not much."

"I could turn it around in two or three days. I got a great pot and acid connection in San Francisco."

"Nobody got acid like back in the city. 'Member window-pane?" asked Rick.

"Yeah."

"Pretty good shit?"

"Yeah. You could turn it over pretty easy up here," said Paul.

"If I get burned it's your ass. Can you wait a couple days?"

Paul shrugged and popped open another beer. "I got plenty of time."

Lively Up Yourself

JANIE WALKED DOWNTOWN WEARING THE MOST CON-
servative clothes she owned. She didn't know where to start, but
she'd look until she found a real job with a paycheck and regular
hours. Store by store, restaurant by restaurant, Janie walked
through downtown Salem and asked at each business if they were
hiring and for what position.

Janie soon realized she would need to invent a past to fill
out the applications. She went to the library where she pored
over phone books from Eugene to find out the name and address
of a high school she might have attended. She did the math to
find what her graduation date would be if she graduated a year
early. She'd call Stella tonight and ask him to be a reference. At
least that part wasn't a lie, just a little stretch of the imagination.
Janie had no doubt that whatever job she got, she'd figure out
how to do it. The hard part now would be figuring out a telephone
number she could use for messages. They still didn't have a
phone, and they wouldn't be getting one any time soon. Doug
probably would let her use his number. He lived close by
and liked her. He tended to answer the phone by shouting in the
receiver *Your dime* instead of *Hello*, but that was the best she
could do. She decided to go home and fill out all the applications
today, and then turn them in tomorrow.

Her feet ached and the walk home was about a mile long.
Through the window of a small bookstore she could see a few
chairs where she might sit and read, and rest her feet before the

long walk home. A string of bells wrapped around the knob tinkled when she opened the door. Inside an older lady with frizzy gray hair pulled back in a long braid and *pince-nez* glasses perched on the bridge of her nose stood behind the counter. She looked up at Janie and smiled. Janie smiled back and browsed the books on the shelves. It was a children's bookstore. She took a leatherbound, illustrated edition of *The Just So Stories* off the shelf and sat in a chair nearest the window.

"Holly, just choose a book and let's go." A woman's voice interrupted the quiet store.

Janie looked up and saw a woman and little girl at the shelf in front of her. The woman looked tired.

"I can't find one." The little girl's voice rose at the end of the sentence in a whine.

Janie looked back at her book.

"There are lots of nice books right here – just pick one so Mommy can go. Look, you're disturbing people."

Janie smiled. "No, it's okay. I'm just looking at this book." She caught the eyes of the little girl. "Have you ever read *Harriet the Spy*?"

"No."

Janie tilted her book down and looked at the little girl. "Well, it might be too hard for you."

"It won't be too hard for me. I'm eight, but I'm a good reader. Where is it? I want to see."

The bookstore lady called from the counter, "It's in the next aisle over – Louise Fitzhugh is the author."

The little girl took off around the corner followed by her mother who mouthed "thank you" to Janie. Janie nodded and went back to her book.

A few minutes later, the daughter carried the book to the counter and her mother bought it. The girl waved to Janie as they left. It was getting late and she had a long walk ahead of her. Putting her book back on the shelf, Janie headed for the door.

The woman behind the counter stopped her. "You have a nice way with children."

"Oh, I just thought she might like that book. It was a favorite of mine when I was about her age."

"Did you read a lot as a child?"

"Oh yeah. I still do."

"My name's Alice." She held out her hand and they shook. "I hope you don't mind me asking – are you interested in a part-time job? I just put an ad in the *Guardian* this morning, but I'm a firm believer in serendipity."

"I'd love to work here."

"I need someone to work full-time weekends and a few hours during the week. It's only minimum wage, but I could give you books at cost. What's your name?"

"Janie Marek."

"It's good to meet you, Janie. Here's an application. Bring it with you tomorrow and you can start then."

"What time?"

"Come in at 11:00 and we'll do all the paperwork."

"Paperwork?"

"Just your tax stuff."

"You don't know anything about me."

"I learned a lot watching you with those customers. Fill out the application and write me a list of your top ten children's books and why they're your favorites. And handwrite it – okay? I'm a firm believer in handwriting."

"I'll bring it with me."

"Then I'll see you tomorrow at 11:00, Janie."

Janie smiled as she walked home in the late afternoon spring sunshine. A flurry of white petals drifted down around her from the trees that lined the way back home. She planned her new life as she walked. She would work at a bookstore and maybe she could take a class at the community college in the fall. She hoped Paul would be happy about the job and all the other things she wanted to do – go to school, have a garden, get a dog, make a baby. Maybe Paul would go to school too, if he saw her doing it. Paul was smart, he could do anything. She had plans for their life together. Maybe they'd get married. The Paul in her imagination worked at a regular job all day and came home at night. He didn't deal, use, or have friends that did. He didn't say mean things and he never hit her. Once again Janie was determined to believe that with enough work on her part Paul would change.

When she got to the house, she saw Doug's car parked in front. He and Paul were on the porch drinking beers. In their new life, Paul was definitely going to need some new friends.

"Hey, baby!" Paul said as she turned up the sidewalk. "Glad you got home before I left."

Janie's smile fell away. "Where're you going?"

Doug moved over on the concrete steps. "Made some room for you," he said patting the place beside him. "Want a beer?"

Janie waited at the bottom of the steps. "No thanks. Where are you going, Paul?"

"I got to run down to the city for a couple of days. Do a little business. Doug's going to drive. I didn't think you'd want to come." Paul clenched his teeth between words. He was wired.

"I couldn't come if I wanted to. I've got a job." She had planned how she would tell him, but it wasn't turning out like she'd imagined. "I thought you weren't going to go to San Francisco anymore."

"Of course I'm going to the city. My family's there. Besides, I got business to do."

"But I thought you were mad at Bill or something."

"You think too much, girl." Paul stroked his Fu Manchu. "So, you got a job, huh?"

Janie felt deflated. "Yeah, I start tomorrow."

"Then you won't miss me much."

"I guess not." Janie let the screen door slam behind her.

PAUL AND DOUG drove all night, stopping only to refuel. By the time they got to Bill's in San Francisco, Paul's head buzzed.

A woman with high cheekbones answered the door and led them to the dining room. She pointed and walked away.

Doug shook his head. "*Night of the Living Dead* in here."

"Bill's women are never very talkative."

Bill sat at the table with Blue. An opened bottle of tequila and two shot glasses half full sat between them. Bill stood when they entered "Look what the cat dragged in! Been too long, Paul." He clapped him on the shoulder and shook hands.

"Hey Bill! This is Doug, the dude I told you about."

Blue looked up at Paul.

"Blue." He hadn't thought about Blue being there. "Long time, man."

Blue didn't smile or speak.

Bill sat down. "Yeah. Come on in and have a drink. Mona," he called, "Get a couple more glasses. You getting to be a big old pussy, man. Driving all the time. When's the last time you got on your bike?"

Paul relaxed as they sat around the table. Glasses came and were filled more than once. They smoked some good pot.

"You still with Janie?" Blue asked.

Paul laughed, trying to make a joke. "Since when did you remember a name?"

"Of course I remember her name. I was with her while you were out screwing my sister. You remember my sister don't you, Paul?"

Bill filled Blue's glass. "Calm down, man."

"I'm calm." Blue said. "So are you with Janie?"

"Yeah, we're still together."

"Just checking. Is she doing all right? Luna didn't do so well with you."

"I didn't do anything to Luna."

Blue got up from the table put his glass down hard. "No,

you didn't. You didn't do shit." Blue grabbed his jacket and left, slamming the door behind him.

Bill shook his head. "Sorry about that. He's been pretty fucked up since she died. Guess his mom's not doing too well. From what he says he had a little thing going on with your old lady too."

Doug's ears pricked up. "Janie?"

Paul shook his head. "Oh yeah?"

Bill sneered. "How long did you leave them out there – a month or two? They were probably threading the needle the minute you left."

Paul sipped his drink.

Bill sat back in his chair resting his glass against his chest. "You were doing his sister, right? Monkey see, monkey do."

Doug laughed. "He's got you there, Paul. You got to admit."

Bill stood up. "Forget about it. Let's do some business."

The Needle and the Damage Done

EVERY MORNING JANIE MADE A CUP OF RED ZINGER TEA, fed Eloise, dressed, straightened up the house, and walked to work. She arrived ten minutes early and waited on a bench outside until Alice unlocked the door. At about seven in the evening she returned home and ate a bowl of cereal at the table with Eloise batting at the spoon. She borrowed books from the store and read late into the night so she could borrow a new book the next day. Seven days, seven books.

She pretended she'd always lived alone. She pretended she wasn't waiting for Paul every minute of the day and night, but she was. She didn't know whether she missed him or not. She knew she wouldn't settle down until he came home. She went to bed at night wondering if this was the night he'd come home, waking her from sleep, wired or drunk or both. When she walked home after work, she wondered if he'd be there and what would happen next if he was.

Friday night, Alice turned the lock in the door and flipped over the closed sign in the window. "What a day! Janie, here's the key for tomorrow. Just keep doing what you've been doing all week and you'll be fine. Do you want a ride home?"

"Are you sure?"

"I'm going to the Heliotrope on my way – you live over near there, right?"

Driving home took only a few minutes in Alice's old station wagon. Janie could see Paul on their front step, a beer can in his hand. Something about the way he sat there made her feel uneasy. She had never mentioned Paul to Alice and she didn't want them to meet tonight. "Alice, could you drop me at the store instead? I need to get some bread. I can walk home from there."

"Sure." Alice turned the corner at the edge of the park.

In the rear-view mirror Janie saw Paul get up and go inside, leaving the door open. She was sure he didn't see her.

At the grocery, Janie bought a loaf of bread and left before Alice could offer to drive her back. She cut through the park to the house. The lights burned in every window. She could hear the stereo from across the street. She should be happy he was home safe, but she had a bad feeling. She crossed the street and went inside.

"Where the fuck've you been?" He was yelling at her before she closed the door.

"I told you I got a job, remember?" Janie put the bag with the loaf of bread on the table. "I had to stop at the store on my way home. When'd you get back?" She put her coat away and walked around pretending his eyes weren't bloodshot, and his words weren't coming out crooked from too many beers. "You eat anything?"

"What is it with you and food? You're always trying to feed me, I'm not hungry."

"I just thought you might be." She looked around for Eloise, but the cat was nowhere in sight. "When'd you get back?" She knew from the way he ground his teeth he was wired, drunk, and dangerous.

Paul's voice sounded ragged and dry. He yelled as if he couldn't hear how loud he was. "Why do you want to know for? I got back when I got back. You weren't here."

"I already told you. I was at work and after work I went to the store and bought this bread –" She held it up. He grabbed it from her, crushing the loaf before throwing it across the room. Janie froze.

There was dried up white foam in the corners of his mouth

and his face was red. "Guess who I saw in the city?" He took her upper arm squeezing it hard. She could feel her pulse under his thumb. "Guess."

"I don't know. Let go of my arm. You're hurting me."

"I saw your boyfriend. Remember Blue?" He twisted her arm so the bone went one way and her muscle and skin went the other.

"Blue was never my boyfriend."

Paul came over the space between them. His chest slammed into her, pushing the air from her lungs and pinning her flat against the wall. One hand held her hair, pulling it hard, so her head tipped back exposing the length of her throat. "Thought you were slick. Thought I wouldn't find out. People laughing at me. Acting like you're all pure and shit. You fucked him didn't you?" His breath smelled metallic of crank.

"You fucked his sister. Did you think I didn't know?" The words slipped out before she thought.

His fists punched every word he said into her ribs and lower back. "Don't. You. Ever. Talk. About. Luna. Again." He slammed her against the wall, knocking her breath away. Then he was crying, falling to his knees in front of her, his arms around her waist, sobbing Luna's name. Saying he was sorry over and over again. She didn't know whether he was sorry for what he'd done to her, or whatever he'd done to Luna. She wasn't sure he even knew who she was. She didn't think it mattered.

Eventually he passed out, pulling her down on the floor with him. He wouldn't let her go. She lay under him until morning. She felt a wet puddle spread around her as he pissed in his sleep. She rolled him to his side and inched herself away, stopping when he twitched or shouted in his sleep. She left him face down in a pool of urine on the kitchen floor and went into the bathroom to get ready for work.

She ran the shower and let the room steam up before stepping inside. She stood under the showerhead, not washing or even moving, letting the water fall over her. A voice in her head

told her she should get out of the house, go hide, get away, but it
was a small voice, not very insistent, and soon it stopped. The
face she saw in the bathroom mirror as she applied her makeup
belonged to someone else. Little had changed since yesterday.
There were no bruises on her face. That was good. She could cover
the dark circles around her eyes. A few nasty bruises marked
her side under her ribs. No one would see those. She was sore, but
she didn't think anything was broken. Her body belonged to
someone else now. She couldn't feel anything.

She dressed silently, tiptoeing around the house. If he died,
this would be over. If he died, this would never happen again.
She felt as if she could kill them both right now. If she knew where
his gun was she would put it to Paul's forehead first and pull
the trigger while he slept. She would kill herself afterward, the
neighbors would call the police, and all this would be over.
If she knew where his gun was, but she felt too tired to look for it.
She would go to work instead, so that Alice could sleep in. She
would feed the cat and after work she'd buy the ingredients to
make spaghetti for dinner. She would put this out of her mind
because there was nothing she could do about it. Paul would be
nice to her tonight. There were never two bad days in a row.
He'd be sorry and she'd pretend to believe him when he said this
wouldn't happen again. She wrote a note: PAUL – I AM AT
WORK. I'LL BE HOME AT 6. THE PHONE NUMBER IS 360-
9553. JANIE. She opened the refrigerator and put the note
on top of an opened can of Coke.

PAUL WOKE UP shivering, wet, and stinking of urine and vomit.
The clock on the wall read 12:15. He couldn't remember when he
got home. He didn't quite remember seeing Janie the night before.
He called out her name, but the house was quiet. The only sound
was the hum of the refrigerator. He started to piece together the
last twenty-four hours. The smell of vomit in the room made him
gag and lurch for the bathroom, but he couldn't stand quickly
enough. It streamed down his chin into his mustache and onto

the floor. He couldn't remember the last time he ate or what he'd eaten. His gut and head ached. He eased himself off the floor, dizzy with the effort, and stumbled into the bathroom. On the floor were Janie's clothes, wet with his urine.

He knew he got home yesterday and she hadn't been here. He'd been mad at her for what Bill had said about her, but he might have cut it loose if he hadn't been so wired. Okay, so he got home in the afternoon and then what? Doug was over for awhile. He and Doug had been drinking. That was evident from the empty beer cans all over the place. He was trying to come down before Janie got home. Thinking too hard made his head hurt worse. He got in the shower and let the water pound on his closed eyes. Where was she now? He wrapped a towel around his waist and went to the fridge – sure enough, she'd popped him open a Coke and left it on the top shelf of the fridge with a note for him. Nothing about what happened, but if he'd pissed on her and passed out in vomit on the kitchen floor, the story was probably not a good one. He'd clean the house up and go do the laundry – give her a call and see what she said. Maybe it would come back to him later. He hoped it wouldn't. He didn't want to know.

THE STORE WAS quiet so Janie brought a book to the counter after she finished dusting the shelves and watering the plants. She couldn't concentrate well enough to read. The words ran together making no sense. She hadn't brought lunch and hadn't eaten since yesterday's lunch. She didn't feel hungry. Her back and ribs hurt. Not terrible. A low, aching kind of hurt. A few people came in and out of the store, looking mostly, not buying. Sundays seemed like the earth spun slower than the rest of the week. People moved slower. She was glad that Alice wasn't here and she could be quiet.

The phone rang in the late afternoon. Janie guessed it would be Paul. She let it ring three times and then picked up. "Children's Garden Bookstore. Can I help you?"

"Hi, baby. You sound all official."

"Where are you?"

"I'm over at the Blue Turtle. Want me to bring you some lunch?"

"That's okay."

"If anything happened last night – if I said anything or did anything – "

"Forget it. It doesn't matter."

"I don't remember seeing you or anything."

"I have a customer. I've got to go."

"When do you get done?"

"At six."

"I'll be there."

"I've got to go."

"Janie? I'm sorry."

When she locked the door, Paul was waiting in the parking lot, leaning against his bike, shades off. He looked worse than ever. His cheeks were sunken and his eyes red. He had a cold sore on his lip. He hugged her, folding her into his heart, but she still didn't feel anything. When they got home she could smell lemon cleanser and a chicken roasting. The night before had disappeared like it never happened. They ate dinner together. Eloise came home and begged for scraps of meat from Paul's fingers. He didn't ask what he'd done and she didn't tell him.

Later, she went to the bedroom to change while he did the dishes. She had her pajama bottoms on when he opened the door. She was reaching for a top as he stood in the door staring at her bruises, dark purple and red on her torso and arms. She didn't look up. He didn't speak. The moment passed. She slipped her top on. He left the room, closing the door behind him.

FOR THE NEXT few weeks Paul controlled himself and, if it weren't for the bruises, Janie had trouble remembering that anything had happened. She wouldn't think about it and then maybe it wouldn't happen again. Paul took care of the house on the days she worked. He dug out a garden area in the backyard for her. He taught himself how to macrame and made bracelets and plant hangers. For the first week he smoked pot but he didn't drink or get wired. By the second week, he had a tall can of beer on the table next to him when she got home from work. He was working on making a bracelet for her with embroidery thread. She'd asked him quietly if he was going to stop drinking. She'd been careful not to make a big deal out of it.

His answer scared her. "I can't."

She didn't ask him again and began watching to see how long the peace would last.

Without planning, she found two more jobs at the mall so, by the beginning of July, she was almost never home except to sleep. Tiny's Sandwich Shop across from Alice's had put up a help wanted sign and Janie was able to work Monday through Thursday from 11:00 to 4:00. On the weekends, Friday through Sunday, she worked at the bookstore from opening to closing. Dave, the manager at McKays Jewelry store, hired her to work evenings from five to closing Monday through Friday. She didn't plan it, but she didn't turn down the work.

Work distracted her. It felt good to have her own money, even though Paul took cash from her purse without asking and she didn't say anything. She didn't want to cause a fight. Paul didn't seem to mind how much she worked, except when he was drinking or wired, then he got jealous and made up stories. Janie learned to always be where she said she would be, at whatever time she was supposed to be there. She never talked to people she didn't know except when she had to wait on them. She suspected Paul sometimes watched her. He knew things about her day he could only know from observation. She told herself it was because he loved her so much. Nobody'd ever loved her like that, she probably just wasn't used to it yet.

PAUL FELT HIMSELF slipping. He couldn't get a front from anybody. He dipped into the product whenever he bought a quantity and then ended up cutting it so far down only the hardcore would buy from him. He couldn't seem to get straight anymore. He wasn't sure when his habit had changed. One day he was Paul Jesse, dealer, cool, respected. Now he was close to fishing through the trashcan, looking for used filters that might contain the residue of crank in their fibers. Smoking pot calmed him down some but it wasn't the same without a beer or two. For awhile, three was his self-imposed limit, then a six-pack would disappear before he realized. To get straight he'd do a little wire – just a taste – and deny it later, when Janie got home. Too much to drink and he passed out and woke up to Janie's bruises. Too much wire and he wouldn't pass out until he drank himself under. He tried the acid cure, but it didn't work like he wanted. Janie told him after a long, bad acid trip that he'd tried to burn the house down. One thing totally confused him. He couldn't figure it out. She stayed. No matter how shitty it got, Janie stayed. Nobody had ever stayed so long and through so much. He kept trying to put it back together. He didn't want to lose her. He began checking on her during the day without telling her. He didn't trust her.

Hard Rain Gonna Fall

MCKAYS HAD MORE THAN JUST JEWELRY. THEY CARRIED china, crystal and silver too. Janie couldn't care less about diamond pendant necklaces, cubic zirconium rings, and fancy watches but with her store discount she had been buying a set of dishes. They were robin's-egg blue with gold trim. Every week she bought a piece and smuggled it home. Paul's need for constant cash made him tight with money. He questioned her about everything. She planned imaginary dinners for the imaginary family she hoped for. She could't exactly see Paul at these dinners. He was more likely throw a plate against the wall than eat food from it. That happened twice this past summer. Once because he didn't want avocado on his quesadilla and once because he did. She was beginning to understand that this would be their life together.

Janie knew she stayed now because she was afraid to leave. Paul could easily kill her when he was high and not even remember it later. There was nowhere to go where he wouldn't find her. He told her that every time he was wired or drunk. He whispered in her ear, so close she could taste the crank on him, "If you ever left me I'd find you. I'd kill you before I let you leave me." She no longer doubted that they would become one of those TV news reports. It was only a matter of time.

The night before she hadn't slept again. Paul wasn't home but that didn't help. Not at all. The worst times Paul came home late and wasted, dragging her out of bed and keeping her up until he passed out. It was Thursday. She worked at Tiny's Sandwich Shop until four and then McKays until nine. She left Paul a note with her schedule and taped it to the refrigerator. He didn't remember things like her work schedule when he had been awake for days. She heard his bike outside and met him on her way out the door. Paul was ten years older than her. Twenty-eight this September. He looked like a man in his fifties.

He smiled at her. "On your way to work?"

Janie kissed his cheek and caught a whiff of wire. "Yeah. I left you a note. What do you have there?" He was holding a wooden baseball bat.

"Check it out. Louisville Slugger. Got it at a yard sale. Going to go play some ball out in Keizer tonight with the guys from the plant. Didn't I tell you I used to play ball in school?"

"No you never told me that. Sounds like fun. When will you be home?"

His face changed – eyes screwed up tight. "Why? You have plans?"

"No. I just wondered if I should pick up dinner. Oh, come look at the tomatoes." She dropped it. In the backyard she pulled foliage away from some plate-sized tomatoes starting to color in the sun. "Aren't they huge?"

He seemed to have forgotten her question and looked relaxed again. Happy. "They look great, baby. Yep. You better get going. Don't plan on me for dinner. I'll see you tonight."

"Okay. I'll be home about ten, unless you want to pick me up."

"We'll probably go shoot some pool and have a couple of beers after the game, but I'll see you tonight." He bent and kissed her cheek. "Don't worry."

At Tiny's she made sandwiches and poured iced teas and sodas. At four, she took a sandwich for herself and ate it in the courtyard. After lunch, she brushed her teeth and hair, and went to work at McKays. Wedding sets were marked down and the store was so busy you'd think all of Salem was getting married. At nine when they usually locked the door, Dave, the manager, was trying to make a last-minute sale to a young couple who wanted to see every ring they had. Janie pulled the iron door halfway down. At nine-thirty the couple left without getting anything.

Dave locked the front door after them. "I thought for sure they'd buy something. Oh well. What're you going to do?"

It seemed to Janie he was moving slower than normal. She carried back a tray of rings and locked the cases in front. It was 9:45. She was going to be late. "I've got to get home. Can I go?"

"I don't like the idea of you walking home this late. Why don't you let me drop you off?"

"That's okay. I like the walk."

"Well, all right. See you tomorrow then."

Janie walked out of the mall and into a summer thunderstorm. If she ran, she might make it home by 10:30. If Paul played baseball in Keizer, and they went to have some beers, he wouldn't be home yet. If she was lucky. She ran across the almost empty parking lot. Dave pulled up beside her in his Chevy Impala station wagon.

He stopped the car. "Hop in."

If she said no, he'd think she didn't like him. He could always let her out across the street from the park, so Paul wouldn't see her. She got in the car.

Through the rain pelting the windshield she could see lights on in the house and a shadow at the window. "Stop here." Her hands were wet and cold.

"Which one is your house?"

"I'm just going to get out here."

"It's pouring. I wouldn't be much of a gentleman if I didn't drive you all the way home."

Paul stood in the doorway with his arms behind his back. Janie got out of Dave's car. Her body felt as heavy as wet sand. Dave waited for her to cross the lawn and open the door. He honked the horn and waved out the window as he drove away.

When she stepped inside, the baseball bat caught her and knocked her backward against the wall.

"That your new boyfriend?" Paul's face was red, veins in his temple bulging. He raised the bat above her head and she rolled to the side. The bat cracked a hole in the wall. He jerked it out, showering the floor with white chunks of plaster. She made it to the door while he fumbled with the bat. Out of the house into the rain, she ran across the street to the park. Too close behind her, she heard the door slam and knew he was chasing her. She tried to get lost in the shadows. She clung to a huge Douglas fir hoping to make herself invisible.

She heard him wheezing in a high sing-song voice, "I'm going to get you."

She darted from tree to tree, away from him, glad for the rain. Without it he'd hear her move. She could see him nearby. She stood still, not breathing. He was close.

"You better hide. Better not let me find you."

She couldn't see him anymore. Then it was quiet. Only water dripping from the trees. A branch snapped behind her.

His voice leered, "Gotcha." He had her by the hair and slammed her face into the tree, pushing it up and down on the rough bark.

She tried to scream, but her mouth was stretched open too far and tore as he forced it into the bark. He turned her around and plugged her mouth with his fist. Janie knew she must be screaming now, but what she heard she didn't recognize.

She pushed at him to get away and slipped in the mud. He pulled her to the climbing structure where children played house.

She was not surprised when he yanked the fabric of her skirt, pulling it down and breaking the zipper. She was not surprised when he pulled her shirt open, biting her breast and pulling the flesh away with his teeth. She was not surprised when he pushed her panties aside, burning her with the metal buttons on his jeans forcing himself inside her. He pounded her body against the wooden play structure until he finally came. He pushed himself from her and walked away.

Janie didn't move. She stayed where she was. She didn't know where else she could go. Later she heard a motorcycle start up.

SHE'D BEEN THROUGH this before. She wouldn't call it rape because it was Paul. The time in the van at least she didn't know the guy. It was worse knowing someone she loved could do this to her. The familiarity frightened her. Her mouth hurt. She felt around with her tongue; it seemed like her teeth were all there, but her face was swollen and the inside of her mouth was too sore and raw to move. She pulled her skirt and shirt around her and went to the house. She was having trouble walking, having trouble taking a deep breath. She would get cleaned up and see how bad it all looked.

Both eyes were swollen almost shut and the whites were red. Her cheeks and mouth were bloody. Janie's hands shook as she tried to dab the blood away and find the source, but it was worse than she'd seen before. She was scared he'd come back before she could get away. She put on a coat over her bloody clothes and grabbed her purse. She was shaking, cold and wet with mud. She walked to the convenience store at the end of the street. She'd call Stella. There was no one else.

The guy at the counter stared while he gave her change and asked her if she was all right. She nodded and took the change. Her fingers didn't work. The index finger lay back limp. She went out to the phone booth. She fumbled with the receiver. Her hands weren't working. She couldn't see the numbers well enough to dial.

A light flashed in her eyes and she made out a cop standing in front of her, his lips moving, but the words were just noise, and then she heard the ocean in her head, and all the strength left her body. The light flipped off and she was falling.

ANOTHER LIGHT, BRIGHTER and in her eyes. Her head felt split open.

"Jane? Is your name Jane Marek?"

She nodded. How odd to hear a stranger say her name.

"Jane, You're at Salem Hospital. I'm Dr. Abadaca. Can you tell us what happened?"

"Nothing happened." There was no way she could explain this. Janie shook her head and moaned.

"Do you know who did this to you?"

"I fell."

"Is there someone we can call for you?"

Her tongue thick, the smell of blood clinging to her. "Stella. Call Stella. Stubbs is the last name – call him, okay?"

"We'll talk when you feel a little better. I'm going to give you some pain medication to help you rest. You'll be staying with us tonight."

Janie noticed a tube running into a vein of her hand. She felt herself falling away and slept.

Desolation Row

A WOMAN'S VOICE MELODIC AND RICH SANG A SONG JANIE didn't recognize. She kept her eyes closed, listening. Her head hurt – face and neck, back and shoulders, arms and legs. She remembered she was supposed to work today and struggled to sit up.

The woman said, "Looks like you're awake."

Janie's eyes were sticky and swollen. She tried reaching up to wipe at them and heard, "Now you leave that to me. Do you remember where you are?"

"Hospital?" Janie's voice more of a croak.

"That's right. I'm your nurse. My name's Annie." A damp cloth rinsed her eyelids.

She opened her eyes and saw a full brown face, the tuck and roll of weight and age pulling at smooth skin. Bright black eyes lined with mascara, full lips covered with orange lipstick the color of convict jumpsuits. A smattering of freckles across the bridge of a straight broad nose. Janie tried to sit up, but her body wasn't responding.

"We called your friend. Mr. Stubbs. You called him Stella? What a name for a big man like that!" Annie had a laugh like a xylophone. "He's in the waiting room. Been here since I came on at seven, waiting for you to wake up."

Janie looked around. "Can I see him?"

Annie looped her arm under Janie's back and scooped her up in the bed, adjusting the pillows behind her. She took her pulse and checked the IV in her hand. "First, let's get you cleaned up a little bit. Then you'll need to see the doctor."

Annie hummed while she sponged away the dried blood. "Your clothes are in that closet, but they're a mess. Maybe your friend can get you something else to go home in."

The doctor came in a little later, read her chart, and examined her, talking the whole time in an extra loud and clear voice, as if she was hard of hearing and a little stupid. "Jane, I'm Dr. O'Connor. Can you tell me what day it is?"

"Friday. I'm supposed to go to work." The words were hard to make.

"Your friend can make some calls for you later. Do you know where you are?"

"Salem. The hospital. Can I see Stella?"

"Do you remember what happened to you last night?" The doctor shining a light back and forth in her eye as he spoke. "The police were called when you went to the Minit Mart on State Street. An ambulance brought you here. Do you remember anything?"

"No. When can I see Stella?" Janie closed her eyes.

"A police report was filed last night in case you decide to file charges against whoever did this to you. I'm assuming you know. You'll be uncomfortable, but there's nothing you'll die from. Not this time anyway. You've got a slight concussion, a couple of broken ribs. Some stitches in your lip and forehead. The swelling will go down eventually. I'll sign your release and you're free to leave as soon as you're dressed. The nurse will give you instructions and a prescription for pain medication. Go see your family doctor in a week. If you have one." He walked out.

Janie looked at the clock on the wall. 8:50 Friday morning.

At 9:25 Stella came in. He didn't say a word. Came to the bed, sat down and put his arms around her. She didn't think she could cry anymore. It hurt so bad when she did, but she couldn't stop.

She asked Stella to call her jobs. And she needed clean

clothes. The clothes she had worn last night were in the garbage. She'd looked at them after the doctor left. Mud and grass stains and blood. A handprint in brick red on her once so-white shirt. She closed herself in the bathroom stall and vomited.

Stella thumbed through the Yellow Pages and dialed the phone. Janie didn't tell him what to say. She didn't know what to say. She didn't interrupt as he spoke with whoever answered the phone – Alice probably, maybe Dave. Stella held her hand, patting it, while she held the cloth over her eyes pretending to be invisible. Stella said his name was Clarence Stubbs and he was Janie's brother. Janie had had an accident Thursday night and was in the hospital. She was doing fine, but she wouldn't be able to return to work. When she was released from the hospital he'd be taking her to his home in Eugene to recuperate. When she was feeling better, she'd call herself. He'd be sure to pass on their good wishes. Once he'd made the last call, Stella kissed Janie on her forehead. "I'll be right back with some clothes."

STELLA DROVE TO the house. Paul's bike was parked in front. The front door was open. Stella sat for a minute taking long deep breaths. He got out of the truck and crossed the street.

He didn't knock. Walked in. Shut the door. The man on the couch only resembled the Paul Jesse he'd once known. He'd aged. His eyes blood-red from too many nights of no sleep. He had a dozen sores on his face and looked twenty pounds lighter. Paul plucked at his droopy Fu Manchu with fingers stained yellow from too many cigarettes. In front of Paul, on the low-slung coffee table, stood a row of empty beer cans, a bag of white powder, bent spoon, lighter, syringe, and a handgun.

Stella took it all in and saw what Janie's life had been the last few months. He didn't blink. "You going to invite me in?"

Paul's voice was rusty. "You need an invitation?"

Stella sat down in a straight-backed chair across from him. "Got anything to drink? My gut's on fire."

Paul went to the kitchen and called back, "Beer or Coke?"

Stella mopped his forehead. He was getting too old for this shit. "Coke'd be fine."

Paul handed him a can and sat down again on the couch. "Janie call you?"

"Nah." Stella took a sip from the can. "The hospital."

"What?" Paul started to get up.

Stella pushed the table over with one kick, dumping everything to the floor. Picking up the gun, he reached over and knocked Paul backward.

Paul struggled to stand up. "What the fuck're you doing? I have to go get Janie."

"No, you don't. You don't have to get Janie." Stella stood next to Paul, their bodies an inch apart. Stella could smell him, reeking of cat pee from the crank. "After all that shit up in Washington. How could you beat her like that?"

"I don't remember what happened. Some other dude brought her home last night. She's fucking around on me. What was I supposed to do. Nothing?"

"Thought you didn't remember." Stella pulled Paul by his shirt to the mirror that hung by the door. "Look at yourself. You're strung out." He let go of Paul's shirt, and Paul began crying, leaning on the door, his shoulders heaving up and down

"I need her back. I want to tell her I'm sorry."

"Aren't you the one always said, 'Sorry don't mean shit?' I came here to get her something to wear. Then we're coming back so she can get her stuff. I'm taking her to Eugene with me."

Paul stopped crying. "She's not leaving. I won't let her."

Stella smacked him open-handed – a bitch slap as he would have called it, once upon a time, meant to humiliate but not to hurt, even though his handprint was red on Paul's cheek. He stuck Paul's gun in the inner pocket of his coat. "You won't be needing this. Don't be here when I come back."

Stella slammed the door and crossed the street to his truck. He started it up and pulled away from the little house. Across the street, a few kids were playing on a merry-go-round. Pretty

soon Ruby would be doing that. Shit. He forgot to get Janie something to wear. He wasn't going back. He'd go by that shopping
center down the street and get her something. She'd need sunglasses too. Her face was a mess. He'd wipe down the gun
and dump it in a trash can behind the store. His stomach burned.
He should eat something. Cookie'd be mad at him if he came
back after a whole day with his stomach in an uproar. He hoped
Janie was going to be ready for what was sure to be an ugly split.
Even if she was ready, Paul was not.

JANIE HELD HER hand still as Annie took off the tape holding
the IV in place. The nurse slipped the needle out and bandaged
the spot, humming while she worked. "There you go. If you want,
you can take a shower while you wait for your friend." Annie
handed Janie a sheet of instructions typed on hospital station-
ery. "Don't get the stitches in your face wet today. Here's a prescription for some Tylenol 3s."

"Thanks."

"I shouldn't be giving you this but I want you to remember."
Annie took a polaroid picture out of her sweater pocket, handed
it to Janie, and left the room.

The picture must have been taken when they brought her
in last night. The harsh light of the hospital examining room lit
up her eyes, already yellow and deep purple, her lip held together
with stitches. Her hair was pulled back, revealing every bark-
scraped surface of her face. Janie held the picture by the corners,
willing herself to take it all in. Look at it. She tucked the picture
into her purse.

Stella had been in the room while she showered. A shopping bag sat on the bed with a note – Back in 15. She pulled
out a long dress, soft cotton and loose. She pulled it on so it didn't
touch her face. Tights, blue hightops, shades, and a blue zip-up
sweatshirt completed her outfit.

Annie stood in the doorway with a wheelchair, smiling.

"I told your friend he could meet us in front with the car. Ready to go?"

Janie shook her head and sat down in the wheelchair. "I want to thank you for – "

"Hush! I've been through this myself twenty-two years ago. Just don't come back, honey. That'd be thanks enough." Annie hummed as they rolled down the hall to an empty elevator. "Your friend, he's a good man."

"He says he's my brother."

"Well, you're lucky to have such close family."

Stella wanted to stop and eat, but there was no way Janie would to go into a restaurant, so they went to a drive-through and ate in the parking lot. She couldn't eat solid food until her mouth healed, so she had a blackberry milkshake. Stella had burgers and fries. When they were done eating, he stopped at a liquor store and picked up some boxes. Then he drove to the house. "Doesn't look like anybody's here, but you let me go in first." Stella helped her out and carried two boxes.

Janie hung back, carrying a box, trying not to drop it. The door was locked, so she gave Stella her key. Her books and little knick-knacks were dumped from the shelves, pages torn and strewn around like confetti. Her clothes were gone from the bedroom closet, and the little bottle of sandalwood oil she used instead of perfume was smashed in the sink. She went to the kitchen. Her robin's-egg blue dishes were smashed. In the other room, Stella was picking up the books Paul hadn't ruined.

Janie got the cat food bag from under the sink and went out the back door. She shook the bag and called, "Elly, Elly, Eloise – come here kitty!" From under the corner of the house Eloise pulled her fluffy gray body up in a long, sensual stretch. Janie carried her inside. "I've got to bring my cat."

Stella nodded. "You want these books?"

"No. Leave it all. I'll be ready to go in a minute." In the bedroom, she got down on her hands and knees by the bed. Eloise rubbed against her purring. Under the bed and a folded blanket were her treasures – the wooden box and the Frida Kahlo book. She put them in a box with Eloise's food and blanket. She brought them to Stella. "Let's go." She took her keys and put them in the refrigerator on top of the last can of Coke. She picked up Eloise and carried her to the truck. She didn't leave a note.

Evil Ways

PAUL HEARD A FLY BUZZING AROUND HIS FACE. HE KEPT his eyes closed, feeling the blood pound against his eyelids to the beat of his heart. He must have passed out on the bed when he got home from – where? He didn't remember. The last thing he remembered clearly was sitting on the porch with a beer waiting for Janie to get home from work. He'd been wired, and then he thought someone gave him a couple of Percocets to bring him down. He'd been drinking, too much from the way he felt.

He remembered Janie's white shirt torn open and rain, something about the baseball bat and Stella had been here. Paul's right hand ached, the skin pulled tight over it. He tried moving his fingers and that hurt worse. He brought his hand up to his face and opened an eye. Christ – what had he done? He forced himself to sit up and struggled to his feet. The room began to pitch and dive, and he fell to his knees and crawled to the bathroom. He locked his arms around the toilet and heaved. When he could move, he splashed cold water on his face. They must have had a fight, she was probably at work. Janie was good like that – dependable. Why did they fight? He knew any reason he had was stupid now, but it hadn't been stupid then. He stood up and wobbled to the kitchen. Blue china dishes lay broken on the floor. He knew he'd done this but couldn't really remember finding her things and breaking them one by one to hurt her.

He opened the refrigerator, and there were her keys on top of the last Coke. When did she do that? There was no note anywhere. He looked all over and then remembered something about a hospital. Janie was in the hospital. He'd put her in the hospital this time. Paul stumbled back to the bedroom and pulled on jeans. He washed his face again and grabbed his wallet. His hand was killing him. The knuckles were swollen, skin torn open. He studied it, memorizing every flap of damaged skin – then punched it through the cheap sheetrock wall in the kitchen. He pulled it out, blood ran down his arm. He wrapped it in a dirty red bandana.

At the store he bought a container of chocolate milk, a Coke, and a pack of cigarettes. The guy behind the register stared at his hand. Standing in the phone booth, leafing through the Yellow Pages, Paul found the hospital's patient information number and dialed. Today was Saturday. He had lost two days. Janie had been admitted Thursday night and released Friday morning. Paul hung up, his hands shaking as he lit a cigarette and called the bookstore.

"Children's Garden Bookstore. This is Alice."

"Is Janie working today?"

"No. Janie's not working here anymore. Are you a friend of hers?"

"Yes. We were going to meet for lunch."

"You haven't heard about her accident?"

Paul's stomach dropped. "No. Is she all right?"

"I think so. I didn't speak to her. Her brother called."

Stella, Paul thought. "Do you have his number?"

"Yes. I have his address and phone number right here."

"Can you give me both? I'd like to send her a get well card." Paul wrote the information on the inside cover of a pack of matches. He closed the flap and stuck it in his pocket before he walked home. He had to clean the house before he called. Try to mend what he'd broken and replace what he could, so when she came home it would be like none of this had ever happened. He'd give her a couple days to forget before he called. A couple of days to miss him. He fingered the pack of matches in his pocket.

A PIANO WAS PLAYING SOMEWHERE. STELLA BROUGHT her here Friday afternoon. Cookie met them at the front door and put Janie to bed. China was happy to see her, but not too pleased about Eloise. Now, alone in her room, Janie could feel China pressed against her side and Eloise purring from the pillow. On the nightstand, a pitcher of water and a glass with a straw so she could drink without it hurting too badly. Flowers and plants filled the windows. Friday she'd gone to bed and slept all afternoon, all that night, only waking up once when Cookie came in with a peach yogurt milkshake and a robe.

Janie sat up, testing the pain. She slipped on the robe and tiptoed to the kitchen. The floor felt smooth and warm under her bare feet.

"Morning, Janie." Cookie sat at the kitchen table feeding Ruby. "How do you feel?"

"Better. Still sore."

"I've got a friend, an herbalist. I want her to take a look at you, if that's okay."

Janie nodded. "Does Stella play piano too?"

Cookie laughed. "No. My brother came over to play."

"I don't want him to see me now."

"He won't." Cookie took a sip of tea. "You'll see him when you feel better, not today though. The thing is – you didn't do anything to feel ashamed of, *chica*, and no one is going to put you down for what happened. What Paul did was all about Paul. It was never about you."

"It doesn't feel that way."

"Feelings are like clouds. They don't last forever."

The piano stopped. Silence filled the room. Janie picked up a glass of water and went back to her room. She left her door cracked open so China could let herself in and out. Eloise lay spread out on the bed, cleaning her gray fur. Janie crawled back in bed.

The sound of someone tapping on the door interrupted her sleep in the late afternoon. "Janie? Are you awake?" Cookie asked.

Janie sat up and yawned. "What time is it?"

"About three. I know you just woke up, but the friend I told you about is here. Can she come in?"

Janie frowned, but nodded.

"Don't worry. You'll like her." Cookie stepped out of the room before Janie could respond.

Janie tied the robe around her waist. She tried to comb her hair out with her fingers and gave up.

Cookie came in first, followed by a woman with curly hay-and-straw-colored hair. She was tall and solid, with tanned skin and blue eyes.

"Janie, this is Marta." From the other room Ruby cried, and Cookie walked out.

Marta carried an old-fashioned leather doctor's bag. In her other hand, she held a woven basket with a leather handle. "May I come in?" She had an accent that sounded European. It reminded Janie of one of Bill's women but warmer.

Marta put her bags on the floor and pulled the wicker rocker up to the bed. She leaned over to pet Eloise, letting the cat sniff her hand before stroking her around the face. "She's marvelous. What soft fur." Marta's face was calm.

"Her name's Eloise."

"Cookie asked me to examine you, but that's for you to decide." Marta sat in the rocker. She pulled a ball of fuzzy yarn the color of a sky blue pink sunset and a pair of knitting needles from her basket.

Janie pictured Lila in Silverton. "You knit?"

"Yes. And you?"

"I was learning, but I had to stop."

"You'll begin again." Marta rocked and worked as she spoke. "I was a midwife in Denmark. I moved here to Oregon about four years ago, and now I raise a few sheep for wool and deliver babies. I delivered little Ruby." Marta stopped rocking. "You should know that I'm not licensed by the state – "

Janie had made up her mind. "I'm not either."

She put her knitting down. "I'll wash my hands."

Marta inspected the stitches and swelling on her face. She gently opened the robe and saw the torn flesh of her breast, the bruises on her thighs and hips, the swollen scabbed knees. She left and came back with a basin of warm water. From her doctor's bag, she produced small bags with different leaves and roots and flowers, and small dark brown bottles of liquid. She filled gauze envelopes with the plants and herbs. After soaking them in the water she applied them to Janie's face, breast, and knees. She described what she was doing as she worked, but Janie heard only the music of her voice. When Marta finished, she covered Janie with the quilt and gave her a spoonful of bitter tasting syrup. "Drink this and sleep. I'll leave more poultices for you to apply again in the morning. Leave these on until you wake up later."

"Thank you."

Marta patted her hand. "Most of the healing will happen under the skin."

STELLA WOKE EARLY on Sunday even though it was his only day off. Ruby was still snoring, her rear-end pointing to the ceiling, thumb in her mouth. Stella pulled on a pair of gray sweats and looked at his sleeping family before tiptoeing out of the room to make coffee. When he thought of the life he lived now, he couldn't believe how lucky he was. He'd married a woman who loved him, and together they'd made a perfect baby girl, a home, and a business of their own. Every morning in the few minutes before his family woke, Stella looked around and said a sincere thank you to the God he knew was listening.

He hadn't slept well last night. Janie'd been here since Friday with no word yet from Paul. Stella knew Paul would show up, one way or another, to get what he thought was his: Janie. He and Cookie had talked about it. Paul was capable of anything when he was strung, and judging by appearances, he was strung out tight and ready to snap. Cookie said not to worry, but

Stella knew better. There'd been no phone calls yet. No drive-by appearances. He could sense Paul out there waiting like a sniper.

Stella started the coffee, looked in the fridge. It was still early. He'd wait to start cooking till Ruby was up – let Cookie sleep in a bit longer. He'd make something soft so Janie could eat breakfast – scrambled eggs with spinach, maybe a batch of cornbread. She liked his cornbread. Hell, he liked his cornbread.

FROM HER BED, Janie heard mixing bowls and spoons clattering. Smelled the familiar coffee Stella always made, and could almost make the last two years disappear and pretend she'd never left. She felt much better. She crept down the hall to the bathroom and snuck up on her reflection in the mirror. Not as bad as yesterday. The swelling had gone down some from her eyes, though they were still bruised, but she could cover them with sunglasses. By the time she dressed and got to the kitchen, everyone was up.

Stella sautéed vegetables on the stove. Ruby sat in her highchair, squeezing sliced banana through her chubby fingers.

Cookie came up the steps from the basement with a cooler. "Found it, Stella. Good morning, Janie." She kissed Janie's cheek. "You look better!"

Stella kept stirring the vegetables but raised one arm like a wing. Janie stepped under it and he hugged her. "How you feeling?"

"Better. I slept and slept. What did Marta give me?"

Cookie laughed. "She gave you back your mojo, *chica*."

Ruby squealed from her chair, rubbing banana on her face.

"Would you wipe her down, Janie?"

"Sure." Janie picked up a damp wash rag and ran it over Ruby's face as she squirmed to get away. "What's the cooler for?"

Stella cracked eggs into the frying pan and whisked them. "We're going on a picnic."

They were ready to leave about noon. Janie wore the sunglasses Stella bought her and borrowed a sleeveless T-shirt and cutoffs from Cookie. Stella packed his car with blankets, some old towels in case they found a swimming hole, Ruby's carseat, and China's bowl. Cookie packed thermoses of iced tea and lemonade, a dozen sandwiches, leftover potato salad and fruit, and chocolate chip cookies to satisfy Stella's sweet tooth.

They drove east out of town, up the McKenzie River through small towns and into the forest. Stella put on a reggae tape and he and Cookie sang along. Ruby fell asleep. China's head rested on Janie's lap. She rolled the window down and a warm breeze blew back her hair. She felt sore all over but she wouldn't let herself think about Paul. For today she'd do her best to keep her mind focused here, in this old car, with people who loved her.

They found a campground with a picnic area on the river. For a Sunday in mid-summer, the place was nearly deserted. Stella picked a secluded spot where shallow water pooled for swimming. They unpacked the car and spread the blankets out in a grassy space between the trees.

Cookie pulled a book from her handbag and gave it to Janie. "My brother Joe brought this over yesterday. He told me to give it to you."

Janie took a worn paperback from Cookie. The pages felt soft and rutted. Some were waterstained. Some barely clung to the glue that bound the spine together. A folded piece of paper fluttered from between the pages. *Dear Jane, I thought you might like this. It's one of my favorites. Love, Joe.*

Cookie tossed Janie a bottle of sun tan lotion. "Put this on so you don't burn."

Smiling, Janie set the book on the blanket and rubbed the lotion on her legs. "Makes me smell like summer."

PAUL CALLED ALL Sunday afternoon from a phone booth. No answer. Either no one was home or they weren't answering the phone. He thought they would answer the phone. No reason not to. Maybe this meant Janie wasn't as bad off as he'd thought. She was probably fine. Maybe still shook up a little. She'd only been in the hospital overnight. Couldn't be too bad if she was out and about already. He didn't like that she wasn't waiting by the phone for him to call. She must have known he would call. Stella and them were probably giving her some ration of shit. Telling her to leave him. Pressuring her. Fucking hippies.

Paul bought a tall can of beer and walked home to fix up the mess in the house. Most of what was broken couldn't be mended so he crammed the garbage full of pieces of things – china and knick-knacks mostly. Janie was always picking up odds and ends at thrift stores and garage sales. She probably wouldn't miss half this stuff. She had too much shit anyway.

He puttied over the holes in the walls and decided maybe he'd paint the rooms like she'd wanted when they moved in. A blue bedroom, he thought, yeah, and a yellow kitchen. That'd make her feel good when she came back. Maybe he'd go back to the mobile home plant – get a straight job again so she wouldn't have to work. Maybe he'd marry her, get her pregnant so she couldn't ever really leave him. He'd have to convince her he meant it. Paul made a plan while he worked around the house, sipping on his beer until it was empty.

At about four, he walked back to the store and bought another beer. A couple a day couldn't kill anybody. He hadn't had a drink on Saturday. He deserved one today. Or two. However many he had. He couldn't remember. He dialed Stella's number twice to make sure he got it right. No answer. Stella had an old lady and a baby. They wouldn't be out too late. Since the house was looking so much better, he decided to stop at Doug's, see what was up. He'd call again from over there. Janie'd be back by dark. Paul had the phone number. Besides that, he knew where they lived.

Hello It's Me

STELLA SAT UP SUNDAY NIGHT READING THE PAPER AFTER everyone else had gone to bed. He was waiting for the phone call to come. When it rang shortly after midnight, he wasn't surprised. He picked it up on the first ring. No reason to pretend he didn't know who was calling. "Hey, Paul."

Music loud in the background and a cash register ringing. "Let me talk to Janie." Paul's voice sounded heavy and drunk.

"She's sleeping. How about you call back tomorrow."

"Where the fuck were you all day? I kept calling."

"We've been home since about eight."

"Look. I got to talk to her for just a minute. You understand, right?"

"Yeah, I understand. You beat the shit out of her four days ago, broke all she had in the way of belongings, and now you want me to wake her up because you're drunk in a bar feeling sorry for yourself–"

"I *am* sorry, man. I just want to tell her. Come on and put her on the phone, bro."

"I'm not your fucking brother and I'm not waking her up."

"Hey, Stella don't get in the middle of this."

"I already am."

"I just want to talk to her."

Stella put the receiver down. Almost immediately the phone rang again. Stella unplugged it from the wall and reached to turn out the lamp.

Janie stood in the doorway wearing one of his T-shirts. She looked about twelve years old, tears running down her cheeks. Stella led her back to her room, tucked her in bed, and made sure the windows were locked. This once, he lied to her and said everything would be all right, and waited until she fell asleep before leaving. He double checked the doors and windows throughout the house before he climbed into his own bed, pulling Cookie close to him. She seemed to store heat the way a stone in the sun did, soaking it up all day to give back to him at night. He buried his face in her neck. She slept deeply. When Cookie was asleep next to him, he felt the weight of their love. Stella stayed up all night waiting for nothing good to come to his door. When it came he wanted to be ready.

CLOUDS SETTLED OVER the valley during the night. Janie began reading the book Joe gave her, but she couldn't concentrate and had to stop. Every time the breeze ruffled her curtains she was startled and had to start at the top of the page again. She didn't sleep much knowing Paul would be calling or coming to get her soon, not knowing what she would say or do when he did.

Early in the morning, she let China out and found Stella sitting at the kitchen table – no paper or coffee – just Stella at the table. He looked up and smiled at her. "You're up early. Want some coffee?"

Janie nodded.

Stella ran water in the blue and white coffee pot, scooped the coffee from a canister on the counter, and lit the gas burner. They were quiet while it brewed, a long time, but neither spoke. For awhile there was just the hum of the refrigerator, the click of China's tags as she crunched kibble from her bowl, the clock whirring at each minute before the hand lurched forward.

"We have to talk about this." Stella poured a cup of coffee and handed it to Janie.

She added cream and watched the clouds float up from

the bottom. "He'll show up here when he's fucked up. He might do something –"

"He already did something, Jane. He'll probably call you today. Are you going to talk to him?"

"Maybe if I talk to him and tell him up front I'm not coming back he'll be okay about it." Janie knew once she said it that she wasn't going back to Paul.

"Maybe." Stella added a spoon of honey to his coffee and stirred. "Cookie won't let me have straight sugar anymore. She's worried about diabetes. I guess honey isn't the same." He took a sip. "Jane, Cookie and I talked, we want you to stay here with us. I don't want you to get worried and think you have to do this alone. I think it's going to get ugly quick."

Janie's hands were cold through the heat of the mug. "Yeah. I know."

"If he shows up, and I'm not here, I want you to call me and the police. Cookie's working today at lunch, but Marta's coming by to see how you're doing. You might be home for a few hours on your own. Keep China with you. Plug the phone in when you're ready for the call." Stella put his mug down on the counter, looked at her steady. "The good thing about the phone is you'll know he's not here if he's calling."

Marta came over late in the morning with her doctor's bag and a knitting basket. She boiled water for tea and brought out her needles and yarn. "Would you like a lesson?"

"You don't have to stay with me, Marta."

Marta looked over the rim of the cup. "But a little company wouldn't be such a bad thing."

"I brought you a set of needles."

Janie and Marta sat knitting at the table. Concentrating on the intricate movement of fingers, needles, and yarn occupied her as she rehearsed what she wanted to say to Paul. She stared at the phone when it rang, dropping the yarn and needles on the floor.

Marta leaned forward and put her hand on Janie's arm. "Take a breath."

Janie walked to the living room as the phone rang, a sound she felt in her stomach and chest. The words she'd practiced in her mind, gone. She sat in the chair next to the phone and picked up the receiver, her mouth dry and hands sweating. "Hello?"

"Hey." His voice sounded quiet, tired.

She waited, wordless for him to begin.

"I woke up on Friday and you weren't here."

"I'm sorry," she said out of habit. For a second she had the feeling she'd grown used to, a persistent doubt that made her wonder if anything had really happened.

"When're you coming home?"

This wasn't going like she thought it would. "I had to get stitches. I had to go the hospital." Saying it out loud made it real again.

"I'm always saying sorrys don't mean shit, but, Janie, I am sorry. I don't remember anything about that night. You okay?"

"Yeah. I don't know."

"It won't happen again. I promise. When are you coming home?"

"Where are you?"

"I'm at Doug's."

"It's so quiet."

"Yeah." A long pause. "Come home."

Janie had been prepared for outrage, anger, threats, but not what sounded like love. She held the phone to her ear.

"I can't lose you, baby. You're my girl." His voice cracked. "I love you."

It felt like hours passed while they each held a phone not speaking.

He sniffed back tears. "I don't know what to do."

"Me neither."

"Come home."

"I can't now." Janie meant the now as in never.

"I'll call you in a couple days. Don't let me down. I love you."

Janie realized after she hung up that he'd misunderstood. The *now* he heard meant she would come back soon. She walked past Marta into the kitchen. Standing at the sink, she stared out the small window at the garden. One word made a huge difference.

PAUL WIPED HIS eyes with the back of his sleeve when he hung up, and slid his shades on before grabbing a beer from the fridge. Outside in the carport, Percy, Zippy, and Doug were standing around the open hood of Doug's car, staring in at the engine. Percy looked up and saw Paul in the window and motioned him outside. Doug held up a finger for another beer and Paul grabbed the six pack and took it outside.

Paul set the sixer on the car roof. "What're we looking at."

Percy popped a tab and took a drink. "Doug says it smells like pancakes when he starts her up. Pancakes or syrup?"

Doug thought for a minute. "More like syrup, I guess."

Zippy nodded his head. "He picked me up today. Smelled like an IHOP on Sunday morning."

Doug scratched his belly. "Makes me hungry just driving around."

Paul nodded. "It's your heating core. Probably got a leak somewhere."

"Think I got to replace it?" Doug asked.

Paul shook his head. "Probably run fine for awhile yet. I might want to borrow it later this week."

"Going to get Janie?" Doug finished his beer and popped open a second one.

"Yeah. Give her a few more days to calm down."

Percy stroked the beer foam from his droopy cowboy mustache. "What's she got to calm down about?"

Paul lowered his shades and peered over the top. "Why's it matter to you?"

Percy shrugged. "Wouldn't want to see her get hurt."

Doug laughed. "Too late, Percy. Had her first trip to Salem General after the game last Thursday."

Percy put his beer down on the car. "You shouldn't've gone and done that."

Paul didn't see the anger in Percy's face until it was too late. Suddenly Percy had him by the ponytail and slammed him face first into the side of the house, rabbit punching Paul's kidneys several times before letting him sink to the ground. Paul didn't fight back or try to defend himself.

Percy wiped his hands on his jeans and picked up his beer. He took another drink. "Janie's a nice girl. Remember how she made us sandwiches that time? I hope this don't happen again."

Paul pulled himself up off the ground and found the hose. Turning it on, he bent over and washed the blood from his face.

AS MARTA DROVE, Janie sucked the peach juice off her fingers. Between them on the cracked leather seat of Marta's pickup sat a paper bag full of peaches. Marta hadn't asked her about Paul's call. She told Janie to leave a note for Stella and Cookie and come pick peaches with her – maybe spend the night at her farm. Janie fed Eloise, wrote the note, and grabbed her bag. They drove to an orchard with a U-PICK sign in front. A warm breeze shook the deep green leaves. Every time she picked a fuzzy-skinned peach, she felt summer resting in her hand. They'd picked silently, filling several buckets before paying at the stand at the end of the driveway. Janie didn't want to go back to Stella's yet, so when Marta asked if she'd like to see her house, Janie said yes.

They drove on a single-lane country road to a gravel drive marked by a mailbox with a rainbow painted on it. Marta signaled and put the truck in its lowest gear, plunging up a steep hill. They passed through an acre or more of gnarled grandmother oak trees with garlands of mistletoe high in their branches. A few sheep grazed on bleached summer grass. At the crest of the hill the drive dipped down and around a bend and Janie saw the place she'd been looking for since she'd left home.

Marta's house and barn were nestled in a curved valley. The only other building in sight was a farmhouse a mile or so away. On one side of Marta's house sat a faded red barn, a lop-sided corral buried on one side by blackberry bushes partly concealing a sway-backed gray and white mare and a goat, and a chicken coop with a dozen sturdy red hens scratching around in the dirt. On the other side of the house were six raised vegetable beds filled with abundance and an old picnic table under a big oak tree. Thigh-high lavender bushes lined the paths around the property. The house was covered in silvery gray shingles accented by a red front door, red window frames, and red window boxes full of geraniums.

From behind the barn bounded a large black dog. Marta got out of the truck and clapped her hands. "Hello Goblin!" The dog wagged its body from side to side and waited for Marta to reach in her pocket for a dog cookie, then sprang off to meet Janie, snuffling around her legs. "That's enough now. I bet you're wanting some dinner." Marta carried her bags to the house. "Would you mind helping me with the chores?"

While Marta fed the animals, she put Janie in charge of watering the vegetable and herb beds and making dinner from whatever she could find in the house and garden. The sun streaked the blue sky orange behind the hills. The scent of herbs and rich composted soil released from the ground. Crickets and an occasional bird song broke the quiet. If she never had to leave, she'd be happy.

They ate together at the picnic table and decided it was too late to drive back to town. Marta suggested Janie stay the next day and they would invite Stella and Cookie to come up for din-ner in the evening. Janie could ride home with them. After cleaning up the dishes, Marta brought her a nightgown of sheer linen with tiny faded blue flowers embroidered on the yoke.

Janie blushed and looked down. "This is so pretty. I can't sleep in this. I'll just wear my T-shirt."

"No. You take it. How will you have good dreams if you don't invite them in?"

Janie took the gown. The linen had been washed until it felt like silk. "I don't know what he did with my clothes."

"Who?" Marta reached out and took Janie's hand.

"All my clothes. I don't know what he did with them."

Marta patted her hand and rubbed her arm. "We can replace things."

Janie was grateful to be understood.

"You'll start over. And now you have my old nightgown. It always brought me good dreams. Now it will bring you some."

Janie hugged Marta and took the gown to the small extra bedrom. She settled in the twin bed under a white blanket and stiff clean sheets that smelled of sun and hay. The house grew still. Janie closed her eyes and waited for good dreams to come.

Miles From Nowhere

PAUL HAD BEEN COUNTING ON JANIE TO PAY THE RENT.
He wasn't working, and dealing hadn't been especially good to
him these days. He'd have to ask her to kick in some cash for the
rent soon. Getting evicted would be a bitch. It'd be hard to prove
to her that he'd changed if he lost the house. The rent wasn't due
until the end of next week so he could hold off asking until she
came home.

Late at night like this, alone in the house, not even the cat
around, was more than he could deal with. He'd grown used to
her. He didn't want to have to ask her to come back again or ask
her for the rent money. But there it was, he'd do it if she didn't
get her ass home soon. Another day and he'd call. A day or two
more and he'd go get her. He couldn't sleep and had no money
for beer or pot or anything. He'd eaten the last Top Ramen this
afternoon. He went to the clock on the stove and stared at it,
trying to remember if it still worked. It took a long time for the
hands to move. It wasn't that late, he decided. Just dark. Fuck
it. What did she expect if she went and left him by himself like
this?

Paul picked up his keys and rode around for awhile. Up a
street and down another. He didn't really think about where
he was headed until he pulled up in front of Debby's house. He'd
seen her once or twice in passing over the last months. She'd
said to him, *No hard feelings,* or some shit. Her dad's car was gone.
Her car sat alone in the driveway. A light on upstairs in her

room. He let the bike idle for a minute and watched her window. Soon the drapes parted and he saw her scrawny silouette. She waved him up, and he turned off the engine and met her on the front porch.

"What are you up to?" She stepped aside to let him pass.

"Nothing. How you been?"

She shrugged and walked past him, calling over her shoulder. "Want a drink?"

In the kitchen, she poured half a glass of rum and topped it off with a can of Coke. He took the drink and downed half of it.

She asked him, "What're you doing here?"

"Thought you might be tired of Jeffrey and ready to deal."

"Oh really? What about your old lady?"

"Look, I saw your light on and thought I'd stop by."

Debby lit a cigarette and leaned back in her chair rocking back and forth on its metal legs. She squinted through the smoke around her face. "You got any wire?"

"I can get some. So, what happened to Jeff?"

"He got stingy."

Paul watched her. She was strung, that's what happened to Jeff. "Can I use this phone?" He nodded to the wall phone by the stove.

"Yeah. Go ahead." She rose from her chair and put her arms around him. "Always a pleasure doing business with you."

JANIE WAS UP early. She and Marta fed and watered the animals and worked in the raised beds, weeding and hoeing next to one another. After lunch, Marta took Janie to the corral and haltered the mare, leading her into the alleyway beween the stalls.

"This is Sugar. She came with the place." As Marta brushed the horse's long curved neck, Sugar blew through her nose, occasionally shaking her head and nickering. "When her ears are up and tilted foreward like this, she's curious and in a good mood, but if you see a horse flatten their ears they're telling you they feel upset or unsociable. Get her a carrot from the garden and we'll introduce you."

Janie went to the vegetable bed and pulled a handful of finger-sized carrots from the ground. She knocked the dirt off and rinsed the bunch under the hose before bringing them to the barn. The smell of horse and grain and hay permeated the air, much cooler than outside. Marta stood in the alley between the stalls with her back to Janie, working the curry comb down the horse's neck and back to the muscular flanks and hips. She started on the other side and looked up at Janie, smiling.

"Come and get acquainted."

Janie approached the horse, bigger than any animal she'd ever been near.

"Just hold the carrots out and she'll take them."

The horse's soft lips moved back revealing yellowed teeth. Sugar took the carrots a few at a time, snorting with pleasure as she crunched them. Janie reached up and touched the horse's neck. Sugar dipped her head, letting Janie rub her soft ears. When the carrots were gone, Sugar placed her nose against Janie's palm and blew her warm breath into it.

Marta pulled hair from the comb. "Shall we take her for a ride down to the creek?"

"I've never ridden a horse before."

"Sugar's a good teacher." Marta got a saddle blanket from the tack room and showed Janie how to step from the fence railing onto Sugar's back. Janie hauled herself up on Sugar's broad back. Marta grabbed her straw tote bag with a jar of water, a pair of garden shears, and two worn bath towels. She mounted Sugar and sat behind Janie and let the mare carry them down through the pasture on a narrow dirt path that wound through blackberry brambles, down the forested canyon to a stream.

Marta dropped the reins and let the horse loose to graze under the trees next to the stream. "I want to gather some fresh witch hazel for your bruises. I'll be back."

Janie sat on a towel, dipping her feet in the water and

listening to Sugar graze. For the first time all day, she thought about Paul. Without his voice constantly in her ear, the fear of his moods, the constant confusion, she could imagine starting a different life. Without Paul, and his voice in her head, she saw her life stretch out a whole other way. The thought of it made her head spin.

DEBBY'S DAD WAS coming home for a few days. Paul rode back to the house, relieved to get away from the constant whine of her voice. She seemed to think they were together now. Sex and a needle, he tried to tell her. That's all it was for either of them, but she wouldn't cop to it. They'd made back money to replace what they'd taken from her dad's safe. He wouldn't find out. The dude must be blind. How anyone could look at Debby's sunken cheeks and yellow skin, the way she picked at her face and ground her teeth, and not know she was strung out? She looked twenty years older than she had a few months before.

Paul couldn't stop thinking about Janie – where she was at any given moment, what she was doing, why she hadn't come home yet. Whatever he'd done it couldn't be that bad or he'd remember it. Couples fought sometimes, Janie should know that. She couldn't leave him over a fight.

He parked the bike at the curb and saw an envelope taped to the door. Ripping it open, he removed a pink form from it. It was an eviction letter dated a week ago. He had three weeks to find a new place. He needed cash.

Paul crumpled the pink form in a ball and threw it on the floor. The house smelled of Ramen and scrambled eggs mingled with cigarette smoke and empty beer cans. He looked around the room. Not much to show for almost thirty years of life. After all that talk of love, where was Janie? He was stuck holding the shitty end of the stick, like always. If she thought she could just leave him, she was wrong. What he needed was a couple of cold beers and a nap.

He tried all the tricks he knew to sleep. Drank a six-pack,

watched TV for hours, smoked the rest of his pot. Sometimes he would be on the edge of sleep only to be jerked back by twitching muscles. Always his mind came back to Janie. He was convinced he'd never be able to sleep until he got her back.

Paul put on his jacket and grabbed the keys from the table.

JANIE STOOD UNDER the lip of a waterfall. It sounded like a thousand windows breaking, growing louder and louder. She woke, heart racing, shaking, and damp with sweat. China barking at the back door, the baby crying from Stella's room.

Stella's voice from the back of the house, his footsteps pounding down the hall. "Call the police."

She reached for the lamp, knocking it over. Stumbling out of bed and into the dark hallway, she could see China blocking the hall between the kitchen and Janie's bedroom. The big dog lunged forward barking and snarling as she grabbed in her teeth a man's arm protruding through the broken glass of the door's window. The hand reaching in to turn the deadbolt was Paul's hand.

He screamed. He stuck his head in through the broken window. His hair loose and greasy around his face. Just a glimpse, like what you see from a speeding car. He beat the dog around her ears and muzzle with his free hand. China held on.

Stella yelled. "China. Give." China let go of Paul's hand and he pulled it back.

Paul yelled something as he ran off, but Janie couldn't tell what he said. His bike started up and roared away. A siren in the distance getting closer.

Janie found the light switch. Blood on the door, dark splotches on the curtains. Shattered glass everywhere. China's bloody pawprints on the floor. China was limping across the floor wagging her tail and panting. Janie sat on the floor.

Stella picked up China and carried her to the sink. "Help me with her, Janie."

A few minutes later, Cookie let the police in and walked with

the baby, hushing her and rocking her back to sleep. Janie stood
at the sink rinsing China's paws under cold water and picking the
glass from them, while Stella cradled the dog in his arms.

Janie answered the police officer's questions the best she
could. Her old address in Salem, what kind of bike he rode.
Not enough. Did she know where he might go? She couldn't say
without getting the whole valley busted. Paul wouldn't be
the only one to want to kill her if she started sending the police
around. They said she could get a restraining order at the
courthouse in the morning if she wanted. She nodded to acknowl-
edge the words but she knew a piece of paper wouldn't keep
him away or anybody safe from him. There wasn't anything she
could do tonight but clean up the mess. China thumped her
tail against the sink and only whimpered a little as Janie poured
peroxide over the wounds. Stella wrapped her front paws with
gauze pads and surgical tape. Janie felt like she'd been cleaning
up after Paul for too long.

PAUL RODE BACK to Salem. At a rest stop outside of town, he
used the rest of the crank he had on him before heading to Doug's.
His mind raced with plans. He'd get a front if he could. No way
could he go back to his house. He'd leave his bike in Doug's garage
and call Debby. She'd drive him around. There'd likely be a war-
rant out for him. If Janie thought she could just walk away and
start some new fucking life, she was mistaken. He'd get her back
or take her out. Either way it didn't matter.

Paul promised himself he'd lie down once this was all
settled. Everything was going to shit around him, and all he wanted
now was to stay wired.

He pulled into Doug's driveway and banged on the
aluminum screen door.

Doug opened up, shirtless, his eyes red, the sound of info-
mercials on early morning TV. "What the fuck are you doing out?"

"I haven't been in yet. Can I park my bike in your garage?"

"What's a matter? You kill somebody last night?"

"Not yet."

Doug held the door open and fumbled in his pocket for keys. "Here."

Paul took the keys and wheeled the bike into Doug's garage. He went from the garage to the kitchen and got himself a beer.

Doug sat on the couch in the living room watching a blonde in a bikini demonstrate a hair removal system. Doug lit a pipe and took a hit, holding his breath. He exhaled and passed the pipe to Paul.

"Can I use your phone?"

"Who you calling?"

"Nevermind, man. Shit, I'll turn you on or give you a little cash."

Doug shrugged. "Go ahead. Phone'll probably be shut off any day now."

He called Debby first and arranged for her to pick him up. Then he dialed Stella's number. Funny how he no longer needed to look at the worn matchbook cover he'd written it on.

Janie must have been sitting right there because she answered on the first ring. "Hello?"

"What the fuck are you doing, Jane?"

"I knew you'd call."

"I want you home. I'm sick of waiting."

"The police were here."

"You think they can save you? You think anybody can save you? It's a matter of fucking time, baby, and you're running out. You think Stella and them are going to stand by you? They're going to dump you like the sack of shit you are, and then what're you going to do?"

"I'm not coming back."

"Tell me this – what did I fucking do that was so bad?"

Her voice got louder, angrier. "Do you not remember the park? You put me in the hospital. You fucked around on me. You took my money. What haven't you done, Paul?"

"I don't remember putting you in the fucking hospital. I think you made that one up to get a little sympathy from your good friends down there."

"It's convenient what you don't remember. Do you remember the playground, Paul? Do you remember what you did to me?"

He could picture how her eyes welled up and looked real blue and for a moment he was sorry for everything. "Look, I told you I don't remember. It can't have been that bad. You know when I'm drinking I don't always know – "

"You don't remember putting my face through sheetrock? How did you explain all the blood in the house? I mean, later on – what did you tell yourself?" She sounded done, like she was all done now, and he couldn't change it no matter what he said. "I don't care if you believe me. I don't care what you do, or threaten to do. I'm finished."

The phone clicked and flatlined. He pressed the receiver and dialed again. No one answered.

I'm So Tired

BY THE TIME STELLA AND COOKIE WERE UP, JANIE HAD cleaned her room and packed her things in a box and a paper bag. She called Marta and told her about the broken glass and China's paws, the baby crying and the police. She asked if she could stay at the farm with her for awhile. Paul didn't know about Marta and she'd be out of Stella's place. Marta said yes. Then Janie unplugged the phone, made coffee, and waited.

Stella thumped down the hall in his bare feet. Yawning as he got a mug of coffee and took the half-and-half from the refrigerator, pouring a bit in before he took his first drink. "Who taught you to make coffee?"

"You did." She looked up at him and smiled.

"Did you sleep at all?"

"Nah. It's okay. I'll sleep later."

"You've been busy." He nodded at the backdoor now clean, the floor swept and mopped, a piece of cardboard duct-taped over the broken window, the curtains soaking in a bucket of soapy water.

"Paul called."

"Yeah. I heard the phone ring."

"He's coming back."

"Yup."

"I can't stay here. I called Marta and she says I can stay out at her place till he stops. If I'm not here maybe he'll leave you guys alone."

"I think it's a good idea for you to stay out at Marta's, but don't count on Paul leaving anybody alone."

"I'm sorry about all this."

"Honey, you didn't do anything but love somebody."

After Cookie got up with Ruby, Stella found his keys and headed for the cafe. He said he'd call Cat and see if she could work so Cookie would have the day at home.

Cookie poured herself a cup of tea. "As long as I'm going to be a lady of leisure, what if I take Janie out to Marta's and we can go do a little clothes shopping on the way?"

Stella handed Janie three neatly folded twenty dollar bills from his wallet. "You pay me back later on."

It took awhile to get out of the house with the baby. Ruby liked to feed herself now and that almost always meant she needed a bath after breakfast, because breakfast was oatmeal and Ruby got it everywhere. Janie took China outside and fed her. Her paws weren't as bad as they had seemed last night. Janie felt an odd sense of hope now that she had a plan. She didn't hate Paul and she didn't love him either. Maybe she never did; she couldn't tell anymore.

Cookie was bathing Ruby when Joe knocked on the front door. Janie peeked out the curtains before she unlocked it.

"Cookie called me to babysit. Why is the door locked?"

"There's still some coffee." She felt shy. She hadn't seen Joe since the party when they kissed. She led him to the kitchen and drained the pot into a cup.

"Thanks." Joe sat down at the table. "What happened?"

"The window broke." Janie couldn't look at him.

"Oh." Joe drank his coffee in silence.

"I really like that book you gave me."

"Great. I've read it–"

"No, not that one." Janie blushed. "I mean the Frida one. I haven't had a chance to read the other one yet."

"That's okay. You've got plenty of time."

"My favorite picture is that one where all her hair is cut off. It has some words in Spanish, but I don't know what it says."

"I speak a little Spanish. You have it close by?"

Janie went to her room and took the book from the box on top of the made bed. She carried it turning the pages until she found the right one. "Here." She held the book out to him.

First he read the words to her in Spanish and they sounded beautiful, like water falling or wind chimes. "It says something like, 'See, if I loved you, it was for your hair; now that you're bald, I don't love you anymore.' That's great."

"Can you write that down for me?"

"Sure." Janie brought him a slip of paper and a pen and watched him as he wrote the words out.

Joe handed her the paper and she read it again before slipping it inside the book and closing it. "Thanks."

"Glad I could help."

"You know Marta? I'm going to be staying at her place for awhile."

"She still have that horse?"

"Sugar? Yeah."

"Maybe I can come out and go riding."

Janie smiled. "I'd like that sometime."

Joe helped them load the boxes into the car and took a squirming Ruby from Cookie. Ruby smiled and patted Joe's face. "See? Nothing to worry about," he said.

Cookie looked at her brother. "Just don't give her any sugar, Joe. I'll know if you do. She can have peaches and yogurt if she's hungry before I get back." Cookie and Janie got in the car. "No sugar, Joe."

"Okay! Okay! Get out of here before she starts to cry or something."

Cookie pulled away from the curb and waved out the window.

They went shopping at a thrift and vintage clothing store

near the café. They left two hours later with a big bag of clothes and stopped by the café with an appetite for lunch.

Cat was wrapping burritos in foil and placing them in paper bags. Her dark hair peeked out of an orange turban piled high on her head. "Hi, ladies. I can't believe Stella talked me into working on my day off. I must be an absolute saint."

Cookie laughed. "Our Blessed Lady of the Guacamole. We just came by to get lunch. We're going out to Marta's."

Cat took a bag to the window. "Hey, Stella, Cookie's here." Stella waved through the window and took the bag to the register.

Cookie washed her hands and tied on an apron. Janie perched on a stool. "Can I help?"

"This'll just take a minute. There's not enough space for three."

Janie watched Cookie make three burritos and fill each bag halfway with chips and small containers of salsa. "I hope Marta's hungry."

Stella came in to the kitchen as Cookie was hanging up her apron. "Just wanted one more goodbye before you go." He gave Janie a hug and kissed the top of her head.

"Where's Janie going?" Cat asked.

Janie realized nobody but Stella and Cookie knew about Paul. Maybe Joe, too—she wasn't sure. "I'm staying out at Marta's for a few days."

"Say hi for me." Cat went back to reading the order slips above her head.

Stella called over his shoulder as he walked to the front counter. "Drive safe and I'll see you later."

PAUL'S BONES HURT – ached like bad teeth. He woke up on Doug's couch unsure of the day, the week. He couldn't remember passing out here or even making it back from Eugene. He did remember Eugene – the window breaking, glass everywhere, that dog of Stella's burying its teeth in his hand. It was swollen now and purple.

Acid rose in his throat and he rushed to the bathroom, puking up black bile. That was happening more and more. It scared him at first, but not anymore. You could get used to almost anything. Like Doug's bathroom. Doug had lived in the same place for a year or so, but it didn't look like cleaning the bathroom had been a regular event. Dirty towels lay on the floor, the sink was gray with soap scum, and the toilet had a permanent stain in the bowl. There'd been a time when Paul had been particular about hygiene. That time had passed.

Paul looked in the mirror. His cheeks had sunken in over the months of cranking and drinking. His skin looked yellowish and lined. Sores popped up on what used to be clear skin. His hair was greasy, his Fu Manchu scraggly. His eyes burned red and bloodshot. Paul couldn't recall looking this bad before. Maybe when he left Mia.

He searched the house until he found a towel but remembered he had no clean clothes. He wasn't sure about the date or day, but his stuff was probably still over at the house. He decided to go over and see if he could get some clothes. He picked up his jacket and left.

His head pounded with every step. He kept his shades on, his head down. At the store, he bought some chocolate milk and checked out the date on the newspaper – Friday. The last day he remembered was Tuesday.

Ladies of the Canyon

JANIE FELT LIKE SHE'D ALWAYS LIVED WITH MARTA. She worked in the garden weeding in the mornings. In the afternoons she was learning to sew and practicing her knitting. It was all very *Little House on the Prairie*, if Laura had been a hippie girl raised by a feminist midwife from Denmark. She felt like she'd come home. She'd started reading the book Joe had given her. She could concentrate again.

Janie felt as if her life had started.Working in the garden always made her feel good, gave her ideas, made her imagine things. Any doubts about leaving Paul had begun to fade with her bruises. She wanted to try something new, start over. It occurred to her that she had a lot of time in front of her. She was eighteen and for the first time that didn't seem so old. She could make up for what she hadn't done the first time around. Like school.

When she went to the house for a glass of water, she decided it wouldn't hurt to call the community college. She was a little embarrassed to admit to a stranger over the phone that she hadn't gone to school since eighth grade – well, really seventh – half of seventh grade anyway, and she didn't have any money. The lady on the phone told her there were free classes for people who hadn't completed high school. They would send her the information today. Classes started in September, a month away.

Janie practically skipped back to the garden, calling over to the berry patch where Marta was picking raspberries.

"Marta, I called a school to send me some information. They'll send it to me here."

Marta came out of the berry patch clapping her hands. "Let's celebrate!"

Janie blushed with excitement and pride. "What should we do?"

"How would you like to learn to drive the truck?"

"Really? I've never had a lesson. I wouldn't want to – "

"You won't break her. And, if you want to go to school from out here, you'll have to learn to drive. I hope you want to stay with me."

Marta put an arm around Janie's waist and squeezed her the way Janie imagined her mother might have. As Marta went in to get the keys for their first lesson, Janie leaned against the truck. She imagined living here with Marta, driving to school in the fall, seeing Stella and Cookie and the baby whenever she wanted. This place would be her home. For the first time Paul was nowhere in the picture of her future.

SWEAT FORMED ON Paul's forehead and at the back of his neck under his hair. The itch and tickle of sweat crawling down his skin made him want to run screaming. Anything to escape this self-enforced waiting. He had searched for Janie at Stella's place. No one was home. He had checked, first watching the house from Doug's car a safe distance away, then walking to the door, like he had reason to be there. Just act like you belong and nobody questioned your right to be wherever you weren't supposed to be. He'd walked around to the back, peeked in through the windows, then left to wait down the block from Stella's restaurant. Waiting. Waiting for Janie to walk out, or in. Waiting for somebody who might know where she was. He felt like his skin was on fire. The hottest day of the year; it must be a hundred, and nothing moving except the sweat at the back of his neck. He wished this was over.

The door opened and Cat appeared, walking toward him on the sidewalk. The windows were all rolled down, and when she got close enough to hear he leaned across the dirty white seats and whistled low. "Ssssss."

Cat glanced up. Her face broke into a smile. "Paul? What're you doing out here?"

Paul looked at her over his shades, eager now to be away before Stella came out. "Get in. I'll drive you home." He pushed open the door.

Cat got in. "Aren't you going to see Stella?"

Paul started the engine and pulled away. "Nah. How you been?" He knew Cat. Knew that she'd had a little thing for him a few years back.

"Pretty good. Where've you been? You look like you've been sick or something. I thought you'd be around by now."

"Yeah. I've had the flu. Plus, me and Jane had a little fight. She ran off before I could say sorry. Hey, you want to get high with me before I take you home?"

She sounded eager. "Want to go to the river?"

With Cat directing him, they drove out of town to the country roads. He stopped at a store for two beers. As they drove on, she jabbered away about nothing, and he asked her questions to keep her going. He parked the car and they walked down an embankment to a stream.

They sat next to the water under a tree, drinking and smoking a joint. When the joint got down to the end he reversed it, put the glowing end in his mouth, cupped his hands around his mouth and blew smoke into her mouth.

She gasped and coughed a little. "I don't smoke much anymore. Mostly at parties, I guess." She stared off at the water.

"You see Janie much?"

"Actually no." Her eyebrows knotted up, puzzled. "I saw her a few days ago with Cookie. I know she's been around, but I only see her when they come in to get lunch."

"How's she look?"

"Like Janie. Like herself. What'd you guys fight about?"

"Same old shit everybody ends up fighting about."

"Why didn't you call her at Stella's and say sorry?"

"I tried, but it's hard to do it right over the phone. Stella doesn't really like me. Never has."

Cat pursed her lips together. "That doesn't seem like Stella."

"He and I go back a long time. Things happened. Mostly my fault."

"Maybe." Cat tilted back her beer, taking a sip. "Are you sad?"

Paul shook his head. "Yup, Cat. The honest truth is, I miss Janie and I'm sorry I fucked up. I want her to come back, but I haven't even seen her to talk to her."

"I hope I don't get in trouble for telling you this – " She hesitated for a minute. "She's staying up at Marta's for a few days."

Paul looked at her for a minute. "Marta?"

"She's got a farm out this way. I can show you."

"You're a sweetheart, Cat. Just show me and I'll go later. See her by myself. You know."

"Yeah, young love."

"Thanks, Cat. I owe you. Hey, and don't say anything, would you? I want to surprise her."

"No problem. I hope it works out for you."

THE MORNING HEAT was intense. Before watering, Janie put on a bikini, determined to work on her tan and study math. She hadn't had much more than long division and basic fractions before she left school. Stella had started to teach her, but then she'd left. Marta wrote out some math problems at breakfast and showed her how to add and subtract fractions. That's what she'd work on first. They'd have another driving lesson when it cooled off in the evening. Marta never made her feel stupid. Janie liked learning from her.

With the garden watered and a basket of cucumbers ready to pickle later, Janie got her math work and pulled a canvas-backed chair into the sun. She rubbed her skin with suntan oil. From the house she could hear an old Joni Mitchell album as she closed her eyes and leaned back in the chair. A song came

on that reminded her of Paul, of waiting for Paul to show
up when they first met, when he'd come to Delores's, when he'd
come to Ernie's birthday party, all the times she'd been waiting
for him, how her heart felt tight and the blood in her cheeks felt
hot and he'd look at her and she knew he could see her.
Thinking of that Paul was like thinking of a dead man. The Paul
she had loved was gone and she missed him. Not that she'd go
back. Every day away from him made going back more unthink-
able. It was like Betty had said when she showed Janie the
owl, how some people you could only love from a distance. Janie
opened her eyes and looked at the paper on her lap.

PAUL TURNED THE tumbler on the wall safe to the final number
and opened the door. He could hear Debby, the water running in
the shower, the fan going. He eased the wooden box of gold
ingots out. Once he did this there'd be no going back, but that was
the point. He'd have a fresh start, pick up Janie, head for the city.
Maybe they'd go down the coast and live around Mendocino for
awhile. He set the box on a table and removed four gold bars from
the velvet-lined box, wrapping each one among the t-shirts and
socks in his backpack. The water stopped running and he replaced
the box, rifled through the envelope of emergency cash. He
pocketed what was left before closing the safe and putting the
painting back in place. Probably end up being good for Debby in
the long run. Once her dad figured out so much was missing
from the safe, she'd get sent back to rehab, or wherever the fuck
she'd been before she got strung out.

He was sitting on the bed smoking a cigarette when she
came out of the bathroom wrapped in a towel water dripping
down her hair and back. She reached for the cigarette and he
handed it to her. "I'm heading out."

Debby said, "I thought I was going with you."

He couldn't wait to be out of there. "No. This dude doesn't
like anybody he doesn't know showing up at his place."

"You've told me that one before."

Paul stood up. "Do you want me to do this or not?"

He could see her eyes weighing the idea of him never coming back with the chance that she'd be wired in an hour or two. "What do you want me to do, Deb?"

"Go on."

He was out the door in seconds. He had the money she'd given him to score and the money he'd taken.

Paul drove the car back to Doug's and parked in front. Zippy and Percy were inside on the couch, smoking a joint, watching TV and drinking red beers from jars. "Where's the third Stooge?" Paul asked.

Doug came out of the kitchen with a plate of eggs and a quesadilla. "My car okay?"

"I parked in front. Got anymore of those?" Paul nodded at the beer and tomato juice.

Percy wiped the pinkish foam from his droopy mustache. "I brought that V-8 instead of regular tomato juice. I like it better. It's got some spice to it."

Zippy belched. "Yeah, but you could just add tabasco if you want spice. Sometimes, I get that clam and tomato juice."

Doug sat down on his plaid recliner. "That stuff is nasty. Clams and beer. Gives me gas just thinking about it." He balanced his plate on his lap and tried the wooden lever to activate the foot rest. "Thing's broke."

Paul got a beer without the V-8 and stood in the doorway watching Robert Conrad tied down to a conveyer belt in a saw mill. "I've seen this one."

Zippy snorted. "We've all seen this one, man."

Paul didn't want to wait much longer. He was anxious to get out on the road. "Hey, Doug. I got a little business proposition for you."

"Let's do it now, man. Big Valley's on next and I got me a thing for that Audra Barkley."

Half an hour later they'd signed over the registration to Doug's Buick and Paul's Panhead. Doug was happy with the trade and Paul was resigned to it. He'd get another bike in California. The last thing he needed was to get stopped. No use taking chances, and there was no way he was messing with court and jail when all he wanted now was to start over, grab Janie, and hit the road. He stopped at Rick's on his way out of town and traded a gold Krugerrand for an ounce of crank and a fresh needle. He'd have to drive all night to get down to the city, if that's where they were headed. He'd do some wire now so he could make the drive and deal with Janie. The rest of the crank he could sell in California to get himself going, rent a place, maybe even get a new bike.

The radio in the Buick worked, and Paul fiddled with the tuner until the Stones came on. His theme song. Things were looking up. Paul merged onto I-5, the Buick swaying from a bad alignment job. Nothing major. It'd make it to the city.

JANIE STOOD AT the sink rinsing lettuce in cold water. The heat had blistered a few of the outer leaves so she tore those yellowed pieces out and dumped them in the compost bucket. She liked fixing meals from the garden. Later, she would look through Marta's cookbooks and find a pickle recipe for the cucumbers in the big basket by the door.

The phone rang and Marta answered on the second ring. Marta turned down the stereo and Janie could hear her voice, calm and reassuring on the phone. "Has your water broken? ... How far apart are the contractions? ... Yes ... Don't worry, Melanie. I'll be there soon."

Janie went to the doorway and watched Marta hang up the phone. "Who was that?"

"I don't think you've met Melanie and Stuart. She's in labor. This is their first child. It might be quite awhile. The first one usually is."

"When do you think you'll be home?"

"Not until tomorrow, but I'll call you once I see how she's doing. You'll take care of things here while I'm gone?"

"Yeah. It'll be fun."

Marta gave her a list of instructions as she got her things together. She kissed Janie on the forehead and got the keys for the truck. She hesitated at the door. "Will you be all right?"

Janie waved her off. "Goblin's here. I'll be fine. See you later. Call me."

As the truck disappeared from view, Janie looked around at the basket of cucumbers. There was nothing to be afraid of here. It would be kind of fun to be alone. She was glad she could help Marta out by doing something for her. She picked up a cookbook and began going through it for an easy pickle recipe. In the fall, she would take sandwiches and pickles for lunch. Maybe she could give a jar to Cookie. Janie found one called *Bread and Butter Pickles* and gathered all the ingredients before she started.

All Things Must Pass

PAUL BROKE UP TWO SECONALS AND STUCK THE PIECES in small chunks of raw hamburger. Every farm had a dog. This one wouldn't be different. He didn't want to kill the dog. Just put it to sleep while he got Janie. He saved a pill for himself for later, when he wanted to come down. He had bought a styrofoam cooler and bag of ice, a few cans of pop, and the meat. He tried to remember what Janie liked to snack on when they went on road trips, but he couldn't. His head tingled from the wire and he felt sweaty. Every now and then his heart skipped a beat. He waited until the sky began to turn purple and the sun hit the crest of the Coast Range. Nobody was out on the road on Sundays in Oregon, but he parked in a wide spot away from where the drive turned into the farm, just in case. No neighbors nearby that he could see. Just a dog probably. Cat said the woman was single, lived out here alone. Probably no guns. Women never had a piece. Just a dog. Like a dog would keep you safe. Paul slipped his hand inside his shirt and felt the warm metal of the handgun tucked there waiting. He climbed over the fence and crept along. He wanted to see what he could, wanted to draw the dog out, if there was one. He heard barking and the tall weeds rustle as a big black dog headed toward him. He ran back to the fence with the dog right behind him. He was just able to make it over the fence before it caught up to him. He spoke softly and threw the chunks of meat over the fence into the dog's path.

It stopped barking, sniffed at the meat, then gulped down all of it. Paul left and went back to his car. He'd wait for an hour to be safe.

JANIE HEARD GOBLIN barking from the lower pasture. She went to the door and whistled for her, but she was too tired to go wandering around in the dark just to find the dog barking at a wayward raccoon. When the barking stopped, Janie decided to take a long cool shower. Goblin would come in later.

Pickling had turned out to be hot work, steaming up all the windows and filling the air with so much moisture that she felt cooked herself. She set up two fans to blow out the sweet spicy smell of the pickles and bring in a little fresh air. The shower felt good. She stood under the head, decreasing the hot water until it was cold. When she got out of the bathroom it was dark.

Janie searched the freezer and found popsicles. Choosing the root beer kind, she sat at the picnic table and unwrapped it. A breeze across her skin cooled her. The scent from the lavender bushes filled the air. Only shadows could be seen now, shadows of trees and their leaves, shadows of the out-buildings. After she finished her popsicle she went inside. She changed TV channels until she found an old movie. *The King and I*. Janie pulled a thin cotton blanket around her and propped a pillow under her head.

Janie stretched out on the couch, losing herself in the film. She left the door open so Goblin could come in when she wanted. Her eyes were heavy and she let them close.

THE TV WAS still on but the volume seemed lower than when she'd fallen asleep. Before she opened her eyes she knew Paul was in the room. She lay still, trying to figure out what to do. Sweat trickled down the back of her neck. Her nose itched. Maybe it was just a bad dream, but then she heard the squeak of the chair across the room and the low rumble of him clearing his throat. She was lying on her side, facing the chair she thought he would be in. She peered through her lashes at him. He wasn't looking at her. He sat back in the chair with his eyes on the TV and his hands in his lap. The room was dark except for the blue flickering light of the TV screen.

"Janie? You awake?" He didn't sound scary. Didn't sound like the guy who'd put her in the hospital.

It felt like her lungs would burst with the pressure of her breath. She couldn't lie still much longer. She didn't want to anymore. She took a deep breath and opened her eyes. "What are you doing here, Paul?" She sat up.

"I thought you were awake. You got anything to drink?" He didn't move or look at her.

"There's some iced tea."

"Does it have sugar?"

Even in the dark she could tell he was wired. "No, but I could put honey in it."

Janie stood and went to the kitchen. Paul followed behind her. She left the lights off and opened the refrigerator door. The light cut a path through the dark room. The cool air from the open door felt good. She pulled out a jar of iced tea and got a glass down. "Why are you here, Paul?"

"Nobody'd let me talk to you. I was going crazy trying to find you." His voice was like a child's.

Janie handed him the glass of iced tea and saw the gun in his other hand at his side. "Why'd you bring a gun?"

"Just in case." He took a drink of tea. The ice cubes clicked against each other. "Get your stuff together, Janie. We're leaving."

"Where to?"

"Back to the city. San Francisco. We can start over again without all these people telling you what a bad guy I am."

"That's not why I'm here, Paul."

He slammed his glass down on the kitchen table. "Then tell me why you left me and don't give me that shit about the hospital. I don't remember any fucking hospital." He rubbed his forehead with his free hand. "You said you loved me. I mean, I took you off the fucking street. I know who you are."

Janie leaned against the refrigerator door, balancing there, choosing her words. "Where would we go?"

"I have Doug's car down there at the bottom of the hill. I can bring it up and get your stuff and we'll go to the city. Remember when we went the first time?" He ground his teeth and rubbed his face again at the temples.

Janie watched him, surprised that she wasn't afraid anymore, or angry. She might be standing here, but none of this had to do with her or anything she'd done or didn't do. This is what Cookie had told her but she hadn't believed before – this was all about Paul. None of this had anything to do with her. She could be anyone and he would be doing what Paul always did.

"Why're you looking at me like that? Quit looking at me like that. Look, my head is killing me. Go get your shit together and let's get out of here."

"Just a minute." She left him in the kitchen and went to her room. On the floor next to her bed was her wooden box. She bent and picked it up. A minute later she was in front of the TV, turning on a lamp so he'd be able to see.

Wagon Train was on. Paul motioned for her to move out of the way. "They're stuck in the desert again. You'd think they'd figure out to carry a map and some water." He pulled a cigarette from the pack in his pocket. The gun lay in his lap. "Get packed. I want to get out of here."

Janie crossed the room and knelt in front of him. "I want to show you something." She took his hand and turned it palm up, placing the Polaroid from the hospital inside it. She watched as he brought the picture of her from the hospital up to his eyes. "This is what you don't remember. I'm not going with you, Paul."

He was silent for a minute as he looked at the picture. "I said I was sorry, Janie. I didn't know what I was doing. I was spun. Baby, it won't happen again. I'm going to get straight and we'll start over somewhere new. I promise."

"I'm not going with you."

He brought the gun up to her chest. "Don't think I won't do

this." His voice shook and he pressed the metal against her heartbeat.

She took a deep breath and exhaled, weighing every word. "I'm not going with you. There's nothing left for me with you. Do what you have to. I'm done running." She didn't look away. She stayed rooted.

He pulled the gun from her chest and raised it to his temple. She knew this would be harder than the other. He was daring her not to stop him. "I'll do it. I'll kill myself right here and now if you don't come with me."

"Whatever you do with your life is whatever you do. It's yours." Janie searched his eyes, looking for someone she used to know. "I'm not going with you, and I'm not ever coming back. You do whatever you have to do and live with it or don't. The Paul I knew is gone, and the girl I was is gone too."

He looked away, looked back at her again, licked his lips. Janie felt peace and strength like she hadn't in so long. She could never change him. She could never make him do or be anything. She didn't want to try anymore.

She stood and turned her back, walking away from him, not sure if what she did was brave or stupid. She called over her shoulder, "I'm going to bed. You can let yourself out or do whatever it is you plan to do." A minute later from her room, she heard his boots thump away, out of the house. The screen door slammed. Janie began to shake. She crossed the room and went outside in the dark, breathing slowly to stop herself from shaking. In the distance she heard the sound of a car driving away.

Dance Sister Dance

OUTSIDE THE KITCHEN WINDOW IT RAINED. THE GARDEN HAD been put to bed for winter a week before. Now, only the cold weather vegetables were still in the ground – kale, endive, beets and parsnips, some sturdier lettuces. Stalks from the long-dead corn crop stood in the downpour. During the night a cold wind had blown the remainder of leaves from the trees. Scraps of russet, carmine, and ochre littered the ground. Janie stood at the stove with a wooden spoon, stirring a pot full of bubbling cran-berries, orange peel, cinnamon, and sugar. She lifted the spoon and waited a moment for the mixture to cool before tasting it. The kitchen was ripe with the good smells of cooking to take to Stella and Cookie's later that afternoon.

Janie had been looking forward to Thanksgiving all week. In school on Wednesday afternoon, she couldn't concentrate on algebra at all. She'd been planning what she'd make. She had collected a shelf full of old cookbooks from junk stores in town and consulted them for ideas.

Even though today was a holiday and she and Marta weren't going to Stella and Cookie's until later, she woke up early and couldn't go back to sleep. Keeping busy had kept her going all week, but that morning her first thought was of Paul. Crazy that she still thought about him. Sometimes it was hard for her to remember how bad it was. Sometimes she felt as if she'd made it all up. Sometimes she missed him so her chest ached and she'd have to hold herself tight to keep from doing something stupid like trying to find him. It felt as if they'd been through a war together, and only he could understand it the way she did. She told herself she should be grateful and mostly she was, but there was guilt when she saw herself living this new life without him. It didn't matter that he chose the life he had, chained to the needle with a monkey the size of King Kong on his back. She wondered if and when these feelings would go away.

Janie spooned the cranberries into a quart jar and secured the lid. She started a pot of coffee for Marta and went to put wood on the fire. China and Goblin lay curled up together on a rug in front of the stove. China thumped her tail as Janie approached. Janie squatted and rubbed China's head. Stella had given her China under a million false pretenses – the poor dog didn't get enough attention or exercise, it would help them out if Janie would take her. China went everywhere with Janie now. She rode in the back of the station wagon to school, to her job at the Red Light, to Stella and Cookie's.

She knew she should be grateful for all this, but today she felt lonely like her fourteen-year-old self, without a home or a family.

STELLA WATCHED JANIE across a table. He and Cookie had the idea of a small Thanksgiving with just a few people, but neither could stand the idea of someone not having a place to go. So sitting on picnic benches at an extra-long table jimmied together at the last minute were twenty-two good friends and family members. Candles down the center of the table dripped wax on the deep purple tablecloth. The light outside had dimmed since the meal began three hours before. Joe was playing something on the piano. The talk had quieted some, but no one was in a hurry to clear the table or move around too much.

Janie sat looking into the flames. She hadn't spoken much during dinner, and when she arrived Stella'd hugged her and had the impression that she was holding her breath. She was coming down hard. In Vietnam there was a saying that pain was weakness leaving the body. If she could live through it she'd be strong, a woman to be reckoned with.

Janie looked up at Stella and took her plate to the kitchen. Minutes passed and she didn't come back. Nobody noticed her leave except him. He rose and kissed Cookie on the cheek, and went out the kitchen door, but Janie was already gone.

IT ALWAYS HELPED to walk. Keep on moving until the panicky feeling diminished. Janie'd been sitting at the table with everybody eating and talking. She felt more alone than she could stand. She left without telling anyone, but Stella had seen her. Stella knew. She walked through the neighborhood thinking of the last Thanksgiving, the one with Paul, how hopeful she'd been and then how disappointed. Even though Paul was out of sight, she couldn't really get away from him. She was still trying to figure out what had happened between them. Because it was between them. Something about her fit Paul, and now he was gone and once again she was left with this feeling that she'd always be alone. Once she'd said that to Marta, and Marta told her that plugging a hole with another person or anything that made you not look at yourself was an invitation to pain. Marta was probably right but Janie'd quit talking about it after that. Paul was no monster and she was no victim. What she'd wanted to say was how like a set they were together. They'd played an intricate game with rules they knew without speaking. She wanted to forget and she couldn't. Joe had asked her out a couple of times, but she said no even though the pull to get lost in someone else tugged at her constantly.

Janie turned the corner and headed back to the house, looking in at families as she walked through dark streets. No way to explain Paul, even to herself. He was to her what getting high was to him. She stood off to the side of the house looking in at the living room, lit with candles. She really wasn't alone anymore. She could hear the pop and sigh of Stella's congas and somebody else playing flute and probably Joe on the piano. Janie walked up the steps and went inside, ready to dance.